Shield Of

By: James M R Ocean

Thanks to all those who believed I could, when I didn't.
To my Mom and Grandma who's wisdom and love light my path.
To my friends whose support is worth more than words can say.

Prologue

He screamed. He screamed so loud he wondered if she heard him. His face burned and the blood that poured from his missing cheek coated his fingers. *She did it. She really did pull the fucking trigger.* He thought as he thrashed. *She shot me and ran away. She took it and ran. The fucking thief!* His free hand reached for the medkit the Germans gave him. He stuffed the gauze where his cheek used to be and bit around it to hold it in place.

He had failed at the task She gave him. This was the first time so perhaps She would be lenient. But the text never mentioned her mercy. Maybe this was his punishment? He pulled out a bottle of rubbing alcohol and popped the cork out. If that was the case. He welcomed it.

He poured the solution onto the open wound and his screaming began anew. He thrashed around in the blood splattered grass, kicking his legs in the air. More gauze pressed against the wound before he pulled out the wrap packets and held them against what was left of his face.

He could still see out of both eyes.

"At least her aim is still shit," he spat foam past his lips and it trickled down his chin into his dark beard. He didn't care though. He looked around for the thief. He'd make her scream ten times as much when he got a hold of her. But she was gone. She'd likely made it back to the French line.

He headed back to the German line and was met at Gunpoint until an Officer recognized him and got his troops to stand down. He didn't speak much German yet, but he was beginning to pick up the language. The officer told him to go to the medical tent once he saw the blood soak cloth against his face. He sneered at the commander and grabbed another soldier's medkit before he headed down the trench. More gauze and more wraps pressed against his face and made him clench his jaw tighter. He kicked over a pail of coals which got a couple of soldiers up and ready to confront him. He pulled the pistol from his side and pointed it at the biggest one's chest.

"Not today," he spoke in rough German with a wild look in his eyes. The big guy looked him over and pointed to his face and gave a nod with his chin down the trench before speaking words he didn't know but he understood the meaning. "Yeah yeah," he tucked his gun away.

He continued down the trench and veered off the once beaten path to a little tent that he'd set up. Her book was inside and she'd know what he should do next. He grabbed the book and opened it to the right page. Letters long since lost to human understanding etched the leathery pages. He assumed the book was made by someone or several people. The regular offering wasn't as hard as it'd been in the past. He leaned over the page with her likeness and let the blood drip from his bandages onto the circles that lit up. Smoke began to fill his tent and before long the pain of his face went away. Replaced by a euphoric numbness.

"Mother," he said, "I have failed you." He tried to weep but found himself unable. Instead, he let out pathetic sobs and hoped it would suffice for the demon he called Mother.

He felt a brush across his cheek and ear. She had become so much stronger since the war started. Since her children were free and brought the world into this madness. The lives that were being wasted made him giggle with glee most nights. With the Order all but gone and the Relics in the German's hands. He could start a new Order. The others had ignored him and deserved to be worm food. They kept him away from his Relic. They were scared of him and he gave them a good reason. He'd find out which of the Germans left the Thief alive and make him suffer for his failures. The new Order would celebrate strength, not hold it back, nor would it hide in the shadows, that people celebrated and cheered, that rewarded them for their sacrifice, or pay for being so insolent. He was Blessed after all. That will mean something in his new Order.

"Child, you've achieved far more than any before you," her voice caressed his soul like ambrosia and he felt light-headed.

"Thank you, mother. I will get the last three Relics. The Rifle is mine. She stole it from me," he began to get frantic. "She shot me and she stole it and I will make her suffer."

The dark tentacle that wiggled from the book pressed more against his cheek and he hissed. Mother's touch wasn't gentle, she didn't realize how fragile humans were sometimes. It pulled the gauze and wrap back and an ichor oozed against his wound. Some of it leaking into his mouth. It tasted like sulphur with an after taste of mint. The pain of the wound stopped and he kissed Mother's hand as it slid back into the book.

"Thank you, mother. You bless me with your miracle," he said

"Never forget who loved you when no one else would," her voice said softly and faded away.

The wound that marred half of his face would make sure that he would never forget it.

⚬

11/8/1919

DEAR MR. HAMILTON,

Thank you for the interesting letter. It does my soul well to hear how things are going back home. And for sending my father's rifle my way. Our rifles are nice but I will likely shoot better with the rifle I grew up using. Even if I have to trade smokes with the French. The Germans put up a hell of a fight in my opinion. Masking crystal will make it hard for the Jerries to spot me. I'll keep my gun cleaned as you taught me, and wrapped. I've already noticed a few people eyeing her up.

Of all the things I've seen since your last letter there is one I must tell you. You won't believe a word of it. I scarcely believe it myself! We went into the trenches Thursday night two weeks back. On the following Sunday our artillery commenced bombarding the Jerry's trenches. After 30 minutes we went over the parapet. My goodness, what a reception the Huns had in store for us! Without exaggeration, some shells made holes about ten feet deep and fifteen feet diameter. It was found impossible to make any advance in our quarter. I dug myself in and waited. It was horrible suspense, as I seemed to be the only man untouched. I learned later of the casualties, fifty three killed and one hundred and eighty-eight wounded

People have often told me in the course of conversations, "it was raining shells" and I admit I took it with a grain of salt. Could not be possible I thought. But having experienced it first hand, I can attest to its authenticity. One shell fell only a yard from where I thought I was covered. The force of the concussion pitched me several yards and I came down into the arms of a barmy woman.

Though I hesitate to call her a woman, were it not for the war, she looks as though she should still have her childish features. But the war has aged and worn even the ruggedest amongst us.

She dropped me into the mud of the battlefield before I had realized what had happened. She ran headlong for the nearest machine gun nest and I thought surely her own death. Yet to my amazement, she fended off the spray with a shield, like knights carried in the stories we used to read. I know it sounds strange, but they glanced off with barely a sound!

The other queer thing about this girl was that no mud or bog hindered her progress. She ran across the field like it was a cobbled road. She smashed the gun with a hammer and killed the gunners before I was on my feet. That's not even the oddest thing she did. She covered our retreat and on her way back she swatted a shell away like it was a baseball.

Our company has since been assigned under her command. Which I was against! A girl has no place on the battlefield. But the more I see her in action, the more I believe she'll help us win the war despite the fact she only goes over the parapet to help with retreats. This past Thursday, she took on a German armoured car, on her own! She bent the main cannon and took off its treads before the crew even knew what hit them. She almost kicked the door off its hinges when the crew tried to escape. She made short work of the situation with a potato masher, but caught a piece of shrapnel in the side. I helped her back to the trench but found no wound to patch, just a bruise!

I have been tasked with teaching her how to shoot. She is many things but a marksman is not one of them. Father's rifle will come in handy and perhaps I will be able to get her to open up. She hasn't said much more than orders to those of us in the company that have been assigned to her. It's better than doing the continual bob work.

Shall be glad to hear from you. I could write more, only am a wee bit tired after seven days in trenches.

Sincerely yours

Chapter 1

1936 Frontline France

R ed flares arched into the air and drifted down against the dark sky.

"Pip! Get the perisher over the ridge," Sergeant Theirs shouted.

"Y-yes sir," I replied looking around, shoving half empty canteens, ammo boxes, blankets, papers, and other things off the tables, looking under benches. I tried to remember where I saw them. My heart pounded in my ears as gunfire echoed all around. *The crate,* I scrambled to the wooden crate, slipping on the mud slick board and grabbing the lock. My hands trembled as I pulled the keys from my pocket and dropped them into the mud.

"Fucking hell." I dove my hand into the icy mud to fish them out. With a few bangs against the crate, I could tell the keys apart again. I dropped the lock and tossed the lid open. It almost hit Private Stevenson when it slammed against the back wall of the trench.

"Careful, Pip. I got enough to worry about from that side of the trench I don't nee-" his head jerked to the side and his blood splattered across the crate contents. His body fell into the mud, his hollow eyes stared into mine as if asking *Why me?* I froze. Stevenson was the one who taught me how to pass for smoking without actually smoking. Now he was...

My heartbeat in my throat, I struggled for air. A shell exploded and sent a wave of mud and clay over the sandbag wall. I huddled to the floor trembling with a scream caught in my throat.

"Pip! For god's sake, you fucking Yankee. Get up or I'll shoot you myself." Sergeant Theirs shouted. After the incident with David's leg, I knew he wasn't one for idle threats.

"S-sorry, sir." I forced myself to my feet and looked into the crate. Blood and bits of brains splattered trench binoculars. I grabbed them and cleaned them off as best I could before propping them up against the sandbags. I peeked over the ridge, over enemy territory. The regiment had captured the hill three days ago with heavy losses, more piled up each day since.

Shadows dipped and moved amongst the trees. Or did they? Was it branches moving?

"L-Left side. I see a bunch of shadows moving to the left near the broken wagon," I shouted.

"Shadows? Or the Enemy?" Private Nora shouted back with her mouth full.

"Might be a diversion to give our position away," Richard added as he chewed on the last piece of his bread and jam. A few more shells landed in front of the trench and sprayed them with waves of dirt.

"I think they have a good idea of our fucking position," Theirs growled. "If you are done, care to get on the gun?" He pointed to a stationary gun they moved during the day.

"Fine," Richard grumbled and popped the last of his supper in his mouth. "Get some ammo, Nora. Charlie, help me with this," he waved the tall husky African over to help get the gun into position.

"There," I said as Nora returned with boxes of ammo. "By the fallen down tree. To the left, there's a pile of rocks. I saw six, no eight people hopping between cover."

"Welcome our guests," Theirs ordered as Richard finished loading the gun.

"Aye, sir," Richard replied and opened fire with a steady stream of lead. More shells fell around them and filled the trenches with more muck and body parts. Something cold slapped my face. It landed on my shoulder and left a sting on my cheek.

I looked away from the binoculars and screamed at the arm laying limp over my shoulder with a few maggots nestled in the wound. A finger hooked the pocket of my jacket and hung on despite my attempt to swat it off. The binoculars fell as I stumbled back. Stepping on Stevenson's hand, I lost my footing and ended up ass first in the mud.

"Damn it Pip. You best not have broken the binoculars. They are worth more than you." Theirs barked. "Go see what is taking Leon so long on the artillery. Andrews! What's Command said about our back up?"

"Fuck all sir, I haven't been able to get through with this hunk of mystical junk." Andrews said and kicked the metal case holding our radio "I told you we should have run a hard line."

I scurried off as the two argued over what command said and what was a better idea. I tried to ignore the stench of piss, shit, and death. Being careful not to step on anyone else. *I shouldn't be here. I am not prepared for this. A week at basic is not enough. Am I going to die here?* My mind raced while I ran. Past others who dared a peek over the edge themselves. *Why would you do that?* I wondered and shook my head.

I passed an unattended can stove that was boiled over, the smell of burnt barley stew gave me a short reprieve from the horrid stench. Until I climbed over a crate of shells into the gun pit. Leon kicked at the large cannon as he swore in Gaelic but switched to English when he saw me.

"Stupid. Fucking. Piece of. Godforsaken. German. Junk. " He shouted.

"Theirs is asking what is taking so long," I spoke up after he stopped kicking.

"You tell him to bring his ass over here and translate for me, or piss off!" Leon yelled back. "I can't figure out how to get a piece of shit to fire."

Some engineer, I thought and looked back at the shell crate. "Who helped you load it?"

"No one," Leon growled and went back to pulling levers and flicking switches.

I knew Leon was a beacon of strength, but didn't expect him to load shells alone, that wasn't an option for anyone else I'd seen..

The gun went off, and I almost shit my pants. It left behind ringing in my ears.

"Haha! It was a magical trigger. Had to hold it long enough." He said and opened the hatch and the spent shell popped out. "Come on, let's stack these close by so we can really give em he-"

A shell landed on a nearby crate that exploded with enough force to topple the artillery gun and fling me back over another. Leon screamed as the gun fell on him.

My body tinged and I ached all over. My hands rubbed over my body to make sure there were no injuries. I winced a few times, mostly bruises maybe a broken rib. It took me a moment to get back to my feet once I got a lungful of air. Through the ringing in my ears, I heard the shelling had slowed. I looked around and noticed a figure hop into the trench further down the line. They broke through and compromised our defences. Flashes filled the trenches and gunfire grew louder as the fighting got closer like a worm of chaos and death. The screams of the dying overpowered my dulled senses I had only been with the company for a couple of months, but they had welcomed me. My comrades were dying, was there nothing I could do?

"Pip," Leon's voice croaked out. "Pip are you okay?"

His voice brought me back and I released the breath I didn't know I was holding. I scrambled over the crates to find him pinned under the fallen gun. "Jesus, Leon. Worry about yourself." I ran over and tried to lift the solid steel cannon off him. I searched for a shovel or something I could use to dig him out.

"You aren't gonna move it Pip. Go get some help." Leon winced.

"I can't. Germans have broken the line. If I leave-"

Leon hooked my feet out from under me as a bullet zipped by my head. I hit the ground hard as a German charged, bayonet ready. My hand gripped a piece of a crate. I used it to block the blade, but it pierced into my forearm.

I cried out as my assaulter leaned onto his rifle. I fought to keep the blade away from my chest as it sank through my arm. "Please, no," I grunted out in German, and my arms trembled. He either didn't hear me or was Russian and didn't understand.

"Fight, Pip," Leon said while he struggled to get his sidearm free. I looked up at the man and saw the hate in his eyes. Like I'd personally wronged him, and he was getting revenge. *It's not fair. I've done nothing to you.* Tears welled in my eyes. *I don't even want to be here.*

The German stepped on my arm and I grabbed the barrel of his rifle as the blade inched closer to my chest. My arm seared in pain but my mud coated fingers couldn't get solid purchase. *Not like this. Not here, please God.* I begged and closed my eyes and screamed out as the blade punctured through my arm.

A shot rang out, and blood splattered my chest, the German coughed out blood and reached for the gushing wound on his neck. Another hit and he fell back to the ground, his blood and brain matter splattered out his helmet. Another shot hit its mark, this time the soldier had enough time to scream in pain before being silenced with another round.

I pulled the bayonet out with a grunt and cradled my arm. I looked to Leon, as more shots rang out. His gun still in its holster, he looked over his shoulder toward the shots. I followed his gaze to see someone running up the trenches. Rifle raised over a shield, he fired off the rest of his clip. He wasn't in german colours or any allied colours I recognized, but he wore a helmet that covered part of his face with feathers on either side.

Backup has arrived, I thought with a relieved smile wiping the tears from my face while I got to my feet.

The soldier swung their rifle back opening a pouch by their hip. Bullets bounced off the shield. The rifle swung forward, catching a clip from the pouch, into the soldier's shoulder before resting on the dip of the shield again.

BAMBAMBAMBAMBAM

A series of shots rang out, indiscernible from each other. More cries in German and the thud of bullets. The soldier leapt into the gun pit and popped off a few more shots before swinging the rifle over their shoulder. An unfamiliar black and white crest stitched to his chest and the feathers on either side of his helmet were black and white.

"Why are you still here? A full retreat has been ordered." A woman's voice came from behind the metal helmet with a gold ring. Just as she finished a series of blue flares shot into the sky.

"Because we just got the fucking order," Leon growled, still trying to get his gun free. "And I thought I'd get tucked in with the cannon to take a nap first." He snapped.

The woman sighed and put her shield down on a crate. "Stop struggling you'll only make your injuries worse." She walked over and grabbed the cannon with both hands.

"You aren't lifting this thing. It took three horses and a dozen men to get it here..." Leon fell silent as the metal groaned under her effort to lift the cannon up off his body. I stared in almost as much awe as Leon.

Movement caught my eye, and I spotted an injured German levelling his gun at the woman. Too occupied with the several tonne gun she didn't notice. Time seemed to slow as I tried to force myself to move. *Dive in the way, shove her free, get a gun and shoot, Fuck, just say something!* I leapt into action and grabbed her shield.

"Look out." I yelled and jumped in front of the shot that rang against the shield with next to no impact. Several other shots rang out as Leon got his gun free. The soldier winced with each shot and slumped into the blood and mud soaked trench.

I leaned against the gun stunned for a moment that I'd managed to do that. The shield, still in my hands, felt much lighter than it should have. It felt comfortable to hold like something I'd used all my life. I turned to the woman whose blue eyes stared wide at me through her visor. I froze as her stare bore into me. *Please don't stare at me.* I couldn't bring myself to say anything as heat rushed to my cheeks.

"A little help here Pip? The lady's doing all the heavy lifting." Leon said as he struggled under the gun.

"R-right" I swallowed and put her shield down before helping Leon free of the cannon. The woman set it back down, but her eyes continued to stare at me while I helped Leon to his good leg. The other foot bent at a grotesque angle.

"What's your name?" The woman asked as she picked the shield up.

"Pepper, Ma'am. I mean Sir. Pepper Gregor," I replied.

She looked me over as if studying everything about me. I felt like an open book to her and it wasn't something that I like. *If you have something to say just say it.* I thought, and my arms trembled. I wasn't sure if it was her stare or the wound that dripped blood.

"We call him Pip, cause he's a pipsqueak." Leon managed a chuckle. I struggled to support his bulky form when he leaned against me.

A shot ran against the cannon, it brought everyone's attention back to the moment.

"You have your orders. Retreat. I will cover you," she ordered and unslung her rifle, she turned to the sandbags to return fire. Bullets ricocheted off her shield.

I took a step and looked back "Should we really retreat? Shouldn't we help her?" I asked despite knowing what was the right answer.

He shook his head. "Lady Unbroken is enough to hold them off. Knights are seriously scary," he motioned down the trench she'd come from "Let's retreat." We made our way down the trench till we reached the former German front line. The bodies from our advance hadn't been cleaned up yet and made the retreat harder.

I stared out over no-mans land and felt my stomach tighten as I helped Leon up. Please let this time be easier. I thought and we made our way out across the field of death. Guided by the streams of blue light that drifted down against the dark sky.

Chapter 2
Relic

WE GOT TURNED AROUND once the flares died off and would have walked back to the enemy trench had others retreating not pointed in the right direction. One handed his rifle to me and shouldered Leon's arm.

"Watch out for harvesters and bog bodies," He said with a grunt. Leon stumbled with his one good leg another soldier took his other arm as he mumbled something. I nodded with a gulp holding the rifle with my good hand, I aimed it over the other with a wince and scanned the darkness for erratic movement.

"You got sacred rounds?" I asked as they lead the way.

"Nope," he replied. "Just need to scare 'em away if they get too close." He grunted and pulled his leg from a muddy hole.

I grumbled watching our flank, the gunfire dying off. My ankle hooked on a branch, and I tumbled into a shell hole. Face first into a puddle of mud and gore. A half chewed face welcomed me from a corpse writhing with maggots and rats. I choked back my meagre supper for a moment before it joined the mix. I scrambled up the side of the hole and desperately tried to clean my face off. I unbuttoned my jacket and would have thrown it in the hole had another soldier not cuffed me in the head.

"Keep your jacket on, moron," he growled.

"But it's covered in-" I started.

"It blends into the dark. You want your undershirt to give you away?" He hissed and continued towards friendly trenches.

He was right. I shivered and fell behind, holding my injured arm close as the cold night bit harder into my flesh.

Snow began to fall as we arrived at our trench. I followed the others who carried Leon to the field hospital. A line of injured ran out of the tent and around one side. Doctors and nurses hurried about assessing everyone who arrived. They gave beds only to those that needed it most, they sat Leon in a chair while a doctor looked his leg over. He made a chopping motion above his knee and the nurse fetched the bone saw and other equipment to amputate.

I gulped and held the gauze they gave me against my arm, wrapping it as best I could with one hand before I put my jacket back on. I had to stand in line with other less injured soldiers. Nurses tossed sets of boots, jackets and torn pants into a wagon out back and a few picked through the remains of the dead or dying.

It appalled some men at first, but I'd learned young that the dead have no use for a good jacket or clean trousers. I walked by and peaked in the wagon and saw a jacket that looked about my size. I swapped mine out and found the new one a little big, but I could live with that.

I returned to my line after a visit to the latrines and no one seemed the wiser. Or they were too wrapped up in their own pain and misery to care about the American who didn't stink anymore.

The line was slow-moving and other than the groaning from inside the tents and the odd time someone called out for help for their buddy it was quiet. This gave me time to think about the knight more. Lady Unbroken as Leon called her. *Who was she? Why was she staring at me?* I thought about asking the guy behind me, but with a bandage over his left eye, I figured he had a bad enough day.

It felt like hours shivering in the cold, the cup of hot stock and tea they'd brought around did little to warm me, or fill my empty stomach. I couldn't tell if being up for several days had caught up to me, or it was the blood loss that made it hard to stand. I tried to lean against the tent and almost fell through.

Once inside a nurse sat me down and hooked me up to a bottle of blood. I stared at it wondering who it had once belonged to. What were they doing now? Did they still support the war?

As the sting of rubbing alcohol shot up my arm I pulled away from the nurse with a gasp louder than I'd like to admit.

"Oh, don't be a child," she pulled my arm back and rubbed the alcohol soaked cotton along my wound. "They got you deep. Lucky it was just your arm and not your gut," she said in a heavy Irish accent. Red hair poked out from her coif almost matched the stains on her apron. The serious look on her face was betrayed by baby fat cheeks, but her nimble fingers were steady as she sewed the wound. Now sat down and more relaxed than I'd been in a week my head bobbed but the pain of each stitch staved off sleep.

Once patched up they gave me some penicillin and I left the hospital, headed for the bunk to get some much needed sleep and maybe a change of uniform in the morning. A bunk was quite an improvement compared to a dirt dugout.

I skipped out on the hot meal and went straight to bed. Just as I laid my head down, a woman with a familiar black and white crest on her uniform came into the bunk and everyone awake snapped to attention. I closed my eyes and turned away.

"Pepper Gregor?" She asked the room, and all eyes turned to me. I ignored it, sleep's embrace was wrapping around me.

"That one there," someone said and a hand shook my shoulder, scattering sleep far from my grasp. I groaned and sat up in my bunk.

"Yeah?" I looked into the dull jade eyes of the woman with short dark hair and soft almost childlike features that made it hard to call her a woman for sure.

"Are you Pepper Gregor?" She asked in a firm tone.

I nodded and looked bitterly between her and my pillow. *So close, I was so close.*

"They have transferred you. Grab your gear and come with me," she ordered.

"Wha-?" I asked not awake enough to process the onslaught of questions that hit my mind

She sighed and rolled her eyes. "Great, he doesn't understand the King's English," her head shook "Parle français?" I blinked "¿Habla español? Mílise elliniká?" She grew more frustrated with each question.

"I speak English," I got out and shifted to sit on the edge of my bunk. "Just don't get why I'm being transferred."

"It's not for me to say. I was just told to come and get you." She fussed with both hands behind her back. "Hurry up, we don't have a lot of darkness left," she ordered and left the bunk.

I looked back at my pillow for a long moment and wondered what would happen if I ignored her.

"Today," she shouted from beyond the doorway.

"Coming." I sighed and laced up my boots before I followed out the bunk. Her boot tapped in the support trench she waited in.

"Where are we headed?" I asked when I caught up. She answered by walking away without a word. *What did I do to be transferred? Who made the request? What unit?* She left more questions unanswered as she guided me out of the trenches and past the artillery and into a nearby patch of forest where a few tents were set up.

"Wait here," she ordered pointing beside the entrance to the largest grey tent and slipped through the flap.

I did as directed and heard a muffled exchange, my eyes wandered skyward through the treetops. The brightening sky looked like any other sky like I could be a million miles from the war until an observation balloon came into view. I closed my eyes and wondered if it was possible to fall asleep standing up. I would've given anything for that.

"What are you doing?" A man's voice broke my thoughts. Dressed in a grey uniform with the black and white crest, he was clean shaven aside from a salt and pepper moustache that made him look mid forties. He carried a small bundle under his arm.

"I, uh I was ordered to wait here." I blinked.

"And you bought it?" He laughed and slapped his side. "That was a test, boy. See if you'll follow orders without thought," he continued. "They'll have you stand there till your legs fall off." He shook his head and slung a towel over his shoulder. "Just go in."

"Are you sure?"

"Of course, they tried the same with me until I marched in and demanded to know what was going on," he replied with a nod and a friendly smile.

I thought about it for a second. *They just want to see how gullible I am?* With a deep breath, I clenched my jaw. *I'll show them gullible.* I thought and marched through the tent flaps.

"Why am I-". I lost my nerve and thoughts when I saw the naked form of a willowy woman stepping from a bath. Her long blonde hair slick to the ivory of her petite breasts, a scar over her left breast and shoulder along with bruises speckled her otherwise flawless body. Her right arm wrapped in grey cloth with red marks. Blue eyes froze me to the ground before I could look away.

"I told you to wait outside." The dark haired woman roared, she pulled a sword and lunged. I turned to leave, but she slammed my face down on the rug covered ground. Before I could utter an explanation, she squeezed the back of my neck tight and something invisible split the ground and grew closer to my face.

"Wait." The blonde woman spoke. The split stopped much too close for comfort. Two maids helped the blonde get dressed. "You are Pepper Gregor, are you not?"

It took me a second to nod my head.

"Speak." The uniformed woman kneeling on my back barked.

"Yes," I squeaked out and cleared my throat. "I am."

"Do you know who I am?" The blonde woman asked.

"Lady Unbroken?" I guessed.

"Correct, do you know what that title means?" She asked now standing in front of me though I didn't dare look up.

I shook my head and the other woman tightened her grip on my collar.

"Out loud," she growled.

"No." I croaked out and reached for my collar.

Lady Unbroken put her hand on the other's shoulder. "Let him up, Sylvia." Her soft voice was full of authority.

Sylvia released my collar after a moment, and I coughed. She shoved her knee into my back to stand herself up. I sat on my knees but still couldn't bring myself to look up. My face flushed and my heart beat in my ears.

"It's a moniker that the troops have given me." Lady Unbroken said. "One that must remain, understand?"

"I've already forgotten what I saw," I replied.

A soft laugh escaped her lips. "No, you haven't. But that's all right so long as you never speak of it." She headed back towards the tub, I kept my eyes on the ground. "I'm sure you have lots of questions. They will have to wait until tonight," she continued and I heard the rattle of a pill bottle. "Sylvia will show you to your tent. Enjoy what rest you can, for tonight the world you know shatters."

I got to my feet and Sylvia shoved me out of the tent. She walked me over to one of the four smaller tents and pushed me into one.

"This is your tent, if I catch you out of there without orders... So help me," she threatened. I wanted to argue but didn't have the energy, instead, I stumbled over to flop on the cot not bothering with my mud-caked boots.

That evening I woke as a woman came into my tent with a jug of water and some towels. She set them on a barrel and left, I rolled over and went back to sleep. If I could sleep until the end of the war that would be fine by me. I woke next when my cot flipped over and it dumped me onto the grass.

"Wha-" I tried to figure out what happened, but it was too dark to make out more than shadows in my tent.

"You didn't even bother to wash, did you?" The familiar male voice said.

"Who's that?" I asked.

"Jonas." The voice replied. "Jonas Edward McClemont. We met this morning."

I recalled the man who persuaded me into the tent.

"The Commander told me to fetch you for supper," he continued. "Though a quick wash and a change of clothes are in order first," he struck a match and lit a lantern on the barrel beside the jug.

"Supper? How long did I sleep?" I asked and blinked at the light filling the tent. "This is the only uniform I have," I added.

Jonas moved over to an armoire I hadn't noticed in the morning and opened the doors.

"Three sets of uniform here. One should fit you well enough," he pulled the first drawer out. "Soap, shaving kit, and fresh ginch in here. I advise you hurry, The commander abhors tardiness." He said before he stepped out of the tent.

It took a moment to gather myself and look around my quarters. Clean linen and a blanket laid on a chest. A chair sat beside the barrel with a mirror beside the jug. I got to my feet to look at the uniforms, standard khaki uniform with the black and white crest on the shoulder and chest. A white owl with a black caduceus in one talon and a mace in the other.

I hurried out of my rank stained clothes and splashed water on my face, armpits and chest. It was ice cold and shocked me awake. I didn't bother with a shave and got into my new uniform once dry. The first one was a little big but it was obvious the other two were for men of greater stature than I.

I made my way out of the tent and followed my nose to the large tent. My hand froze before it grasp the flap of the tent when I heard muffled voices.

"Permission to enter?" I asked hoping I was loud enough.

"You may enter." Lady Unbrokens voice replied.

I pulled the flap and stepped inside to find Jonas, Sylvia, and Lady Unbroken sitting at a round hardwood table.

"Reporting for duty Sir." I stiffened and saluted.

"At ease Pepper." The Lady spoke. "We are not on duty yet. But you are late for supper and missed out on soup," she motioned to the empty seat beside Jonas. I moved over to sit down just as a cart was rolled into the tent with four plates covered in metal domes.

The maids that rolled the cart in placed a plate in front of each of us and removed the dome. Steam wafted off mashed potatoes, corn, and a hamburger steak with thick gravy. My mouth had watered at the smell, now my stomach growled ferociously. I picked up the fork and knife to dig into the steak first.

"Ahem." Jonas coughed and caught my attention. He held his hand in my direction, his other hand held Sylvias, and hers held onto the Lady's. The Lady's free hand laid on the table beside me.

"Sorry." I put my utensils down and held their hands and bowed my head over the delicious meal. The steam wafted over my cheeks.

"Dear lord," The Lady prayed. "We give thanks for the meal we are to receive, bless the hands that made it possible. We are thankful to rise another day. We pray that we can continue your work and that our nights work bare fruit." With the prayer finished I pulled my hands back and dug into the meal. It was the best thing I'd had in my life. I thought the hot meals the army provided were good, but it didn't compare to this. It was quiet at the table as the others ate with more reserve than I could muster. I was almost done when a basket of fresh fluffy buns was placed on the table. I used one to clean my plate of the last streaks of gravy.

"So, Pepper," Jonas spoke once I finished. "Bit of a queer name. Where's it come from?" He asked and sipped at a mug of coffee.

"Uh, well... It's a bit of a long story." I tried to dismiss.

"We have some time." The Lady encouraged.

"It's a name my mother liked," I replied

"For a boy?" Sylvia added with a raised eyebrow and pushed her plate away. Half her corn and potatoes still left.

"No." I sipped my water hoping they'd change the topic but Jonas and Sylvia stared waiting for more. Lady Unbroken continued with her meal. I put my glass down. "She was sick when she was pregnant with me, a fever my father told me. It took her mind and almost took her life. She had wanted a girl." I sighed and shrugged, it felt strange to be telling them this, but I couldn't stop.

"Didn't think to change your name?" Jonas asked. "Or go by something else?"

"I did. But it caused mother extreme distress when anyone else was around. So I just sucked it up. I mean it's a weird name, but there is a lot worse that I could have to deal with."

"Wise words." The Lady spoke.

"Spoken like a man beyond his young years," Jonas added and raised his mug.

"It happens when you spend twenty years looking after a deranged mother," I replied. Jonas and Sylvia looked at each other.

"Twenty years? How old are you?" Jonas asked

"I'm twenty-six." I said before I could stop myself, I knew what was next.

The Lady looked at me with her piercing eyes and I stared down at my cup of water and wondered if I could drown myself in it to get away from it. She knew.

"How did you take care of-" Sylvia began.

"He's a fucking dodger." Jonas accused and got to his feet knocking his chair over.

"I... I did what I had to. My mother would have died if I left her." I explained.

"So you just let others take your place in the draft, so you could stay close to mommy?"

"It's not that simple. No one else would take care of her." I explained.

Sylvia took the longest and quietest sip from her mug and leaned back in her chair.

"You're a coward." Jonas glared at me.

"I am." I snapped back. "I shouldn't be on the front lines. I'm not a fighter, a killer. I'm not someone you want at your side." I slumped back into my seat as the image of Stevenson's dead stare flashed before me.

"Sylvia, Jonas." The Lady addressed them without removing her eyes from me. "Go get ready."

"But-" Sylvia started. The Lady raised a hand.

"Now." She said so coldly that a shiver passed up my spine. Jonas shoved off the table and headed out of the tent. Sylvia nodded and stepped back from the table to follow.

The tent sat still for a moment as The Lady's eyes beckoned my own, I resisted, but it wasn't long till her gaze held mine and I found myself adhered to the seat.

"You may think you do not belong here. But had you not been here, you may have gone your entire life not knowing how Blessed you are," her words soothed the pounding of my heart.

"Blessed? N-no way. You must be confused. I'm not even religious." I shrugged and drew my eyes away from hers for a moment to look at my empty plate. "This was the first time I've prayed before a meal in years."

"You will learn faith along your path to becoming one of the Blessed Knights." Her words drew my eyes back to hers. She held them another moment, then got to her feet. "Sometimes the tests for Blessed can be wrong, but I know that's not the case this time." She walked over to her armour spread out across a table and picked up her shield. "You proved it last night."

She glided back to the table and held the steel flat iron shield with a bronze cross embossed into it to me. A nook sat on either side of the top where a spear could be held.

"Go on. Take it," she said. I looked up at her, then to the shield. My hand reached out cautiously and took it, prepared for it to be as heavy as it looked. But it was light, much too light to be steel.

"Is it made of Vosbril?" I asked, bouncing it in my hand. It was almost imperceivable how light it was.

She shook her head. "No. It's forged from bronze and steel in the fourteenth century," she sat back in her seat. "It is also proof that you are Blessed. Only the Blessed may lift that shield." She motioned with her glass before taking a sip. "It may even be your chosen Relic," she said with a shrug. "Something that we will find out in time. For now, I will induct you into the Order as an Initiate."

"What? Don't I have a say in the matter?"

"Absolutely. You can join the Order as an Initiate and become Jonas squire when he is knighted. Or you can continue your life outside the order. Returning to the front lines to serve your time as a soldier, then your extra time for dodging the draft." She crossed her legs at the knee and locked her eyes on mine again.

I placed the shield beside the table and considered my options.

"Can I have some time to think it over?"

"No." She sipped her wine and leant back in her seat. "We have an important operation tonight, and I'd like you to be part of it. But I won't force you. As a child of God, you have the freedom to choose."

Being strong armed isn't much of a choice. "What's the operation?" I asked.

"Classified," she said as she swirled her wine. "But time sensitive. So, I'm afraid I will need your answer now."

"I... uh, what... um." I swallowed and scratched at my cheek.

"If you can't decide, I will take that as a no." She got to her feet and picked the shield up. "You may stay the night as the maids have yet to clean your uniform. In the morning, Sylvia will return you to-"

"I'll join." I spat out and thought I'd regret it at once. But a warm smile graced her lips as she looked down into my eyes. Something about it told me I'd made the right choice.

"Good." She stepped away from the table and Sylvia returned along with two maids. One cleared the table as the other moved over to the armour and got it ready with Sylvia. "Go speak with Jonas. He'll get you armed and ready for tonight's mission.

I left the tent and looked into the clear night sky with a sigh. The smiling crescent moon seemed like good omen.

"It's not as bad as you think." Jonas voice chimed beside me and made me jump.

"What?" I turned to see him still in uniform but with a helmet with goggles on it, a lantern at his belt with an eerie blue glow. A thick camo cloak hung off his shoulders the hood bundled behind his neck.

"I was just saying." He said and shrugged two rifles back onto his shoulder. One's barrel was covered in tattered cloth. The other I recognized as The Lady's rifle from the night before. It's pale wood a stark contrast from the standard issue rifles. "It's not that bad. I won't have you shovelling shit in stables or carrying my drunk ass home too often," he laughed. "But I do like my boots to shine." He grinned and motioned to the crisp brown leather boots laced above his ankles. "Until I'm a knight, you'll be shadowing us and learning the ways of the order." He slapped my shoulder. "Who knows maybe you'll become a historian instead. I've heard a rumour of a quill Relic." He chuckled.

"What's a Relic?"

"Ah, you didn't get the full introduction eh Dodger? Well, let me sum up as much as I can. We're the Order of the Blessed." Jonas explained and put his right fist over his heart. "Divine people, chosen by God to blah blah, something religious, amazing weapons, leaders of humanity, lots of responsibility." He flapped his hand to mock talk as he rolled his eyes and hung his head. "To be straight with you, the Blessed are people that can use the Relics, items of magic that are quite powerful, with minimal negative effects."

"Negative effects."

"Yeah, like Lady Therese's shield and Sylvia's sword, er what's left of it," he said with a shrug. "Or the rifle." He said in an eager tone and a grin. "That one's mine though." The words left an uncomfortable knot in my stomach. "These are yours." He dropped a helmet with a pistol in a holster on the ground in front of me.

"Thanks." I put the helmet on and just got the holster on my belt when Lady Therese and Sylvia came out of the tent. Jonas snapped to attention, and I followed suit. Therese held her hand out as she examined us both. Jonas unslung her light rifle from his shoulder and handed it over to her.

"Let's get a move on." She ordered.

"Yes Sir." Jonas and Sylvia said in unison.

"Yes Sir." I followed a second late. Therese lead the way with Sylvia close behind and Jonas took the rear leaving me in the middle as we left the camp.

Chapter 3

Circle

My feet slowed as the trenches came into view.

"Keep moving Dodger," Jonas said. "We've got a way to go yet." He finished and shoved me forward. I bit my tongue and straightened up as we marched past the guns, where soldiers stacked munitions. Down to the command bunkers and into the back room, where a map of the surrounding area sat on a table surrounded by several men. They paused their grumbling as Therese walked into the room. All of them nodded to her, except for the bald man with a white moustache at the far end of the table. He narrowed his eyes while Sylvia, Jonas, and I stood along a log wall.

"Gentlemen," Therese said as she stood at the open end of the table. "Major General," she addressed the bald man. "I should congratulate you on your victory the other day, however brief it was. It cost many lives and left this regiment in need of reinforcements that won't come for more than a month." She finished as she took off her gloves and dropped them onto the table.

"Our intelligence said they moved troops out of the area," the old man said. "We planned to-"

"Hand the victory over to the Russians?" Therese interrupted as she leaned on the table. The old man mimic'd her posture, and the others shifted away from the table.

"Listen here girl, I don't need your advice," he growled.

"Not if spending lives needlessly is your goal," Therese replied.

The room went silent as no one dared to make a sound until the groans of a sick soldier being carried through the support trench eased the tension.

"Intelligence reports can be wrong, it's unfortunate we lost so many." Major General said, breaking the tension further. "We are planning for a counter attack in the morning. With your help we should have little problem fending off-"

"Major General Noboa, you seem to forget that my squires and I are not under your command," Therese said.

"If you aren't going to help then why in hell's name are you here?" Noboa shouted and slammed his fist on the table.

"I didn't say I wouldn't help," Therese said pushing off the table. "I will head for a patrol. When we get back, I will look over your plans and advise you how we will help." She picked up her gloves and walked out. Sylvia followed and Jonas ushered me along behind her.

It wasn't until we were out in the trenches again that I realized how quiet and shallow I was breathing. I forced myself to take a deep breath and coughed at the smell of the trench.

"Noboa is an idiot. Why do you give him any leeway?" Sylvia asked as they headed towards the front lines.

"Because he's an idiot that listens to command," Jonas said. "She can talk to General Vanar or the Field Marshal and get him to listen."

"Despite his eagerness, he is a good man," Therese said. "He wants this war over as much as any of us do. Though his methods are stale and foolhardy."

I listened to the exchanges between the knight and her squires but only answered questions directed at me with a shrug. *This is all beyond my scope. Generals, Field Marshal, I'm used to dealing with Sargents or lieutenants at most.* I had hoped to keep myself distracted but with each step we grew closer to the front trench. My feet grew heavy and began to drag until Jonas kicked me in the ass. I caught up to Sylvia and kept close for fear of another boot.

"Why are we going to the front?" I asked.

Sylvia glanced over her shoulder with knitted eyebrows.

"I mean, what is our mission? I haven't been told what we are doing."

"I am going for a patrol," Therese said loud enough for me to hear. "You three are to watch my back for any harvesters or other monsters of the night."

"What about sniper fire?"

Jonas laughed. "Not gonna be an issue."

"They'd waste ammo and give their position away," Sylvia added.

I didn't understand what they were talking about, but we'd arrived at the front lines and I lost my string of questions.

Sylvia propped up a ladder as Therese spoke with a commander.

"There is one in a shell hole here," he indicated on a paper map. "Two more here and a few scattered further down the line."

"Thank you," Therese said with a hand on the man's shoulder. He tucked the map away and saluted. She turned back towards us. "I'm going north for one by the fallen tree," She said and put her foot on the ladder. "Then I'll head south along the trenches. Jonas keep your goggles on. Sylvia keep the ladder close and Pepper follow their lead."

She climbed the ladder and with a few steps was gone into no-mans-land. I couldn't believe it. She walked out as casually as a Sunday stroll. Rifle over her shoulder and shield on her arm. I waited to hear the shots of snipers, but they never came. The crunch of her footsteps on the thin sheet of snow faded into the night.

Jonas pulled his goggles down and snuck a quick peek over the ridge.

"She's got the first one." He said and stepped back taking a trench scope out of its side pouch. "Let's go," he headed down the trench. Sylvia picked up the ladder and motioned for me to follow.

Jonas darted down the trench, and poked his scope over the ridge for a moment, then moved again. I kept low and watched Jonas as he moved about the others in the trench. I looked back to Sylvia occasionally; she kept the ladder under her arm as we moved.

"What is Therese doing?" I asked after an hour.

"Lady Therese." Sylvia corrected. "She is collecting dog tags," she finished and looked me in the eyes.

"What? Dog tags?"

She nodded and blinked a few times before she looked away. My stomach tied into a knot, and she motioned for me to follow Jonas. We passed a group that played cards beside a man under a mud stained blanket, dead or asleep I wasn't sure.

"There has to be more to this," I said as we settled again. "She said that-"

"Lady Therese," Sylvia interrupted. "When you talk about Lady Therese use her proper title."

"Uh, all right. Lady Therese said it was an important operation. Dog tags don't really feel that important."

Jonas yanked me to his side as he peered down the trench scope. "You talk too much Dodger." He said and took a glass out of his goggles to hold over the trench scope. "Look." He pulled me to it.

I looked through the scope expecting to see only darkness but was met with a bright green haze of the horizon in stunning detail. I'd seen night scopes in the past but they didn't compare.

Therese knelt beside a body muttering as she snapped the tag from its neck. Her hand moved over the person's face.

"Lady Therese reads the rites to those that have fallen, abandoned on the battlefield. She gives those souls the chance at peace. If you think that isn't worth something, then you've got a lot to learn," Jonas said.

Therese stood up and looked in our direction before she waved a hand full of dog tags in the air.

"She's waving," I said.

"What?" Jonas shoved me to the side and put his glass back before he looked out the scope. "all right, we are getting close," he said and thumbed the latch on his lantern, a blue mist began to waft from the opening.

He handed a small gemstone, that sparkled with reds and yellows like fire, to Sylvia and I. "Keep this on you." He said, more to me. Sylvia tucked the stone into her pocket.

I stared at mine for a moment then tucked it in my shirt pocket. The mist formed a fog that settled along the trench. We moved down the trench a few more times, each time the fog grew thicker until I doubted Jonas could still see anything through the scope.

He kept on his toes as we moved but I noticed that the other soldiers were becoming less alert. I bumped into a soldier that startled for a second like I'd woken him from a nap on his feet. *I guess it is possible.*

"What's going on?" I whispered to Sylvia. She held a bare finger up to her lips.

"Okay, that's the signal," Jonas said and pulled his scope back. "Up you go." He motioned over his shoulder as he sat beside a soldier and plucked a cigarette from the mans hand.

"Uh, what?" was all I got out before Sylvia had the ladder up against the trench and started to climb. "What about you?" I asked Jonas as he pulled a lighter from his pocket and lit the stolen cigarette.

"I'll be here when you get back." He said with a smirk. "Though you better hurry, Sylvia won't wait forever." He pointed to the ladder as Sylvia stepped off.

My heart pounded against my chest. *Why? Why am I going back again? This is the third time this week.* I grumbled, swallowed and tried to steady my hands as I reached for the ladder. One rung at a time, I climbed automatically until my hands were on the snow dusted surface.

Sylvia was all I could see in the blue tinted fog. She stood with a hand out which I took and she helped me up but her eyes were trained on something beyond the fog.

"Stay close." She said and drew her sword. Or what was left of it. It looked more like a jagged dagger with a wide handle. We made our way through the fog, only the crunch of snow under our feet accompanied the beating of my heart in my ears.

The fog grew lighter until it was ripples at my ankles and we were left with the shroud of a cloudy night. I stuck close to Sylvia until the sickening snap of a bone and the crunch of flesh almost had me jump onto her shoulders.

I spun to see the shadowy figure of a beast with extra arms and glinting yellow eyes. Two arms pulled a mans leg off and flexed it a few times. Then brought it to a mouth of tiny sharp teeth that ground against the knee in a grotesque sampling of flesh.

I turned to run back to the trench but Sylvia grabbed my hand.

"Hold. It's just a harvester." She said like that would calm me.

"I know what a harvester is. They eat people," I hissed trying not to draw its attention as it lips smacked on the foot of the leg.

"They eat *dead* people." Sylvia corrected. "They only kill people they feel are a threat to their meal."

A grunt came from the battlefield as another harvester tore open the rib cage of a woman. It pulled out her intestines and examined them with its one big eye like a ring of sausages then coiled them over its arm and tucked it into a basket it dragged along.

"How are you okay with this?" I reached for my gun, but she stopped me.

"I'm not. But they aren't our mission." She reminded and got close enough I could smell the mint from her tea as she looked me in the eye. "Don't move fast. They'll take it as a threat. Let's go," she ordered and pulled her hand off mine.

I followed her and mimicked her slow movement as we continued in the dark. The snow covered most of the field's carnage.

Finally, we came up to the battered remains of a stone tower, likely something from the middle ages. It was a wonder the thing still stood.

Therese knelt before a half standing wall her hands folded in prayer with several dozen dog tags laid out on the wall.

Sylvia put her sword away and stood beside Therese with her hands folded and head bowed. I looked around the ruin and moved my hand back to my gun in case a harvester decided that warm flesh was better than cold.

"There is no need to be hostile here," Therese said as she got to her feet.

"Why's that?" I asked.

"This is sacred ground... harvesters, demons, even the tainted bog bodies can't approach this tower." A hollow smile graced her lips. "You need only fear mortal man here," she finished.

"I think the war has proven how much I should fear mortal man," I grumbled. The corner of her mouth curled into a genuine smile for a second.

"That is true." She replied, and the night fell silent. "Come, we have an appointment to keep." She motioned for me to follow as she walked into the empty archway of the tower. "Sylvia, keep an eye out. Just in case."

"Yes sir," Sylvia said and pulled her busted blade free from its scabbard again. It was so strange to see. She had two colts on her, but always reached for the broken blade. I shook my head and followed Therese into the broken building. She paused at a boulder and looked back at Sylvia who nodded. Therese pushed the several tonne stone free to reveal a door of solid oak. It looked none the worse for wear, despite having a boulder rest on it for who knows how long.

She turned to face me as I looked down at the door on the ground. "Pepper. When we get inside, I need you to hold your tongue, no matter what," she instructed.

"Inside? Inside where?" I looked around. We were already inside the tower. There was only outside to go.

She pulled a ring of keys from her satchel and sorted to a silver key with a white owl head, turning to the door she knelt beside it and slipped the key into the iron lock. The thunk of a bolt pulling back followed a jangle of the key. She lifted the door and it lead into a dark hallway that went straight down into the ground.

I was dumbstruck, magical doorways? That's the kind of thing you hear in legends and myths, not real life. Magic existed sure, but minor things, radios, coffee pots, truth seats, scopes, or lanterns.

Therese stepped into the doorway and stood up on the other side, she held the door open as Sylvia urged me forward.

"Where does this go? Why is it so dark? Stop shoving me. What's going on?" I had so many questions but she wouldn't listen. Therese grabbed my leg and pulled me down through the door. Holding me upside down or at an angle I couldn't wrap my mind around it. I hung from her hand above a dusty stone floor. White flames popped to life atop torches on the hall behind us.

I crashed to the floor as the door dropped closed behind Sylvia who headed down the hall and peeked around the corner. She waved us forward when I got to my feet.

"Whe-" I was about to ask but Therese's hand slapped over my mouth.

"Remember. Not a word. It is for your own safety. I assure you," she reminded me. "Not. One."

I nodded, and she pulled her hand back.

"Now, stay close to me." She ordered and headed down the hall. Sylvia had already gone down the next corridor and waved us forward as we rounded the corner. I looked back but couldn't see the door we'd come from. When one torch ahead of us came to life another behind us died.

The knot in my stomach doubled the moment I was pulled into the hall. I took several deep breaths to calm my pounding heart, but it did little. I almost choked on the lump in my throat when I swallowed. So I kept close to Therese as she ordered, she said my world would shatter. *Are the legends and myths true? Is there more to the world than we see?* I wondered if this was what she meant?

We wandered countless hallways and down a half dozen staircases. Dust clung to everything and the must of underground hung in the air. I began to wonder if there was an end to the path when we came to another oak door. Therese stepped up to the door and pulled out a golden key with a circle on it.

"Stand beside me once we are inside," Therese ordered as she locked eyes with me. "Right beside me, understand?"

I nodded, and she took a long deep breath before she unlocked the door and stepped inside. I followed close behind her and Sylvia stayed by the door.

The room was lit with an eerie full moon glow from the ceiling, its edges came down in front of three rows of curved benches broken into four sections to form circles. The walls were of solid marble and the floor was smooth cobblestone. Another door sat on the far side of the room. But otherwise, it was bare.

"Looks like we beat them here," Sylvia said.

"Good," Therese said as she stepped into the circle.

I followed and stood beside her, I looked up trying to see some stars or maybe get an idea where we were, but the moonlight was so bright I couldn't see past it.

There we stood in silence for several minutes. I had just gotten my heart under control when the other door's lock clicked open. My heart raced as I wondered who or what was on the other side of the door. I kept my breathing under control and my legs from turning to jelly as the door opened.

My blood ran cold as a half dozen German soldiers filed into the room. Their commander took a knights helmet off and handed it to a soldier before he stepped into the circle of light a gloved hand pushed his slicked blonde hair back. The moonlight glinted off the steel and gold of the pristine armour as the young soldier stood beside him.

"Hallo Frau Therese." The Commander said without glancing in my direction, he walked up and held his hand out.

"Rheiner" Therese nodded and shook his hand. "Bleiben wir bei Englisch für unseren neuen Initiierten," and pointed to me. I blinked hearing her speak decent German. She was wrong, but I couldn't correct her.

Rheiner looked me over and smiled in a way that did not comfort me, his powerful frame and strong jawline were imposing even if it wasn't his intent. "So, you found another one as we lost one." His eyes shifted to the shield. "I hope we are still on good terms Frau Therese."

"Ah, yes." She said sliding her arm free she handed it to me. "Hold this for me, Initiate."

I took hold of the shield and slipped it to my side, but Therese pulled it in front of me. I felt a little safer behind the shield until I noticed everyone's eyes were on me, wide with awe, I raised the shield higher and tucked my chin behind its crest. *Please don't stare at me.*

"So you have." Rheiner mused for a moment. I couldn't bring myself to meet his steel-blue eyes.

"I'm sorry to hear of your loss. Was it Raoul?" Therese asked. Rheiner looked back to her.

"No Raoul is manning the lantern. It was Peter."

"Peter? The one with the Torc?"

Rheiner nodded.

"What happened?"

"Zakeem." Rheiner sneered at the name and spat on the ground as did his soldiers and Sylvia. "That bastard you warned us about. He's gone mad, a rabid dog."

Therese nodded and sighed. "I take it you didn't capture him?" Rheiner shook his head. "So he is in the wind again." She chewed on her lip. "We will deal with him as he shows up. If we waste time hunting him now, we'll lose our chance to end this war."

I didn't believe what I'd heard. *End the war? Is that even possible? Twenty years of bloodshed brought to an end. It just didn't seem so simple.* Therese dug into her satchel and pulled out two envelopes with wax seals on them.

"Here is the communication and the list of names." She reached into the satchel again. "And the tags I found," She pulled out a shoebox that jangled, a heavy sigh escaped her lips as her eyes lingered on the box before she held it out.

Rheiner tucked the letters into the inner pocket of his jacket and took the box with both hands. "Vielen Dank Frau Therese." He brushed a hand over the box. "The mothers of Germany and her allies thank you for closure." He turned and handed the box to one of the other soldiers a woman with a bow slung over her shoulder. He whispered an order, and she nodded stepping back holding the box.

"Sadly I cannot do the same for the mothers of Britain and her allies. I was not involved in the assault last night. But, I will get the letter to General Torben." Rheiner continued after clearing his throat "With any luck, we can see a ceasefire in the coming months." He said patting the letters.

"It's a huge step in the right direction," Therese said with a smile.

"Assuming this one lasts." One of the German soldiers grumbled louder than he intended, another elbowed him in the side.

Rheiners steel glare made the man straighten and lower his gaze. Rheiner cleared his throat again. "Sorry, Frau Therese. Rest assured, this one will see the end of this war. And with god's blessing, all wars." He made the sign of the cross over his chest.

"From your lips to god's ears Rheiner," Therese said and also made a sign of the cross.

"Yes, well we best not linger," Rheiner said. "Till we meet again Frau Therese," he bowed. "Bleib sicher." He finished with a wink and a smile.

Therese nodded and gave him a salute. She took the shield from me as Rheiner plucked his helmet from the soldier beside him. He headed back but paused to cuffed the one who spoke across the face. A trickle of blood ran from the man's lip but Rheiner said nothing to him. The rest followed, and the locked thunked behind them.

Therese sighed and turned around to the door we'd come from. Without a word, she headed back. Sylvia motioned for me to follow as she took up the rear, locking the door behind us as we walked back through the empty hallways.

I had so many questions. Who were those Germans, why were we talking with them? What communications? What about ending the war? Another cease fire? Who was Zakeem and what did he do to earn such a scornful reaction for everyone?

Chapter 4

Abandoned

We arrived at the exit after a shorter walk than before and fewer turns. Which just added to my list of questions, *It took twenty minutes to get to the circle. How did we get back so soon?* but I held my tongue. Lady Therese opened the door to a soft glow against the wall of the tower and the crackle of wood. *More questions.* Lady Therese and Sylvia exchanged a furrowed brow frown that told me this wasn't something they expected..

"Out," Therese ordered. Sylvia grabbed my arm and stepped through. The shift in gravity took my feet a second to reorient and made my stomach flip. She pulled me behind a wall and pressed a hand to my chest.

"What's goi-"

"Shh," She hissed.

Lady Therese pulled the boulder back over the door and turned to the empty archway.

"Stay here," she said in a quiet tone and stepped beyond the doorway. An act that still made me tense up for the shot to end her every time.

I noticed a flickering light on the wall opposite of me and followed it back to a peephole. Sylvia moved over to peek around the door frame and I turned to look through the peephole.

A blonde man sat shivering alone in the dark with his hands over a fire. His uniform was stained with mud and blood, his or another's I couldn't tell. He poked at the fire encouraging it to grow with a white stick. After putting the stick down, he blew on his hands and held them closer to the fire. Close enough for the flames to lick his palms but he didn't pull back or even wince.

"Hail friend." Lady Therese said as she approached the man from the side so he would see her.

"You ain't mah friend," the man said with a rough southern American accent. His hands rubbed together more, and his teeth chattered.

"Perhaps not, but we are allies." Lady Therese said and pointed to the colours on his uniform, then to her own. Her voice was smooth and calm like she'd practiced this a hundred times or more. She approached him like he was a stag that would bolt if she moved too quick.

"Huh, you don't act like it," the man grumbled. "No one does." He stoked the fire again with what I realized was a bone. The flames grew higher, he dropped the bone into the burning pile and held his hands closer. The flames danced against his palms and I winced away, expecting to see his skin blister and boil. When I glanced back they were unharmed in the flames.

"It's dangerous to have a fire out here in the dark. Come with me, I'll get you back amongst friends," she said stepping within a few feet of the man. "You can trust me." She held her hand out to him.

"He said you'd say that." The man's words made Therese stiffen. For a moment, she didn't move a muscle. With a tentative step back, she scanned the desolate waste around the broken tower. I saw the terror in her eyes and wondered what was going through her mind.

"Who told you that?" Therese asked and rested her wrist on a handle at her hip. *A weapon? Like Sylvia's maybe?* I glanced over at Sylvia who watched things unfold too. When I looked back the man glared at Therese and I gasped as his eyes flickered with flames from within. *Was he a demon?*

"You know. He was the only one to help me. He didn't abandon me. Like the rest of you did." His nose flared. He picked something from the snow up and held it tight in his hand as he got to his feet. The fire rose with him. "You left me for dead like the rest of them!" He pointed towards the trenches where I could see the fog still lingered.

"Lady Therese." Sylvia sprinted out past the door frame.

"Stay back," Therese ordered. Sylvia stopped in her tracks and pulled her blade free. The man's eyes shifted from Therese to Sylvia and back. His chest heaved and his breath came out in steamy waves despite his shivers.

"He said you'd leave me behind again. Or kill me to take it back." He looked at his hand clenched tight around something I couldn't make out.

"He's wrong. I don't want to kill you," Lady Therese said. "I want to help you, please hear me out."

"You're lying!" He shouted, and the fire grew to match his shoulder. "He told me you'd lie. I saw what you did to him."

"She didn't-" Sylvia added.

"Shut up and DIE!" He roared and the flames in his eyes grew brighter. He waved his hand and the tower of fire shot out as if an extension of his hand. Sylvia dove to the ground and the flame arched over her. She was up just as fast and charged.

"Wait, Sylvia," Therese shouted. But it was too late, Sylvia slashed at the man. I thought she'd missed, but blood soaked the man's uniform and sprayed against Sylvia's arm. It burst into bright blue flames and scorched his uniform. Sylvia screamed as the flames arched up her arm. She dropped and rolled on the snow covered ground. The man's uniform burned open to reveal the healed wound, or more accurately the burn mark that sealed it from shoulder to hip.

"Sylvia" Therese ran to help.

I stepped back and forced myself to take a breath. *What am I doing? I can't just sit around. I have to do something? But what can I do against that?* My heart pounded against my chest as I searched for something to work with. The fire grew brighter beyond the wall and a couple bangs rang out. I looked back and saw blue flames erupt from the man's calves.

Therese lowered her revolver. "Please, there is no reason to fight." She begged. "If you would just listen to me."

Handgun. I pulled mine free and stepped from the door frame.

"Hey!" I shouted. "Hey, asshole." I ran along the wall to get him looking further away from Sylvia. She had put the fire out and her hand searched in the snow.

He turned on me with a wide firey snarl, flames licked out past teeth as black as coal. I felt the heat despite the distance as I levelled my gun at him, and my foot caught on something under the snow. I fell face first into a frozen puddle. I pushed up and looked back while blood poured from my nose, to see a shell lodged in the ground, it was half my size.

The man's laugh turned my blood to ash. "Don't worry little man. I'll end it for you." He took a deep breath. I curled into a ball, what else could I do? My death was here and all I could do was pray the shell went off before the flames got through my clothes. I tensed as the heat surrounded me.

"Stay down." Therese's voice ordered as she tackled and rolled a few feet with me. She got up and held her shield against the flames.

I pushed up. "There's a shel-" she shoved me back to the ground.

"Down!" She ordered again.

The shell went off with an ear shattering explosion that lit up the sky like day. It would wake anyone in the nearby trenches as the earth rumbled. Dirt and debris flew threw the air and rain down tainting the snow coated landscape.

It took several seconds for me to realize I was still alive. The ringing in my ears wasn't the call of an angel and nor were the spots in my vision the light at the end of the tunnel.

The shell had decimated what was left of the tower and the surrounding area. I couldn't see Sylvia but the man got to his feet slowly on the other side of a crater. Most of his uniform had been burnt or blown off. His lean muscular form was covered in fresh burn scars, his hair mere singed patches.

A tug on the back of my uniform brought my attention up. Therese stood tall and unscathed from the explosion.

"To your feet Pepper," she ordered and tugged at my uniform again. She closed an eye as her breath caught. "Now," she added through clenched teeth

I scrambled to get back on my feet and holstered my gun while I looked around. The shell had carved a hole in the earth, but from where Lady Therese stood there was an undisturbed slice, aside from the fresh dirt.

I stood slack jawed and wide eyed. *Was that a miracle?* I tried to ask but stumbled over my words and only got out "Wha."

"Later," she replied. Her eyes moved and I followed them to some shifting dirt on the edge of the crater. "Check on Sylvia," she ordered before she unslung her rifle and placed it on the ground.

I looked from her to the burnt man who held his head. *How were they alive?* I wondered looking around for an explanation while I skirted the crater towards Sylvia.

Lady Therese walked straight through the crater. "It need not be like this," she pleaded, "We can help you," she continued like she was trying to coax an injured animal. "We didn't abandon you. How can I show you I'm not lying?"

I dug the dirt off Sylvia in quick handfuls until she could push herself up and gasp for air.

"Are you hurt?" I asked while I dug more and brushed the dirt off her.

"What?" She shouted.

"Are you all right?" I shouted back. She thought for a second and nodded.

"I'm alive." She winced and held her chest. "A few broken ribs never killed anyone."

"Unless it punctures your lungs or gets infected," I added and scooped some snow up to hold against a burn on her arm. She hissed through clenched teeth but didn't pull back.

"Just pray it doesn't come to that," she replied. "Lady Therese?"

I looked past her to the crater as chunks of fire burst around Therese's shield without so much as a singe to the metal. "She's okay."

"She's always okay," Sylvia grunted and stumbled to stand.

"You're injured, stay down."

She shook her head and stumbled another step forward before she fell to her knees. Her hand dug into the dirt and she pulled the broken blade out. "Not yet." She gritted her teeth and got to her feet again taking a slow breath. Tears formed in her eyes but she looked skyward and blinked them away.

Her gloved hand lurked forward and snatched something from the air with a ting. She winced, a whimper escaping her throat.

"In the crater," she ordered and jumped down.

I dove in as a bullet bit the ground nearby. "Who's shooting?"

"Allies, here." She handed me her satchel. "Pop a flare off so they can see." I dug into the bag past a notebook stuffed with photos, bandages, a collection of tags and found the wide mouthed gun and shot it into the night sky. The bright flare gave more light than the burnt man did. His flames sputtered across the ground and caught fallen trees, tattered clothes, and bodies on fire. Spark sputtered around him as the shots focused on him, none landed. He threw a ball of flames at Lady Therese's feet and the stones melted forcing her to take a step back. Then turned on the trenches.

"All of you will burn!" He roared and took another deep breath, flame shot from his lips across the desolate field. It arched across the trench and caught some troops, a lantern burst and the fire spread. People screamed and ran while others tried to douse the flames with piss buckets or blankets. Others threw ammo and explosives away from the spreading flames.

"Stop this," Therese ordered, the man turned back to her. "They are not your enemy."

"Everyone is my enemy," he replied. "They all left me to die, or tried to kill me. Now they will all fear me," he said when flames enveloped his entire body. "I am a god!" he laughed.

"Where's your gun," Sylvia said as she climbed back over the edge of the crater. "Shoot him."

"Uh, bu-" I dropped the flare and pulled my gun out again. "Bullets don't work on him."

"Just do it," she said and winced as she got to her feet. She headed towards the trenches.

"You don't want this," Lady Therese said. "A legacy of pain and fear? You can do *so* much good. Please, before it's too late."

I stood in the crater and took aim, a few deep breaths. He hasn't noticed me. *Centre mass.* I closed my eyes and pulled the trigger. The shot kicked back and knocked me off my feet and a bolt of light screamed from the barrel into his shoulder and spun him to the side. Jonas never told me they were Blessed rounds.

I blinked as blood poured from his shoulder and he almost dropped what he'd been holding. He looked at his arm, then glared death at me. His eyes were lost in the cloak of fire but I still felt them on me.

"You dare," he raised his arms, all the flames grew into pillars on the battlefield.

I scurried back, the soft ground making it hard to get traction. Sylvia rushed the man from behind slashed his hand clean off. The fires died. She spun and buried her blade in the man's back. Blood dripped from the invisible blade that stuck out his chest.

His eyes looked the blade over confused repeatedly as if to ask where it came from, or why it was there. He looked to his hand on the ground and coughed up blood, he gasped for air and let out an agonized cry. His remaining hand gripped the blade and tried to pull it out.

I hurried over as Sylvia pulled the blade back. He slumped to his knees coughing up more blood.

Lady Therese stepped up to him while tears ran down his scarred face, she brushed them away as blood foamed from the wound in his chest. "It's okay," she cooed to him and knelt with him.

"It's" he gasped. "It's cold. Mama, it's... cold," he sputtered. Therese cradled his head in her shoulder petting his head.

"Shhh, it okay. You are safe now." She said and whispered something to him, his form went limp and I watched him take his last breath.

Sylvia kept her back to the man as she cleaned the hilt of her blade and grumbled.

I stepped closer and reached a handout. "Are you-"

"I'm fine," she snapped then stuffed her blade back into the sheath with a jerk and walked over to the burnt man's hand

Therese laid the burnt man on the ground and brushed her hand over his face. I looked down at this man who had been burnt, shot, stabbed and felt betrayed by his fellow man. My stomach sank into emptiness as I looked over the field wondering how many others had died feeling the same. My throat tightened, and my legs trembled before I could take a few ragged breaths to control things.

Sylvia's hand slapped to my chest. "Here." I held my hand out, and she dropped a brass lighter into my hand.

"What's this?"

"It's a Relic," she said. and unclasped her cloak to cover the naked burnt man.

"His Relic," Therese said as she finished her prayer over him. She stood with tears falling from her eyes and blood on her shoulder. "Go get Jonas. We won't leave our brother for the harvesters."

Chapter 5

Even

Jonas and I returned with a stretcher for the burnt man. We got back to the trenches as the sky began to brighten. The man was heavy and though I struggled I kept up with Jonas as we made it back to the grove. Lady Therese asked Sylvia to go ahead so the maids were ready when we got there.

We laid the stretcher on a table and stepped back as the maids prepared the body. They said nothing when they pulled the cloak away or washed the blood from his burnt face and chest. But I could see the horror in their eyes. Lady Therese pulled Jonas aside.

"Go to the airfield, prepare for us to leave tomorrow morning." He nodded and jogged away from the front lines. "Sylvia, please radio ahead to Rome. Let them know we are coming."

"Yes sir," Sylvia said, she headed to the large tent.

My eyes drifted from Lady Therese to the maids washing the burnt man's body and coated his twisted skin in a thick layer of sweet floral scented goo. It came in half-sized quarter casks.

A hand squeezed my shoulder. I straightened my stance.

"Relax Pepper," Lady Therese said. "It's okay to mourn."

"Mourn? He tried to kill us." I replied.

"True. But he wasn't always like that. He was a child at one point, loved and was likely loved too. He laughed, played and hoped for a good life," she sighed. "But this world has a way of corrupting." She patted my shoulder. "When they finish, come see me," she said, then limped towards her tent. She was trying to hide it but every few steps I noticed a shift in her gape

I watched as they wrapped strips of linen around his body. One maid came over to me.

"What was his name?" She asked with an Italian accent, notepad in her washed hands.

"I... I don't know," I replied after thinking back a moment. "Check his tags?"

"He didn't have any. I thought Lady Therese gave them to you."

I shook my head.

"How sad." She left me to help the others wrap his head. They pulled a sheet over him and left.

I stood with the remains of an unknown soldier, one of countless. This one was lucky enough to get buried. How many others were picked apart by harvesters or worse? Lady Therese words echoed in my ear and a lump caught in my throat. I swallowed it down so I could speak.

"I'm sorry," was all I could get out. It felt paltry and almost hollow, though I meant it. I took a deep breath and headed to Lady Therese's tent. A maid rushed out of her tent as I approached. Soft cries of pain came from inside the tent and I wanted to rush in but remembered last time.

"Permission to enter?" I asked as a nurse brushed past me with her arms full grey bandages. There were some hushed words and a pause.

"Enter."

I pushed the flap back and stepped in to see both Sylvia and Lady Therese with nurses tending to them. One wrapped the grey cloth bandages up Therese arm and shoulder while another re-set her fingers. A third ground up some herbs into a paste and put them on blisters across her shoulder.

Sylvia had her own batch of grainy paste being spread over her arm and thigh while a maid stitched her side. A chunk of bloody metal sat on a plate beside her. Once finished, she clipped old stitches from Sylvia's shoulder.

Light scars dotted Sylvia's olive skin. She held her hair back with her free hand. Her unscathed leg bounced while the nurses worked quick.

Lady Therese turned once her black and blue torso was wrapped in grey bandages. Red runes came to life as she took a deep breath. "That's better." She sighed and let a maid continue wrapping her hand and wrap the smeared paste.

"Now then Pepper. After a night like this, you likely have a few questions," Therese said and motioned to a chair.

"No," I replied and sat down.

Lady Therese and Sylvia exchanged a look with raised eyebrows then looked at me. "You don't?"

"No, I have more than a few fucking questions." I snapped. "For starters," I reached into my pocket and pulled the brass lighter out. "What is a Relic? Why are they important?" I said and tossed it to the floor. "Who were those Germans? Who is Zakeem? What's this about ending the war? Why did we let the harvesters have some people but not that man?" I pointed out the tent. "The magic door, those hallways, that room, your shield, that blade? Just... what to everything!"

Sylvia laughed for a second but a wince cut it short.

Lady Therese smiled towards Sylvia. "I'd say we shattered his world." Sylvia nodded. "When they are finished, can you make us some tea? This will take a while." Sylvia nodded again and Therese turned back to me. "First off, pick that Lighter up. It is a Relic and you will treat it with dignity." She ordered.

I looked at the lighter on the rug then to her. Her blue eyes locked on mine, daring me to challenge her.

"Yes, sir," I said and bent to pick it up. I put it on a nearby table because I didn't want it back in my pocket.

"Second. Return the stone Jonas gave you. It will need to charge so we can use it again." She motioned back to the table.

I patted my pockets and found the stone. It was dull and grey now. "Add that to the list of questions," I said and put it by the lighter then sat back down.

"That is fair." She replied. Sylvia slipped a shirt on and headed out of the tent with the maids.

"Now. Where would you like me to start?" She asked and stepped over behind a curtain to slip into a shirt and a fresh pair of pants.

I still think pants look weird on women.

"The beginning seems like a great place."

"Hmmm, well the beginning could be hundreds of years ago with the first Relic, but I'll start as close as I can." She returned to her seat.

"I was eight when the order found me. They were travelling through my home near the Baltic sea. They were on their way to Sweden, but Andreas, he was the rifleman then, saw me release a wolf from one of my father's traps."

"A wolf? That's dangerous."

"For most, yes. Have you never noticed that animals react well to you when they don't to others?"

I shook my head. "I'm a city kid, not a lot of animals around."

"No stray dogs or cats?"

"Nope, more like rats and cockroaches."

"Did they give you trouble?"

"No."

Therese closed her eyes for a second and tilted her head as if that made her point.

"Being in tune with animals is a common quality of Blessed. So Andreas and two others stayed to test me. I passed, and they paid my parents. That was the last time I saw them." She paused, on purpose or to collect herself I couldn't tell. But I felt like I should say something.

Sylvia returned with a tray of tea and a couple bowls of warm oatmeal. My stomach grumbled at the sight and I ate while Lady Therese continued.

"I became a squire and worked with different knights to find out which Relic would choose me."

"Which one did you end up with?"

"None. No Relic chose me. I could use them all, but not like their Chosen. Which, while rare, is not unheard of. Sometimes it just takes more time with Relics for them to choose you."

I sipped my tea with a maple aftertaste. It was odd, but comforting I assumed they used it because pure sugar was scarce. I began to wonder what this story had to do with any of my questions.

"They were doing the same with Zakeem."

Sylvia spit at the name. *That's what it has to do.*

"He was a boy from Egypt and hated the cold. But excelled with the rifle. He kept saying that it was his chosen Relic. But Andreas kept saying he wasn't good enough and sent him to work with another Knight. Looking back, I guess this is where it started." She sighed.

"The war broke out when I was thirteen and though the knights didn't participate at first. It didn't take long. Shortly after my fourteenth birthday, we were on the front line, but only to help the allies defend and withdraw. It was frustrating, to say the least. There were a lot of fights back then," she sipped her tea.

"Zakeem was always on the side for attacking. There was a lust for blood in his eyes and I think Andreas recognized it. You see, Andreas had a darkness about him in the moment he pulled the trigger. But he pulled himself back from it. It was a tool for him, not a fuel to keep him going. Anyway, I digress." She said with a wave of her hand.

"We finally got the chance to assault a German hill and..." Lady Therese drew a ragged breath. "I was with Andreas, providing cover.

I don't know how it went down for the others. But as I killed my first man Andreas got hit, not by a fluke. They knew exactly where we were. He shielded me told me to be quiet, I stayed there until dusk." Lady Therese paused and lifted a shaky cup to her lips. The sip helped steady her.

"They all died. Zamira, Micheil, Kidane, Avery, Lorie, Kori, Sarjeet, Izabella, Shelly. Names that mean nothing to you, but were family to me. All dead."

"And Zakeem killed them?" I asked.

Therese let out a snort of laughter. "No. But he did betray us. The Germans knew we were coming and prepared. They wanted the Relics. I found the Sword shattered a few feet from what was left of Commander Zamira. They couldn't lift the shield, so they sent Zakeem back for it." She paused again, this time to top up her cup of tea.

"Did you kill him?" I asked

"He wouldn't still be an issue if she had." Sylvia pointed out.

"Right." I blushed having been so caught up in the story I forgot my question. "Well, what did you do?"

"I didn't think about it at first, not until I realized how composed and unscathed, no blood or dirt on his uniform. I was a sobbing dirty mess and had Andreas blood crusted my clothes. I demanded an explanation. To his credit, he did not lie to me. He confessed and complained about the snipers forgetting to grab the rifle when they confirmed Andreas' death."

"So you shot him, right?" He sounded like one of the few that deserved a bullet.

"I tried, but the Rifle is very dangerous. Even in a Blesseds hands, it can backfire as much as hit a target. Andreas would only allow me to fire when he touched the rifle too. I pulled the trigger when he lunged at me. I hit him, but the round came back and almost killed me." She pulled the neck of her shirt back to show the scar on her shoulder.

"As he screamed I ran for my life, back to allied forces. Who were too scared to approach me at first." She laughed and shook her head. "I can't blame them. A blood soaked child coming from no-man's-land with a shield, a broken sword and a rifle as big as herself." Her eyes lingered on her tea a moment.

Jonas walked into the tent. "The airfield will have two planes fueled and ready for the morning." He said.

"Two planes?" I asked

"We are taking the body to Rome. Where it will be cremated, and placed in the Knights vault. All Blessed are given this honour."

"Even though he tried to kill us?" I asked.

"Yes, *All* Blessed are given this opportunity."

"Even the Germans?"

"All Blessed."

"Even Zakeem."

She paused and her eyes locked onto mine and I regretted mentioning the name. "That is not for me to determine." She said and grabbed a slice of toast from the tray Sylvia brought in.

"Right, well if you are just breaking the boy in. I will head to the range." Jonas said and picked up a piece of toast. "Be gentle with him ladies." He laughed.

The rest of the morning Lady Therese answered my questions. She explained how Sylvia and Jonas became squires. A church near the heel of Italy found Sylvia. Jonas lifted the shield after she stopped performing first aid on a man when he Medics had arrived.

Captain Rheiner was the leader of the German Knights. He'd been hunting Therese for years when he got more Knights. When Sylvia showed up the two captured Rheiner and explained their plan to him. It took meeting a few times to convince him to work with Therese.

He knew of commanders in both the German and Russian chains sick of the war and wanted to end it. But were too scared of losing face if they called for surrender. Therese knew of a dozen commanders with the Allies that felt the same way. The letter she gave over was for those Commanders hoping for a cease fire and to start peace talks.

I went to bed with a strained headache. There was still more to explain about the Relics, but Lady Therese said that would have to wait for Rome. The wind rustled the walls of my tent as I crawled under the covers.

I awoke when a maid brought in a jug of water and towel sitting up once she left. With the splash of warm water on my face, I looked in the mirror to see I needed to shave. It wasn't a daily hassle for me, so I didn't mind. I pulled the shaving kit out of the armoire with a fresh pair of underwear and pants, after a quick wash and dry I put them on.

With soap lather in hand, I rubbed my face. It wasn't the regular stuff, this had a soft cedar scent. I put the razor together and dragged it along my cheek a few times. The simple ritual helped my headache. It distracted me from the craziness of the days' events, from the sight of the burnt man's corpse, from the fear of the coming night.

The flap of my tent opened and Sylvia stepped in with a basket hooked on her arm. I froze as her eyes landed on me, half naked with half my face covered in suds. They did a quick once over and my cheeks flush. I hoped shaving kept it from being too obvious, I turned away from her gaze to grab a towel and slung it over my shoulder. At least it offered me some cover.

"Uh, sorry." She said with a smile. "I should have knocked."

"That's all right," I lied. "I was just shaving." My eyes returned to the mirror, washed the razor and took a deep breath.

"I can see that."

"What can I help you with?" I asked.

"I wanted to make sure you didn't miss supper," she said. "And I did some baking today, I thought you'd like some fresh biscuits." She pulled the cloth back on the basket revealing a dozen fluffy golden buttermilk biscuits.

"You know how to bake?" I continued to shave and side eyed the biscuits.

"No."

I stopped and looked from her to the food and back again. "Are they magic biscuits?"

She laughed and shook her head. "Heavens no, Magic food tastes horrible. It nutritious but you won't want to eat it."

"Okay?" I said and glanced between the basket and her face again. The corners of her lips curled in the slightest smile and her light green eyes tried to sparkle. It felt cold though like she was too jaded to find much wonder in the world. But she was trying, and that made me smile too.

"It's something I picked up last night." She added and plucked a couple of biscuits to put them on top of a napkin and set on the nearby table.

"Last night? Was that before or after the patrol and attack?" I finished shaving and splashed water on my face, drying it with the towel.

"It's something Daniel did back home to calm down. Seems it still works."

I blinked at her explanation. "What?"

"The Blessed man from last night. His name was Daniel." She said.

"How do you know that? Did you find his dog tags?"

She shook her head and her smile faded. "When I take a life with my sword... I learn about them, memories, personality, skills." The fingers on her left hand twitched until she rubbed them with her other hand. "I never picked up a guitar but I could play eight or nine different songs."

"That's..." I searched for the right word.

"Snazzy?" she replied and her eyes looked away.

"Horrible." I corrected. Her eyes returned to me. "How... how do you cope with it?" I turned to my shirt and slipped it on, buttoning while she spoke.

"I do what I can. Daniel liked to bake. It was one of the few times his mother wasn't drinking." She said and rubbed her hands more.

"Wow, that's... a lot to take in." I said and turned back to see tears streaking her cheeks.

"It is, and I don't know how I do it every day. It's a struggle, I remind myself I bake not for myself but for Daniel. I play guitar to soothe Alicia and Bram," she brushed the tears from her face. "And I have no one to confide in because Lady Therese thinks we are blessed, but I feel we are cursed." She said as she sobbed

Sylvia had been many things in the brief time I knew her. A strict commander, a dedicated follower, a calculated killer, but at that moment I realized she was as scared as me, if not more. As sick of the war as I and I'd only been here for a few months.

"I'm sorry." She sniffled. "Daniel was rather emotional and blunt." She tried to clear the tears from her eyes. "I don't normally do this."

I stood there for a long moment racking my mind. Then offered her my towel. "I'd like to say it'll be all right, but I don't want to lie to you," I said trying to keep my own tears back. "But we've got each other to count on. If you ever need to let out some steam, or talk, or try new baking recipes, or whatever. I'll do what I can, even if it's just be there."

Sylvia took the towel, drying her face with a laugh. "Come now, I'm the Squire. I should say that to you, Initiate." She smiled and rubbed the snot from her nose on the towel then handed it back.

"Yeah, but you've been at this longer. So my shoulders are free of bullshit."

"That's not what the truth seat showed us last night." She laughed and handed the towel back.

"Wait what? You guys had me sit in a truth seat?" I asked, feeling offended.

"We needed to know about you." She smiled, and I rolled my eyes.

"Couldn't have just asked me?"

"Would you have told us as much as you did?" I shook my head and pursed my lips. "That's why we did it." She giggled, and the sound tickled my ears, I couldn't help but smile.

"Well, I guess with Daniel's help, we are even." I chuckled and tossed the towel over the armoire door.

"Yes, I suppose we are." She smiled again. "Come, let's head for supper."

Chapter 6
Mines in the Field

THINGS MOVED RATHER fast after that. Supper was potato soup with onions and buttered cabbage. Dessert was bread with raspberry jam, a standard ration. Then onto another patrol, this time I shadowed Jonas

"Best get used to being my squire," Jonas said with an air of playfulness. I took it as a joke, but he made me do everything but wipe his ass. He joked about getting me to do it, it better have been a joke.

We moved down the trench all night as Jonas spoke in private to commanders. He made me stand outside the offices and got in my face if I stepped a few feet away to warm up by a fire. It was usually something about military bearings or chain of command. But Lady Therese had said we aren't part of the military, so I didn't get why he got so perturbed.

When they called stand-to Jonas had me sit with the ammo monkey's, the youngest recruits that no one trusted with a rifle, although I was ten years their senior.

The hair on my neck stood straight for the whole hour as it always did. Once the stand down was given, we made our way to a lorry, I climbed in the back and Jonas spoke to the driver. It had been a long night, and I was looking forward to something hot to eat and my cot.

I tucked my hands into my pits as the engine fired up, Jonas jumped into the back and slapped my thigh as he sat beside me. "You are in for a treat today Dodger." He leaned back against the canvas wall and the lorry rumbled down the road.

"Why's that?" I asked after he didn't continue.

"We are heading to Rome. You get to see the Knights hall first hand. Took me a year to see it when I first joined and we took the train there."

"I've been on trains before," I replied.

"We aren't taking a train this time," Jonas smirked. "We're flying."

"Is it some kind of Relic?"

Jonas shook his head and pulled out his flask and took a sip. "No. It's the marvel of man's creativity."

"An Aeroplane? I thought they only used those for scouting or raids?"

"Far from it my boy. Like all of man's innovations, it's been used for a number of years now. Dropping bombs, dog fights, scouting and transport of critical information. I tell you planes are the future of humanity." He said tucking his flask back in his jacket.

"H-how high do they get?"

"Thousands of feet in the air." He looked out the back of the truck. "So high that people look like ants."

"So you've flown one?" I asked. My fingers fidgeted with a button on my jacket.

"No, Lady Therese and Sylvia have been trained. The hope is that after the war we Knights can get around the world quicker than ever before. Maybe even to North America." He shrugged.

The squeal of the lorries breaks made me jump.

"Here we are," Jonas said and jumped out the back of the truck, I followed onto a fog covered road. The truck rumbled off and Jonas lead me down the foggy road. As the sun rose, the fog began to lift and the open field came into view. Engines roared to life, I turned to see a few dozen planes lined along the side of the field. Two with their engines rumbling sat at the far side.

A procession carried Daniel's body to a hatch in the back of one. Sylvia climbed into the cockpit of the airship, while Lady Therese already sat in the other.

"Come on, we're late," Jonas said, and we ran the rest of the way. Someone came out to meet us with thick jackets and hats that had goggles. I noticed Sylvia's plane had the familiar target painted on the side but Lady Therese's plane was bare of any military marks, just the Owl crest on the tail.

"What are you doing here Lieutenant Bishop?" Jonas said with a casual salute to a man in his forties. He looked like he was headed to the other planes just being spun up that lined the airfield.

"Flying escort." The man replied before jogging to a plane with a blue nose.

"I wouldn't want anyone else," Jonas replied and turned to me. "You get in with Therese," He pointed as we headed towards the planes.

"But-" I started as the roar of more engines drowned out my words

"Can't hear you," he tapped his ear "Get going." Jonas shoved me towards the white plane with black stripes. He climbed up into the gunner seat and gave a pat to Sylvia's shoulder. Their engine picked up, and the plane pulled away.

"Come on Pepper," Therese shouted over the engine.

I took deep breaths and pulled the goggles down and tried to swallow my fears.

"You've got this" I whispered to myself and climbed up into the second seat. I couldn't call this one a gunner seat as there was no gun.

As I sat down Lady Therese revved the engine and the plane lurched forward. I gripped onto the seat with one hand and the other gripped a handle. My stomach dropped into my seat and I leaned forward as the plane rumbled. The hand on my seat came up and covered my mouth, I fought to hold my lunch back.

"It won't be so bad when we get in the air," Therese said as the plane lifted off the ground. My stomach bounced off my seat and came back up. I heaved what little I had and then dry heaved a few more times. For the first time, I was happy for the mud that caked my boots.

"Are you okay?" Lady Therese shouted.

I nodded my head and spit onto the floor of the plane. "I think I'll live."

"There is a thermos of chamomile tea under your seat. It should help." She said

I lifted my head and glanced over the edge of the cockpit just as another plane zipped by us. I clenched my eyes tight and hid my head and shook it furiously. *No no no no no.*

"Thanks," I groaned. "I'll get to it."

"Don't drink it too fast. We've got a full day of flying and no pit stops." I nodded again and fought with my stomach to keep it from heaving any more. The cold air brushed my cheeks and swept the stench away, the thick wool jacket kept me warm despite the chill. It took me an hour to settle with my stomach. The occasional dips and shaking didn't help. By the time I sat up and looked out over the bright white clouds below our escort had turned home.

The fields of clouds stretched far and wide, it was serene. Aside from the roar of the engine, but I could drown out its steady tune. I dared to look down at what looked like the softest wool or rolls of creamy icing.

"Feeling better now?" Lady Therese asked.

I looked forward and saw her rosy cheeks below goggles that framed her blue eyes in small mirrors. She tapped her chin, it took me a second to get what she meant. I wiped my mouth with the back of my sleeve and nodded to her.

"The first flight is always the hardest." She smiled. "Before long you'll be flying yourself."

"You think so?" I asked and looked down at the clouds again. A hole in them made me realize just how high up we were. Roads stretched through fields like threads on a quilt dotted with grazing animals. My vision blurred and my stomach did another flip. I closed my eyes and leaned back into the seat taking deep breaths until it passed. I looked up at the bright blue sky, so clear and crisp. Then I reached under my seat, not daring to peek over the edge again, and pulled the thermos out.

"You want any?" I asked and poured some tea into the lid and took a gulp.

"After you have some."

I refilled the cup and put the cap back on when the plane shuddered violently. The cup slipped and splashed over my coat and lap as the engine sputtered and then died. The sting of hot tea was secondary to the silent dread that surrounded us.

"What... what's going on?" I asked.

"I'm not sure," Sylvia replied as she pulled levers and flipped switches. "The gages aren't moving."

"Are we going to crash?" I stood up and looked over her shoulder.

"No. I'll get it back," she said and turned the key. The engine rumbled for a second then sputtered dead again. "Damn." Lady Therese said and her hands went back over the instrument panel that I couldn't make sense of.

"What's the problem?" Sylvia shouted. Her plane a few dozen feet from ours.

"It's just a hiccup," Lady Therese shouted back. "We'll be okay." She added and turned the key again. This time the engine didn't make a sound. "Shit. We have to land. You go ahead. We'll catch up."

"Land? Land where? Is there an airfield nearby?" I asked.

Sylvia and Jonas exchanged looks. "Not till you are safe on the ground," Sylvia replied.

Lady Therese nodded. "Find something to hold on to Pepper. It's going to get bumpy."

I sat back and started to pray. "Please god. If we make it back in one piece, I'll be a good Christian, go to church, protect the hungry, feed the poor, clothe the beggar and donate to the children." Something about the prayer seemed off, but I didn't have the sense to correct it.

"Last ditch idea." Lady Therese said and pointed the nose of the plane down. The roaring wind drowned out my scream as we sank into the clouds. Her hands continued to work the panel. She smacked it and gave it a kick but still nothing. We punched through the cloud and barreled towards a thick forest. Lady Therese pulled hard at the stick and the nose pulled up and my heart jumped into my throat. We rose almost back up but levelled off before the clouds.

"Do you see a good place to land?" Lady Therese asked as she looked to the right.

"What's a good place?" I asked and looked left and behind us. "Like a road?" I asked as I spotted a dirt trail behind us.

"No, they are too rough, like an open field."

"There is a barn over there." I pointed. "Gotta be something right?"

"Hopefully." Lady Therese said, and the plane listed in that direction and pointed the nose down for a few seconds.

I tensed until we were level again. The trees grew closer as a field spotted with cows came into view just beyond the barn. I went back to the only thing I could do. Head down and hands pressed tight together. *Please god, I know we've never spoken and I've not been the best person. But I only stole to feed my mother. I worked extra that week to pay it back.* I had no idea what I was doing, but it was all I could think of.

"I hope you are praying for a smooth landing and not that we just survive," Lady Therese said.

"They say there are no atheists in foxholes, I believe that is true in a falling plane too," I replied.

"We aren't falling."

"The ground is getting closer and we don't have a way to stop it. This is falling!"

"It's just a Sunday glide," She joked, but I heard the tension in her voice. "There's the field." She pointed ahead where a grassy field waited with dozens of cattle grazing.

"What about the cows?"

"Hopefully, they are smart enough to move. Shit, we don't have the momentum." She pushed the nose down for a moment and I gripped the seat between my legs as the treetops banged along the underside of the plane. A loud thunk reverberated through the machine.

"I've never known a smart cow," I shouted back and clenched my teeth, then tucked my head low as the barn passed a few dozen feet below the plane. My breath caught and I waited for the worst. Our tires touched the ground, and we bounced, my face slammed into the back of Lady Therese's seat. I pressed my back against my seat and pushed against the frame to prevent a repeat. We bounced again and rumbled along the field as cattle moo'd in protest and their bells rattled when they scattered.

We came to a stop a dozen feet from a fence and both let out a huge sigh of relief.

"You okay?" She asked.

I nodded. "My face has been better but nothings broken," I replied and pried my hand off my seat to pull the broken goggles up to rub my eyes. Lady Therese got to her feet and waved her arms. Sylvia's plane rumbled around us once and then flew off.

Lady Therese let out a sigh of relief and sat on the edge of her cockpit. "See, told you. Nothing to worry about." She smiled and unstrapped her cap pulling it off with her goggles before she ran her hand through her hair, it unfurled and bounced down her back. She looked at me and bit her lip to stifle a laugh "You really lost your breakfast." She smiled and covered her mouth.

"Lunch, I didn't have breakfast this morning," I said and stood up from my seat, brushing what I could off my jacket before I took my cap and goggles off.

"Here," She pulled a handkerchief from her pocket. "How did you get it on your cheek?" She asked leaning closer to brush my cheek.

"I wonder how I get myself anywhere sometime." I sighed and took the handkerchief from her and brushed it over my pants after I unzipped the coat.

"Well, the tea almost makes you smell nice." She smiled and pulled her rifle and shield out from the cockpit. "We should go introduce ourselves and see where we are."

"Introduce ourselves? To who?" I looked around but only saw cows that kept a wide berth from us.

"There is a farmhouse near the forest. Hopefully, someone is home," She said and unzipped her jacket, she stepped onto the plane wing and then down to the ground.

I tucked her handkerchief into my shirt pocket and stepped onto the other wing and down into a cow patty.

"Ah, fuck!" I pulled free and wiped it off on the grass. "This day is just getting better and better," I grumbled.

"Careful, there are mines in this field too," Lady Therese said with a fit of giggles.

"Thank you, Sir." I groaned and jogged to catch up to her. Our feet rustled through the otherwise silent morning. I imagined the farm would look beautiful on a sunny summer day. The grey clouds and dying leaves did little to raise my spirit.

A tune caught my ear and pulled my gaze to Lady Therese as she smiled and crooned. It was something familiar but I couldn't remember the words or where I'd heard it, in passing somewhere? It brought a smile to my own lips as I enjoyed the melody.

Chapter 7

Unseasoned

The family was home and though Lady Therese had to explain who we were at the business end of a rifle. They welcomed us and gave us a ride into town. Therese tried to pay them but the father wouldn't take her money. Saying something like 'service to the church is its own payment.' He spoke three words of English so she had to translate everything from French for me.

We got to the nearby train station as the train pulled in and were on our way to Rome within the hour. We settled in a booth near the front of the train car.

Lady Therese sighed as she settled back in her seat. The shield tucked between the wall and her legs. "It will take us a week to get to Rome."

"That long, Sir?" I said. A man approached our booth keen to make use of the empty seats. But his smile faded when he saw our uniforms and he continued with a polite nod.

"Yes, that means less time for R and R, if any. They will be done by the time we get there." Lady Therese finished as she watched the people milling around in the station.

I raised an eyebrow and followed her sad gaze she wasn't looking at anyone in particular though. "Any time from the front is a welcomed reprieve if you ask me, Sir," I added.

"How right you are. I suppose a week long train ride through the country will be nice." Lady Therese replied without taking her eyes off the crowd.

The whistle blew, and the train crawled from the station, gathering speed.

"So what can I expect when we get to Rome?" I asked once we were on our way

"Depends when we get there. We'll miss the funeral and report. We may just turn around and have to go back. If not, I'd like you to try the Relics we have at hand and do some training. I might let you spend some time exploring Rome. Italy has some wonderful cuisine." She grinned. "There are libraries and architecture to explore, pretty much anything you want."

"What do you do?"

"There is a gelato store I always stop at near the Vatican, then it's off to read reports."

"Reports? On what?"

"Issues that might need our attention more than the war."

"What could be more pressing than the war?"

"A vampire breaking its contract, Yeti's terrorizing people, trolls straying from their nests." She said in a hushed tone.

"Wait, Vampires? Yetis? Trolls? Those are all fairy tales."

"That's what people are led to believe." Lady Therese continued and she leaned against the window frame.

"But you claim they are real?" I yawned.

"Yes. Cover your mouth," she said in a maternal tone, I felt a childish flush of embarrassment.

"We knights are supposed to protect people from monsters," her wistful gaze stared out the window while shadowy monsters danced and disappeared as quickly as the train's light created them. "Though I wonder who the monsters really are," she sighed.

"Pretty sure trolls are monsters," I chimed in.

"They can be nasty if their nest is threatened." She shrugged and put a finger to her lip when A woman paused beside our booth and hushed her two children. She looked over the seats before she gave a cautious glance to our booth.

"Please, feel free." I stood up and moved to sit beside Lady Therese.

"Oh, I wouldn't want to impose." She dismissed but her son slipped from her hand and plopped down across from Lady Therese, his blue-green eyes stared up at her.

"No trouble at all." Lady Therese motioned for her to sit.

"Thank you. It seems all other booths are full." She sighed in relief and she sat down. then lifted her infant from the basket she cradled and cooed it back to comfort. The strawberry blonde boy looked no older than six with a curious and innocent stare. His eyes shifted from Lady Therese to me and back to her and her sword.

"Have you two finished your term?" The woman asked with a smile.

"Uh, no." I looked to Lady Therese who seemed caught up in a staring contest with the boy. "We are..."

"On leave." Lady Therese answered without breaking her glance. "Headed to Rome to lay a colleague to rest."

The woman's eyes went wide, and she stammered. "O-oh, m-my. I'm terribly sorry to hear that," she pulled her son closer, forcing him to look away from Lady Therese while she protectively pet his head.

Colleague felt like quite the strong term to use for a man whose name I only knew because Sylvia held a part of him. He was as much a stranger to me as anyone else on the train.

"Thank you." Lady Therese gave a melancholy smile then sighed as she leaned back in her seat again. "You should catch some sleep Pepper."

"What about you, Sir?"

"We'll take shifts. You look like you need it more than me."

Part of me wanted to argue with her, I could stay awake. But the train bench was soft, and I found my eyelids growing heavier with each minute. I folded my jacket up like a pillow and rest my head on the bench's corner.

I woke a few hours later when the train pulled into the next stop. The scent of floral soap filled my nose as I stirred. I opened my eyes to see Lady Therese smile down at me.

"Enjoy your sleep?" She asked. It took me a second to realize my head was in her lap. I shot bolt up.

"S-sorry, sir. I don't know how I-" She put a hand out to stop me, but it didn't stop the flush from burning across my cheeks and up to my ears. I wished the train was in motion so I could jump free.

"You almost fell into the aisle," she explained. "So I let you lay down and get proper rest. Though sleeping that hard could be a problem." The corners of her lip curled in a warm maternal smile.

People shuffled off the train as I rubbed the sleep from my eyes, others trickled on shortly after. The mother was asleep with her infant back in the basket and her boy asleep across her lap.

"You can catch some sleep now Sir," I said and straightened as the train started again.

"How about we get a bite to eat first?" She said in a way that reminded me of my mother.

My stomach growled loud enough to make the young boy stir.

"I'll take that as a yes," she teased. "Go get washed up and I'll get us a seat in the dining cart." She finished before she picked the Shield up and headed towards the back of the train. I wondered if she went anywhere without the Shield as I left for the bathroom.

I splashed water on my face and neck for a quick wash. When I opened the door to leave a man with a red scarf up tucked up over his nose blocked the doorway. For a second I thought the train was being robbed. But his black suit was far too nice for a train robber, and this was Europe. That kind of thing didn't happen, did it? His grey eyes looked from me to a silver and gold pocket watch he held in the palm of his hand. The silver cover was embossed with a bird and had detailed etchings around the frame. He snapped it closed and glared from under a black fedora with an intensity that made me hesitate.

"It's free now," I said and squeezed past hoping to get away from him.

His eyes narrowed, and I felt the sneer even with his scarf covering his mouth. A cold shiver tensed the muscles through my body. He brushed past without a word and headed towards the front of the train.

I let myself breathe again unaware that I had held my breath, and watched him walk down the car. He didn't look back or pause as he walked into the next car.

Something about the man sat wrong with me, like a soreness I couldn't massage free. I did my best to shake it while I made my way to the Dining cart where I found Lady Therese sipping tea as she stared out the closest window with a worn letter in her hand.

She looked the furthest thing from a knight. Sure she was in a crisp uniform, and had a regalness about her. But with her hair down and gentleness to her face I would find it hard to picture her on the battlefield, had I not seen it for myself. She smiled to everyone despite the sadness in her eyes. If it was mourning for Daniel or a longing for something else I wasn't sure.

As I sat down across from her, she tucked the letter away and pushed a menu in my direction.

"What can I order?" I asked and tried to make sense of the menu.

"Whatever you want. Dinner is on me." Lady Therese said with a smile and took a sip of her tea. I shuffled closer and kicked something under the table.

"Sorry." Lady Therese said. I looked under to see her pull her shield back under her seat. I guess she doesn't go anywhere without it.

"It's okay," I said and tried to make sense of the menu. Duck Cumberland? Curry of Lamb Madrase? Pennepicure Pie? I understood a word in each of these but what they were was beyond me.

"Everything's so fancy. What's Mountain Trout Au Bleu?" I asked.

"That's just trout. Nothing too fancy about it." She shrugged and gave a nod to the waiter.

He made his way over with a tired smile. "What can I get you?" He asked with a notepad in hand

"I'll have what she's having, and a Cider," I said and handed him back the menu. He nodded and headed to the kitchen.

"You don't know what I'm having." Lady Therese said with a raised eyebrow.

"I don't know anything on the menu." I shrugged. "You seem to have good taste."

"Do I?" She smiled and locked eyes with me. I swallowed and my posture straightened.

I realized why she had this effect on me. It reminded me of when my mother had her moments of clarity. She could stare right into my soul with practiced ease and read my every thought like the Sunday Times. I looked away and cleared my throat.

"I.. I mean the meals back at camp have been fantastic. So I figured you know what's good here." I looked at the silverware that sat on the table waiting. I thought there was supposed to be more? But a simple fork, knife and spoon sat on either side of a plate that had seen its years.

"The rations are beyond my control. But the steaks were a treat. I am glad to hear you enjoyed it."

"It was the best meal I'd ever had."

"Really, Well you are in for a real treat then." She smirked.

"What did you order?"

"You'll find out when it gets here."

"Not one for giving time to prepare I see."

"Spontaneity can show the true character of man," She made it sound like an old quote

"Who said that?"

"Me," She smiled for a second. "I believe in testing Initiates. Seeing where they are weakest, so I can focus on their improvement."

"Where do I need to improve?" I asked, and the Waiter returned with my Cider. I thanked him and took a gulp of the cool sweet beverage.

"I can't say for sure. Jonas believes you ask too many questions when you are given orders. Sylvia thinks you lack the necessary grit to be on the front."

I knew Jonas thought of me as a fool at best or disposable at worst. But to hear what Sylvia thought twisted something inside of me. I could brush the sting from Jonas's opinion but Syliva's lingered and soured my drink. I couldn't help but wonder what Lady Therese thought. I chewed on my lip for a moment before I spoke. "What do you think?"

"I think you are unseasoned. A soldier struggling with the rules of society and the reality of the battlefield. Your mother meant the world to you and with her gone, you need to put your dedication in a new direction." I expected to feel indignant when she spoke of my mother. But her words hit a note that made me squirm in my seat. "If you dedicate yourself to the Order I believe you could turn into quite the respectable Knight."

I was about to reply when she leaned back in her seat, covered plates were placed before us. The waiter removed the covers to reveal a tiny roast chicken with potatoes and asparagus. Therese thanked the waiter before tending to her meal, she picked up her knife and fork to cut into its leg. Her hands looked rougher than any woman I'd met, yet still lean and agile.

"Chicken and potatoes? Not exactly what I'd call fine dining," I chuckled and cut my potatoes with a fork.

"It's a quail."

"Quail?" I spoke around the potato in my mouth. "What's that" I poked the bird with my fork.

"Don't speak with your mouth full." Therese scolded in her maternal tone. I pursed my lips as she shook her head. Her scolding had an annoying level of endearing to it. "It's a wild chicken. They taste better, try it."

I poked at the tiny roast bird a few more times before I cut a piece off, a tiny piece, and took a bite. It tasted like chicken. Chicken roasted with garlic and lemon. Buttery with a crisp skin.

"Well?" Therese asked as I savoured the taste.

"What?" I asked as I cut off a bigger piece.

"What do you think?" She smiled.

"I told you, you have good taste."

Chapter 8
Bloody Messenger

I ate the next piece and the next until the bird was nothing but bones.

Lady Therese ate with the level of grace she often displayed, our conversation lost to delicious food. Once I finished my drink, I leaned back with a content sigh. My legs stretched out, bumping into the Shield again.

"Sorry" I pulled my leg back.

Lady Therese dismissed it and she sipped her tea again.

I looked at the shield under the table for a long moment before I spoke again.

"So, what Relics are there?"

"Hmm?"

"Like what are the different Relics? I know of your Shield, the Sword, the Lighter, I think you mentioned a gun? Rheiners Helmet is one too right?"

She nodded and put her teacup down.

"Yes, his Helmet is a Relic," she said. "There are a little more than a dozen Relics. Aside from the five you've listed. There's the Sickle, the Needle, the Hammer, the Compass, the Bow, Torc, Gauntlet, Spear, Rings, Whip, and the Horn. That's not to say some haven't been created during the war."

"How do you create a Relic?"

Lady Therese shrugged. "No one knows. It's usually by chance. A Master Swordsman's desire to learn all the sword styles created the sword for instance. A few have been intentional like the Rifle and the Compass. But both creators died while presenting their work."

"Oh wow. How did they die?"

"Senoir Jonatán Madrid was killed demonstrating the Rifle," she said in a frank tone. "No one is sure if it's because of the Rifles curse, or if it was a suicide," she leaned back in her chair. "The first shot set his shop on fire and the second tore through his heart."

"Jesus. That's gruesome."

"Indeed," she shrugged. "Talha El Nour, on the other hand, died of heart failure. Though his mind was going in his old age. He created a gold and silver compass that could point to Relics and Blessed."

"Sounds like that could come in handy."

"It did. It's how they found me. The Relics chosen Blessed can find the exact spot of any Chosen or Relic. And it's quite discreet too. To most, it just looks like a pocket watch."

The tense chill returned and made the hair on my neck stand.

"A pocket watch?" I asked as Lady Therese sipped the last of her tea.

"Yes. Most wouldn't think twice about it."

"Does the pocket watch have a bird symbol on the silver side?"

Lady Therese locked eyes with me and this time I couldn't look away. Her eyes narrowed and her lips pursed, she chose her next words carefully.

"How do you know that Pepper?"

"I-I've seen it."

"When?" She asked in a bone chilling tone.

"H-here" I chattered and did everything to look away from her gaze. "On the train." I wasn't sure if the trembling came from the sudden coldness in her demeanour or the hints of fear that marked the edges of her voice.

"What?" Lady Therese pushed her seat back and stood up, revolver in hand. She slid the shield out from the table with her foot and kicked it up to her hand with practiced ease. The motion and the sudden presence of the gun made several of the other diners gasp and scatter.

"Why didn't you mention it earlier?" She practically growled

"I- I didn't know it was important" I stammered out and stood up too.

"Show me where you saw it."

"A man in a Black suit had it."

"What did his face look like?" She pressed me for more info and tucked her revolver back into its holster but kept a hand on the handle. It did little to calm those who had already seen it.

"I- I couldn't see it. It was hidden behind a-"

"Red scarf." Lady Therese finished and my eyes went wide. I knew it. Something was off about him. It wasn't just my imagination. That gut feeling I had about him came back and weakened my knees.

"Who is he?"

"Zakeem. He's following us." She said and her teeth clenched. "We have to find him before we reach the next station. Where is your gun?"

"Back with my bag."

"Ugh, Pepper. Never leave yourself defenceless." She shook her head and took the lead back to our seat. We stopped to check every person in a black coat, hat or shirt along the way.

Lady Therese grabbed a passing Porter. "How long until we reach the next station?" She asked while I pulled my bag down to dig my gun out. I tucked it into my waistband.

"Ah, twenty minutes Ma'am. I'm sorry we are a little behind schedule." He said.

"Tell the conductor to continue at half speed." She pulled him closer to whisper just loud enough I could hear. "There is a wanted man on board and if we reach the station, he'll get away."

The terror in man's wide eyes was clear. "R-right away Ma'am, I'll get him to stop the train before we arrive in the city."

"No, He'll catch on and escape into the night. Half speed only and be discreet about it."

He nodded, so she released him, he straightened his jacket then made his way towards the front of the train faster than I viewed as discreet.

"Nathaniel?" The Mother we'd sat with spoke up now that she was awake. She looked around wild eyed. "Nathaniel, where are you?" She stood up from her seat. "Have you seen my boy?" She asked, desperation in her voice.

I shook my head and looked to Lady Therese. She sighed and shook her head too. "No, but I'll help you look for him." She said with a smile. "Pepper you look towards the back of the train. If you come across either of them, do what you can."

"But-" I started, Lady Therese raised her hand to stop me.

"No time for it. Go." She said and took the mother's hand. "Where might he have gone too?" She asked and lead the woman towards the front of the train.

"Okay, Pepper you can do this." I coaxed. "He was headed to the front of the train. So you just have to find the boy." I went back from car to car calling for him and asking if anyone had seen him. After a few cars, I began to think it was a lost cause.

"I saw him." A girl about Nathaniel's age said after I asked her father.

"Where did you see him?" I asked.

"He was with a man in the last car." She pointed back.

"A man?"

"Yeah, in a white fur coat. He had a red scarf covering his face."

I closed my eyes and let out a strained sigh. Of course he was. A lump tried to choke the words from my mouth.

"Thank you, sweetie." I managed and looked to the back door of the car. I made my way over and each step took more effort than the last. My heart pounded in my ear, it took me a minute to remember to blink and breathe. I opened the door to see it wasn't the last car Just a half full luggage car. I still hand time, I looked back, should I get Lady Therese? But what if he hurts the boy or gets away in the meantime? I slapped myself.

"Man up." I grabbed my pistol and checked the round in the chamber before I pressed forward. I peeked into the window of the last car. The empty passenger car caused the knot in my stomach to tighten. It just screamed of a trap.

I saw Nathaniel speaking to the man in a white fur coat. Where did Zakeem get that? The boy seemed all right, in fact, he smiled and laughed as he licked a red lollipop. Zakeem put his hand on the boy's head. I couldn't wait any longer.

I threw the door open and shouted. "Zakeem." He tilted his head while he pet Nathaniels. He glanced back at me and I saw his wild silver eyes. Like a rabid wolf, hungry for blood.

"How disappointing, you aren't who I was expecting." He turned and snapped the compass closed. He spoke with a lisp and a middle eastern accent.

I kept my gun in hand, but hid it behind my back; I didn't want to frighten the boy as I stepped forward. My eyes locked on Zakeem, watching for any sudden movements. My jaw clenched so tight it was hard to speak.

"Nathaniel's mother is calling for him," I said and held my hand out. Nathaniel pouted and looked back to Zakeem.

"Always respect your mother, child. She'll love you more than anyone." Zakeem said and released the boy with a pat on the head. "You go with Mr. Greggor." He waved.

He knew my name, he knew who I was when we crossed paths. My jaw clenched tighter and I glared down the car. I gripped the handle of my gun tighter. He was going to answer some questions once Nathaniel was safe. So help me.

"Come, Nathaniel," I spoke as soft as I could through clenched teeth trying to keep him naive of the danger.

"Can I keep the lollipop?" Nathaniel asked Zakeem.

Zakeem laughed and knelt beside Nathaniel. "Of course. You run off now. Don't want to worry your sweet mother too much." He gave the boy a gentle push. "I'll visit you again soon." He looked back to me and I could feel his smug grin beyond the scarf. *Not if I have anything to say about it.* I thought.

"Okay," Nathaniel said and walked down the train car, not a care in the world as he licked at his lollipop. I was almost jealous of him. But I didn't dare take my eyes off Zakeem. He danced the compass back and forth between his fingers.

I took Nathaniel's hand and backed into the luggage car. I closed the door and set the gun down.

"Nathaniel I need you to wait here." I picked him up and sat him on a stack of luggage near the far side of the car. "I'll take you to your mom in a moment okay?"

"Hmm, can I keep the lollipop?" He asked holding it out.

"Yes you can. Just stay there." I picked my gun up and went back. This time I levelled my gun at him. Both hands, centre mass. I reminded myself.

"Okay Zakeem, what are you planning?" He stared silently out the back of the car. "Don't think you'll get away this time." I marched down the car ready for a fight.

But not an ambush.

Zakeem tackled me from a bench, smashed my head through a window and slammed the gun free on a seat. It hit the floor with us.. He reached for it. I kicked it across the car. I swung and felt a crunch under my knuckle when I hit his face. He stumbled back to his feet. I scrambled to mine ready to throw another haymaker. He pulled a luger and had it in my face before I could. I froze, staring into the infinitely dark barrel of the gun.

"So brave, so stupid. I should put you out of your misery." He pressed the barrel against my cheek and leaned in close. "Has she told you what she did?"

"She told me what you did," I growled and felt warmth trickle down the side of my neck. "You betrayed the Order," I growled.

"Hah, I brought about change. The meek always fear change." He laughed. "Stand up." He motioned with the gun and stood back.

I got to my feet and pressed a hand to my head and winced. A gash on the side of my head made my hair slick with blood. "Murder is change?" I replied. If he was going to kill me, I'd rather die with some moral high ground, its all I had.

"Yes," he hissed. "A changing of the guards." He motioned me back towards the baggage car. "A new era where Knights don't serve, but rule. People should pay us for protection. We have the power, they can't do much to stop us. Have you seen Therese in action?"

"*Lady* Therese." I corrected as I backed up.

"Hah, that whore has you trained well. You bark even when someone doesn't use her false title."

"She is a knight. It's the right title."

"It is, but she never earned it. There are no more Knights. Just idiots squabbling over titles. And one day I will kill her."

"Not if we kill you first." My back pressed to the door of the car.

"Hah, Therese's tried for years, Jonas is too arrogant, and Sylvia wouldn't dare. That leaves you." He laughed more. "And you've never even killed a man, I have nothing to fear from you." He pushed the gun into my stomach and I took a breath, bracing for the shot to come.

"I, on the other hand, I hold your life in my hand. I could take it at any moment."

"So why don't you?" I snapped.

He shrugged. "Maybe I want to let the next generation of Blessed make the call. Open the door."

It took me a second to realize what he meant. Then I reached behind me and fumbled to open the door.

"Maybe, I want you to give that bitch a message." He tugged down his scarf and I saw why he wore it. The cheek on one side was missing exposing the row of teeth in a sadistic one-sided grin. Beyond that was marred with burns and part of his ear was missing. "I'm coming."

He smiled a twisted and horrific smile that would haunt my dreams for years. He kicked me in the stomach and I doubled back into the luggage car. I hit the floor and knocked a stack of baggage over. I struggled to get out from under the pile as a loud 'thunk' made the car shudder. By the time I was on my feet Zakeem's uncoupled car trailed behind us by several feet. I watched as he walked back to his coat. It shimmered back to black, and he faded into the night.

Chapter 9
Iron and Diamonds

I MET LADY THERESE in the dining car with Nathaniel's mother. He ran to her and she swept him up in a tight embrace tears staining her cheeks. She checked him over thankful he was okay before she scolded him for doing this again, threatening to take him over her knee.

"You're injured." Lady Therese said. She stepped closer brushing her hand up my neck to find the wound. I winced and pulled away.

"Yeah, I got in a fight with Zakeem," I said and grabbed a cloth off a table and held it against my head.

"He let you live? Why?" She tilted her head.

"To pass on a message. He says he's coming." I sighed and sat on the table's edge.

"Thank you for finding my son." The boys' mother said and wrapped her arm around my neck.

"Careful," I warned trying to keep my blood from staining her clothes. "But you're welcome."

"Oh my, what happened?" She let go of Nathaniel's hand to sift through my hair.

"Uuuh," I looked to Lady Therese who shook her head. "I tripped."

"You tripped?" The mother raised an eyebrow, skeptical of my excuse. It was clear she was used to shoddy excuses and could see right through them.

"Y-yeah, I tripped and knocked over some luggage, right, kiddo?" I turned to Nathaniel who nodded as he continued on his half finished lollipop. His mother pushed my head back and dabbed at the wound with a new cloth.

"He knocked a bunch of bags over. It was funny." Nathaniel replied with a giggle and made sloppy crashing noises.

"Well, you will need stitches. Lucky for you, I am a nurse." She smiled at me. "I'm Melissa,"

"Yeah, lucky." I smiled back. "I'm Pepper."

"Pepper? That's a strange name for a man."

I resisted rolling my eyes. Instead, I gritted my teeth as she pressed against the cut harder. The train's whistle blew, and it came to a stop in the station.

"Since you are in capable hands," Lady Therese said. "I will tend to other issues." Her jaw clenched and she headed back the way I'd come from.

"He's gone," I said.

She paused. "How unfortunate." She seethed and clenched her fist so tight her leather gloves squeaked. I couldn't tell if it was because of my failure or his escape. I hoped it was the latter.

We got off at the next stop. Melissa got the station's first aid kit and sewed my head up. Lady Therese kept Nathaniel occupied; he had a tendency to wander off it seemed, though his sister slept soundly in her carrier. I offered to pay Melissa.

"It's the least I can do for you," she said with a shake of her head.

When she left the station, Lady Therese sat me down on a bench.

"That was foolish Pepper. Zakeem is not someone you should tangle with."

"Tell me about it," I replied and pointed to my stitches.

"I am being serious. He's deadly. You should have come and got me."

"He had Nathaniel, I didn't want him to get hurt."

"At what cost?"

"He's just a kid," I replied, my stomach clenched and I shook my head, dismayed that I had to explain myself.

"Yes, a regular boy," she corrected. I raised an eyebrow. She paced across the station platform while she continued. "You are Blessed, a chosen child. You don't realize how special that makes you."

"Is that why we carried Daniel off the battlefield but left others?" I added and crossed my arms.

She sighed and paused her pacing to look from the platform to the surrounding streets.

"If you saw a piece of iron on the ground. Would you pick it up?"

I blinked. The question seemed quite out of place.

"I don't see what-"

"You wouldn't. Even though Iron is useful and used in so much of the world. You couldn't bother to pick up a handful. Right?"

I didn't get what she meant. But I nodded along to get to her conclusion faster.

"Now, what if you saw a diamond? Would you pick that up?"

"Yeah, Diamonds are worth a lot," I replied.

"Because they are rare. Rarity makes up most of their worth." She turned and smiled at me. "You are a diamond, rare and beautiful with great potential."

"And none blessed are iron?" I asked, my hands dropped to my sides as my mouth hung aghast at her explanation.

"Yes, they are useful and important to the world."

"But not worth as much as us?" My hands clenched though I tried to hide it.

"It's not fair. I know. But we are chosen for a reason. It's something to consider. I do my best to serve the people. Help and protect them. Give them closure and help their souls move on. But we could spend all day every day carrying corpses from that forsaken battlefield and make no progress. Ending the war is how we help the masses."

"But we give Daniel a burial with Honors after he almost killed us?"

"He is a diamond, Pepper. He deserves some level of respect in death."

"I'm not sure how I feel about that," I admitted after a moment of silence.

"It is something I struggled with too. Commander Zamira was very strict about it. But after Zakeem got everyone killed, I learned the value of a Blessed. Hopefully, it won't take that much for you to learn." She gave me a solemn smile and stood after the whistle for the coming train rang out in the night air.

Chapter 10
Council

We took turns sleeping the rest of the ride to Rome; that was thankfully uneventful. When we got to Rome, it was a brisk sunny day.

Sylvia met us at the station with a car that took us across the river to a church near the Vatican. It was a large stone church, two stories tall with a domed third ceiling. Beautiful stained glass windows and I was told about a mural on the far side. I couldn't pronounce the name but Sylvia told me it was a church dedicated to the father of Mary who was a saint.

When we got out of the car, Lady Therese scanned the streets and buildings suspiciously. A single car drove by but there weren't any people walking on the sidewalk, and it was quiet. Far too quiet for a large city. I was about to ask about it when a barking dog broke the quiet. Therese shrugged, and we walked into the church without a word.

I wanted to ask Sylvia which Mary she meant because I could think of at least three off the top of my head. But they ushered me towards the back of the church and past a door hidden in the stone framework of the building. Down a set of stairs that curled deep into the earth, a hundred feet or more. The hum of electric lights followed the patter of our footsteps.

We emerged in a bunker that went on for hundreds of yards. Dozens of men and women in light grey uniforms hurried about. Some with clipboards others pushed carts with crates and equipment. A woman wearing a babushka came up and presented a clipboard to Lady Therese

"Sylvia," Lady Therese turned after she took the clipboard.

"Yes, Lady Therese?"

"Take Pepper to the armoury. He lost his gun on the trip." She said.

"Yes, Lady Therese." Sylvia said and pressed her hands together and bowed. She turned to me. "Come on." She motioned.

"I- I didn't lose it." I tried to correct as I followed. "We got attacked, it got knocked out of my hand."

"It's all right," Sylvia said once we were out of earshot. "We aren't exactly hurting for gear." The right corner of her mouth curled into a comforting smirk. "How was your trip?"

"Aside from being attacked by Zakeem?"

Sylvia and several workers spit on the ground. I blinked, taken aback by the universal hate for the man.

"Does everyone do that?"

"Pretty much,"

"Well, it was long and boring, but the food was good." I shrugged. "Did I miss anything?"

"Nothing much. We've mostly been waiting for Lady Therese to show up." The muffled sounds of rifle fire distracted me a moment. "I got to spend some time with my family. They moved to Rome after I joined the order." She explained.

"What about Daniel?" I asked, trying to catch her gaze.

"They entombed him the day after we arrived."

"What about the version with you?"

"Oh," her eyes shifted to see if anyone was around us before she tucked a strand of hair behind her ear. "It's been... all right. Everyone loves the baking I've been doing. Even if they don't know why." The rifle shots got louder the further we walked.

"I believe that."

She opened a door, and I stepped into a room that stacked from floor to ceiling with weapons. Swords, spears, crossbows, with packs of bolts, and gun's, racks and racks of guns. Enough to arm a battalion to the teeth and have some leftover. Most of them I recognized but there were strange guns. One looked like a rifle that would take two men to carry.

Another shot rang out louder and brought my attention to a gun range where I saw Joans discharging a shell. He plucked a new round from the box before him and carefully examined it turning it over in his fingers.

"Let's get you something simple," Sylvia said. I nodded and watched Jonas toss the bullet into a pile of unfired rounds behind him, then pick up another.

"Simple is good." I replied.

"You should get some range time too, you almost missed Daniel completely." She smirked and walked over to the worker who stood before the racks of weapons with a clipboard. "Hey Tanya, can we get a standard Colt?"

"Yes, Ma'am," Tanya saluted and walked around a corner just as another shot rang out.

"I don't have great aim." I shrugged. "The people I've hit I'm sure were flukes."

"We'll change that. You'll be a crack shot with some practice."

"Right now?" I asked as I watched Jonas discarding another two rounds. I wondered what made them inferior to him.

"Not likely. The council has been impatiently waiting for you and Lady Therese to show up," she remarked and her smile faltered with a sigh.

Tanya came back with a case and put it on the table in the middle of the room.

"Here you go. Regular rounds?" She asked holding up a small box.

"For now, but we'll need Blessed before we leave," Sylvia said and pushed the case towards me.

I opened the case and my eyes went wide. A clean gunmetal grey Colt M1911 was nestled in the box along with two magazines. I didn't know much about guns. But this one always stuck out to me. It's how I identified officers when their ranks were defaced in mud or hidden in shadows.

"This is an Officer's side piece," I said in awe.

"Yes, well, it's our standard. It's reliable and reloads faster than a revolver." Sylvia said and opened the box of bullets. "I trust you know how to load it?"

I picked up the magazine and grabbed a handful of rounds to thumb in. "Yeah, Captain Theirs made me load his mags a few times." I finished as Jonas walked into the room slung rifle over his shoulder.

"Good, you're here. The council has been waiting for you and-"

"I've already told them Jonas." Sylvia interrupted.

Jonas narrowed his eyes at her but she ignored him and grabbed two more mags and a holster. She handed them to me as Jonas walked to the door.

"I'll get the car ready then."

"It's already warmed up from picking them up. But you can warm my seat up." Sylvia added. I snickered which earned me a glare from Jonas. I turned back to fill the magazines.

Jonas left with a huff and slammed the door behind him.

I glanced at Sylvia who tried to keep a straight face but her lips grew into a smile which made me snicker and then we both broke out laughing.

"What's so funny?" I got out between laughs.

"I don't know," Sylvia replied and wiped a tear from her eye. "I don't question laughter." She smiled and calmed down. "We best get going." She added and gave a pat to my shoulder. "Try not to lose this one."

I nodded and tucked it into the new holster, the extra clips I dumped into my pocket. Then I followed her back the way we came.

Lady Therese was already in the garage when we got upstairs issuing orders for the workers. Jonas leaned against the car with his arms crossed and tapped his foot as we approached. He got into the back seat, Sylvia moved to the driver's seat and motioned for me to sit in the front passenger seat. Lady Therese saw us and handed the clipboard off before she joined us.

"The council is impatient" Jonas snapped once Lady Therese closed her door.

I glanced at Sylvia who smirked and I fought to keep my snicker contained.

"The council is always impatient, if you jump every time you'll never touch the ground." Lady Therese said without a glance in his direction. Sylvia started up the car, and we headed out.

"Would they be such a pain with more Knights?" Jonas asked.

Lady Therese sighed. "In time they will have more Knights." She shifted in her seat to face him. "For now, none of you are ready. You show promise, which was good enough before the war. But times are different." she gave his knee a comforting pat.

"They are more desperate, with Zakeem hunting us to Rome." He replied.

Sylvia pulled us out of the garage and down the empty street. "Enough," she said with a sharp tone. "This meeting isn't about you. It's about Pepper."

I couldn't tell if the uneasiness in my stomach was from hearing her words or the lack of even birds flying around, or maybe it was the rough road we were on. I gulped, Sylvia glanced at me and I felt Jonas' eyes on the back of my head.

"Me?" I took a breath to keep my heart from pounding hard enough for them to hear. "Why me?"

"To see if you will be chosen by the Lighter." Lady Therese replied.

"What? I don't want that. It's Daniels."

"Who?" Jonas asked.

"The Blessed we burned and entombed," Sylvia replied.

"Oh yeah, I forgot about him."

I wondered how long it would take me to forget his scarred remains, or the burning rage.

"I suspected as much." Lady Therese said. "However. The council is impatient, as Jonas said. They hope you are chosen so they can fast track Jonas' Knighting."

"Why would they fast track it?"

"Because I deserve it," Jonas said.

"You've fired the Rifle one time," Sylvia said with a mocking laugh and turned a corner. Where people lined the sidewalk. It was like we'd driven out of a hidden part of the city. "A Knight can have only two squires under them. If you find your Chosen Relic, you will be a squire," she explained glancing between me and the road.

"So why don't they make you a knight instead?"

"Because she's fucking crazy." Jonas shot back from the back seat. Sylvia slammed the breaks and my face almost hit the dash. She drew her blade from the sheath tucked by the gearshift.

"Enough!" Lady Therese shouted loud enough I thought the windows might burst. She glared at Sylvia with a heat that made me want out of the car. She turned on Jonas next, grabbing his shirt and almost pulled him from his seat. "This, is why you aren't ready. You are too eager to start fights and be disrespectful. Starting fights doesn't prove you are a man," she said and shoved him back against the door.

Jonas tried to suppress his scowl unsuccessfully. I saw Lady Therese challenge his glare with a much deadlier one until he looked away, in the side mirror. I glanced at Sylvia who struggled to hold back the broken blade in her hand. With a grunt, she managed to wrestle the blade back in its sheath. I'd never seen Lady Therese mad and hoped I'd never see it again. Her years of battle had developed a glare that rivaled Daniels flame. Sylvia raised a finger to her lips as she put her sword away.

There was no worry about me saying anything. If the floor could swallow me up, I'd have been happy to escape. I stared forward quietly waiting as the tension in the car grew until we started again. The rest of the ride was quiet except for the rumble of the car's engine and the occasional curse under Sylvia's breath at other drivers.

We pulled up to a several storey red brick apartment building.

"Sylvia." Lady Therese broke the silence.

"Yes, Sir?"

"When we get inside, go see Stephan."

"Yes, Sir" Sylvia nodded.

"Jonas."

"Yes?" I heard him shift and stiffen in his seat.

"Check your shit at the door. I won't have you stepping out of line in front of the council. Am I clear?" She turned and locked eyes with him. He gave a quick nod. "Pepper,"

I tensed at my name. "Y-yes Sir?"

"Relax, you have nothing to worry about." She said with a familiar warmth in her words.

"I'll try, sir," I replied. But knew it would be next to impossible.

Inside it seemed like a regular apartment. A little quieter than I was used too, but I began to think Rome was just a quiet city. We went up the centre stairs to the top floor and down a long hall with only one door at the end. Inside Sylvia broke off from us, she headed to a single door and we walked over to a set of double doors. Lady Therese knocked and waited a moment. She looked at Jonas who shrugged and then knocked again.

"They've been asking for you every day. They should be here." Jonas said.

"Lady Therese!" Sylvia screamed from the other room. I turned and reached for my gun just as the double doors burst open. Lady Therese stepped to shield me from the splinters. Jonas leapt back over a few desks in a single bound and unslung his rifle as a half-dozen people covered in blood and viscera bowled into Lady Therese shield.

"Get clear." She shoved me back. I fell on my butt and slid across the floor like a curling stone.

How did Zakeem beat us here? I wondered. Jonas leapt again and stuck upside down on the ceiling, he levelled his rifle. One bright shot and a body hit the floor followed by another and another.

I got to my feet as Lady Therese shoved the horde back and pulled a pick hammer from her hip. With a flick of her hand she crushed a woman's head, the blood and brain matter sprayed up across the wall. A few got past her and ran after Jonas and me.

I pulled my gun out and in a panic put a few rounds into the one after me. It stumbled to the floor and lingered for a second but lunged with fingers chewed to sharp bones. I caught its necktie and pushed it back. It snapped its teeth and spit blood on my face. Red veins pulsed in its pupils. I shoved back with all my might and wedged my gun into its mouth.

With that shot, the creature went limp. I felt an angry rush pass through me. It hungered for more and tried to take control but with a shudder, the feeling was gone. I pushed the body off me and took aim at another that Jonas had injured while it crawled on the floor. It took a couple of shots to hit its bobbing head, it too slumped against the floor. The rush happened again; I growled to shake it off before I got to my feet.

Sylvia came out of the room she went too with a man's arm over her shoulder. "We have to leave."

"But the council." Lady Therese said as she stomped on the neck of a man biting at her leg. It snapped but he didn't stop gnawing until she brought her hammer down on his skull.

"Those are the council members," Jonas said and fired another blessed round. "We need to worry about the Rifle," he added then dropped from the ceiling.

"I can get it." Sylvia said and stumbled with the man who hung limp against her body. I ran over to her and scooped the man up over my shoulder. He was lighter than he looked.

"I'll get him back to the car," I told Sylvia and we made our way back to the stairs. She got tackled by a dark blur when she went through the door. I stepped out with my gun in hand expecting to see Zakeem. The figure shuddered before it turned to ash on the invisible blade that stuck through its chest.

"What's going on?"

"Later," Sylvia waved the ash away. "Get Stephan to the car."

I looked back and saw Jonas running our way along the ceiling. I ran down the stairs as fast as I could. Across the main floor and threw my shoulder into the front door. It didn't budge. I tried the handle, but it wouldn't turn. Banging came from another door on the main floor. I turned and looked for Jonas. I could hear him struggling but couldn't see him. He wouldn't be any help. It was down to me. I laid Stephan down on the ground by the door and checked my mag. I had two shots left. I grabbed another as one door began to splinter. I put myself between Stephan and the monsters.

Another door burst open and they poured out running full tilt at me. I didn't have time to breathe and close my eyes. I fired. Two rounds, one monster down. I ejected the mag and slapped in the next one. More shots as they got closer. I slammed the butt of my gun into the face of one that got close and reached for my next mag as I fired off the last few rounds. I kicked another monster and slammed the last mag home. Pain shot up my leg as one dug its teeth in. I killed the monster and I limped back a step with a quick glance down. Thankfully It didn't get through my pants.

A monster lunged for my throat and his face exploded over my chest.

"Get the fuck out!" Jonas shouted and unloaded the rest of his mag to clear a circle around me.

"The doors locked." I shouted back. Then shot the closest ones down. Jonas aimed at me and I dove. His glowing shot hit the door handle and punched a baseball-sized hole.

"Out, now!" He ordered.

I scrambled to my feet and shot a creature that crawled after Stephan. He groaned as I lifted his arm over my shoulder and kicked the door open. It resisted, and I put my heel into it this time. It shuddered open; I put our weight into it. It opened enough I could squeeze us both out. I dropped Stephan on the stone steps of the building and dragged him the rest of the way.

As I pulled him into the back seat, I noticed sirens in the distance and getting louder. I jumped and readied my gun as the door I forced open fell off its hinges. Sylvia ran out sword in hand and a rifle slung over her shoulder, Jonas followed close behind. Lady Therese emerged just as the smell of burning hit my nose. Smoke billowed above the building as Lady Therese climbed into the front seat.

"Drive."

Sylvia slammed into gear and the car shot forward. We passed a street with a firetruck and a few police cars screaming down.

"What just happened," I asked once Sylvia slowed down, I struggled to keep Stephan sat up.

Sylvia looked to Lady Therese, but she didn't move. I wasn't sure if she didn't hear me or just didn't want to answer.

Jonas pulled out a box from under Sylvia's seat. "Isn't this ironic?" He said and put the first aid kit on Stephan's lap.

"What is?" I asked, directing my attention to something else.

"Nothing," He chuckled and pulled out a small vile and uncorked it before he waved it under Stephan's nose.

Stephan coughed and jerked his head away. "Oh, what the hell?" He spoke with a soft greek accent and sat up. He brought his hand to rub the back of his head. "Jonas? Where am I?" He looked around with a brief nod to Sylvia and Lady Therese, though he gave me a confused once over.

Lady Therese turned back to us and his eyes widened as much as mine at the blood that splattered her scowl. Now she looked more like a warrior than a lady.

"Stephan, what's the last thing you remember?" She asked.

"Ah, I was talking to a young girl. She was shivering constantly and had a high fever. Her father didn't speak a language I recognize." He winced and rubbed the back through the long dark wavy locks at the back of his head.

"Where's the Needle?" Lady Therese asked next.

"With me. Why?" Another fire engine roared past us. "What happened to the council?" His brown eyes followed the truck.

Lady Therese sighed and turned back to the front seat.

"Therese." Stephan reached a lanky pale hand out to her shoulder.

She pulled free of his grasp. "They're at rest now." She replied.

Chapter 11
Blindsided

The drive back was quieter than one would expect after a shootout with rabid half human monsters. Sylvia double backed, took extra turns and extra long ways on the route back. She settled us under a busy overpass and turned the car off. Other than the murmur of life beyond the cars confines, it was quiet.

"If we are being followed," Lady Therese was the first to bludgeon silence with her words. "We must prepare as soon as we get back," she added.

"If you let me use the rifle, I can take care of tails." Jonas pouted like a petulant child, though he kept watch out the back like a faithful hound.

"If you see any, I might let you." Lady Therese sighed.

"You can't be serious," Stephan said with a groan still rubbing the back of his head. "I can't patch that if it backfires even with the Needle."

"It won't back-" Jonas started

"I know." Lady Therese said and pointed. "Head down that street."

Sylvia turned the car back on and directed it in line with her orders.

"What happened?" I asked. "What were those things?"

"The council." Jonas said.

"No, they weren't." Lady Therese said.

"They sure looked like them." Jonas shot back.

"They looked possessed," Sylvia said as we slowed for a man crossing the street. She never let us stop completely.

"Possessed? But the building has runes." A pillar of smoke came into view beyond the buildings that surrounded us. "Had runes," Stephan corrected.

"Fuck." Jonas interrupted and punched his seat.

"She's right, though it was unlike any possession I've seen." Lady Therese said with a tilt of her head.

"I think they were Wendigos," Sylvia suggested

"That's impossible, they only exist in North America," Stephan said matter of factly.

"But they fit the description. Cannibalism and self-mutilation, they sounded more animal than man when they attacked."

"Doesn't change the fact they don't exist in Europe," Stephan said.

"What if someone brought them over?" Lady Therese asked.

"That's not... that shouldn't be possible. Spirits can't stand moving water. They'd have killed themselves if they sailed over."

"What if they flew?"

"That's not..." The little blood that returned to Stephan's face drained away, his eyes grew wide in realization and horror. "St. Louis." He gulped

"What about the city?" I asked.

"Not the city. The plane. It has been done. I never considered it would be a bridge for spirits" Stephan said and leaned his head against the back seat.

"So Wendigo's. What do we have to combat them?" I asked.

"We've never encountered them." Lady Therese said. "So we just have to hope our normal tactics work."

"Normal bullets seemed to put them down." I offered. Everyone fell into another moment of silence. I wasn't sure if it was to contemplate my words or if they had even heard me.

"We are getting low on fuel." Sylvia chimed in.

"Jonas, any tails?" Lady Therese asked.

"No, I think we are in the clear," Jonas said and turned to sit in his seat.

"Take us back to the bunker." Lady Therese said before she lifted the rifle over the back seat. "Jonas. Be careful with this."

Jonas blinked in disbelief. The stacked two-barrel flintlock rifle seemed freshly polished despite being from another century. Jonas nodded and took the rifle with both hands and held it tight, almost hugging it. Like someone might lovingly hold a baby or a puppy.

"Are you sure about this Therese?" Stephan asked.

"The council is dead. We need as many Relics in play as we can get." She fumbled around a moment.

"So he's a Knight now?" I asked.

"No. He's still a squire." Sylvia replied and glanced in her rearview.

"Says who?" Jonas asked with a scowl.

"Me." Lady Therese said as we turned into the garage.

We took a freight elevator down to the bunker's main hall. Lady Therese's knuckle tapped on the back of her shield. It was the only sign of her nerves or impatience with the slow clunking machine. When the door opened Lady Therese let out a sigh of relief and her taps stopped. She stepped out and spoke in a voice that boomed in the cave.

"The council has been destroyed. All hands, prepare for an attack. Elders, find your units and issue arms as you see fit."

Everyone froze and stared wide eyed at her for a moment. They exchanged furrowed looks of disbelief between themselves unsure of what to do next despite her orders, a few muttered in disbelief.

"This isn't a drill. MOVE!" She shouted.

People dropped what they were doing and sprang into action. What I'd thought was a sleepy group came to life. Crates creaked while being pried open, rifles clattered when handed out. Boxes of ammo clanked to the ground and popped open. Belts of bullets jangled around orderlies who ran to doorways that swung open to reveal heavy guns. Weapons I thought were ornate displays along the walls got plucked up and handed out.

Jonas excused himself to head and get the pack of special ammo he'd been preparing from the armoury. A man in his mid-sixties ran up to Lady Therese.

"There hasn't been an attack in over five hundred years. How can you be sure?" He argued and crossed his arms.

"I can't be." Lady Therese said as she marched through the hall. Her scrupulous eyes watched all those that she passed.

"Then why-" Lady Therese stopped and turned on the man before he could finish.

"Because I will not have us share the council's fate." She shot back and leaned into the man. "If I am wrong and nothing happens so be it. If I'm right and we aren't prepared..." She looked around. "Then all is lost."

The desperation Lady Therese's eyes or the determination in her tone shook the man. He stumbled back and nodded hurried to his charges and got them fitted with chest plates with high collars. Chain-mail sleeves and helmets that sat low enough to keep their necks safe.

"Stephan, you head to the Vatican, if things get bad you must evacuate the Pope and any who will listen to you. Take Sylvia for some added insurance."

"All due respect Lady Therese," Sylvia replied before Stephan could speak. "I'm not leaving."

Lady Therese looked to Stephan who's eyes shifted between them his mouth slowly closing as he stepped back. She sighed and shook her head. "Your stubbornness is frustrating and endearing." With a nod to Stephan, he headed off towards the back of the bunker.

"What can I do?" I asked having stuck close to Lady Therese and Sylvia.

"Stay in the back Pepper." She turned to me with a sad, expression. "Without your Relic you can't lead, and with no gear or proper training you're likely to be in the way."

Her words hit me hard. I was a burden again. To her, the others, I had begun to feel like I belonged but I was still too new. I looked at Sylvia for some kind of encouragement.

Her eyes softened as she regarded me. "It'll be okay. You can help from the back with Jonas." She smiled as sweetly as she could but it felt hollow. Like a lie, you tell children to keep them from throwing a tantrum. Was I just a child in their eyes?

"Alert Stephan if things go bad." Lady Therese said with a hand on my shoulder.

"And run away with him?" I asked with bitterness in my voice that surprised me.

Lady Therese turned to face me head-on and I prepared for her to tear into me. As she stepped forward I closed my eyes and tensed for a slap.

Her arms wrapped around me and pulled me close.

"Choosing life is nothing to be ashamed of." She whispered in my ear and held tighter. "Above all the order must survive." She said louder when she leaned back. "Get in contact with Rheiner."

"B-but he's German." I stammered, embarrassed at my tantrum.

"More than that, he's one of us." She stood back with her hands on my shoulder. "He understands what the Relics are really for."

I didn't get what she meant. I knew she trusted Rheiner, though I didn't get why. She gave my shoulder a pat and a smile that quieted the rebellion in me. Jonas came back, but I didn't want to leave her side. Everything in me told me to stay, to help, to do something. But it was too quiet and her smile was too loud.

A bang reverberated in the halls of the bunker and everyone froze. A distant roar followed and people doubled their efforts.

"Jonas. Take Pepper and provide support from the rear." Lady Therese said and pushed me his direction.

I hesitated. I still didn't want to go. I wanted to stay and fight. I searched for some support between Lady Therese and Sylvia and even Jonas, but Lady Therese was right.

Jonas grabbed my arm. "We don't have all day Dodger, let's go." He tugged me away before I could think of a reason for me to stay.

A crash came from the elevator and the doors shuddered while we retreated behind everyone. Away from the danger, something I should be happy about. But when I saw everyone prepared for what was coming, it made me sick with shame to be this far back.

My knees wobbled as we settled behind a cement barricade. I leaned my forehead to the cool stone and took deep breaths. *You can't always run*, I told myself. Lady Therese's words echoed in my ear as I reached for my pistol. Another bang rattled the elevator doors even more. *I have to stand up, help those around me.* I took a few more deep breaths, stood up and took my first step towards the front. *I would help.*

The elevator door burst open followed by another roar, but this time it reverberated in my bones. I'd expected more monsters like before, or maybe a werewolf. Instead, I stared wide eyed at the frame of a lion the size of a transport truck with a mane as black as death. Obsidian ram horns glinted like a crown on its head. Bone white spines pressed out its skin along its spine. Its jaws dripped with a fluorescent green ichor that sizzled when it splashed to the ground. Thick leather bat wings sprung from its shoulder and flexed out against the bunker's walls and ceiling. The beast swallowed that side of the bunker with its form. Its tail slashed through the air and carved out trails in the stone with the foot-long spikes that dripped with the same green ichor as its mouth.

My stomach hit the floor and the voice that urged me forward was quiet.

"Open fire!" Lady Therese shouted. A hundred tiny rounds of salvation replaced the beast's darkness. The beast's roar drowned in the symphony of destructions the guns replied with. My legs gave out, and I hit the floor as I watched the beast get torn apart.

Jonas grabbed my collar and pulled me back behind cover.

"Follow your fucking orders Dodger!" He shouted and shoved me to the stone wall with the rifle pressed tight across my chest. He glared at me as I struggled.

"I.. I want to help." I finally got out as I fought back tears.

"Then do as your told." He said and pulled the rifle back as the firing stopped. "Here," he handed me a pair of shoes. "Get these on." I blinked and looked at the shoes and then his now bare feet.

"What about you?" I asked. He pushed the shoes in my hands. My shoes were much too small for him.

"I don't need em anymore." He smiled and caressed the rifle with an unsettling twinkle in his eye and a smile that made me want to sink into the stone.

"You still need shoes," I remarked and peeked over the barricade to see the beast in a bloody mass on the floor.

"I'll get some after we're finished. You might need the Gecko Grippers to run away." He said with a smirk and then coughed. I noticed others were coughing, and it was quickly getting worse.

"Its blood is gas!" Sylvia shouted and a couple of orderlies opened up crates to reveal large crystals. A wall of wind shot up from the floor between them and kept the gas circling back on itself. But there were over a dozen others caught on the gas side of the wall. They coughed and gagged at first, screamed as their skin burned and peeled off, the exposed muscles turned black. The vomit and foam that poured from their mouths and noses eventually gagged their screams. I watched in horror as their forms struggled and spasmed even when they were bloody husks on the ground.

"Thank fuck for Cardea Crystals," Jonas said as he got to his feet.

"Is it over?" I asked.

"I doubt it." Jonas said. He knelt and looked down the sight of his rifle. "Get those shoes on." I scrambled to take mine off. His were several sizes too large, but I tied them tight hoping that would do the trick.

Lady Therese held her rifle over the shield, like she expected more. Sylvia held her sword with both hands close by.

A scream echoed in the cave, I looked over the barricade to see someone stomping. Then swatting at something before it came into view. It looked like a hairless rat with two tails and a couple of tendrils poking out its back. Each time the tendrils grabbed her she winced. Another climbed her body and another. Her uniform became pocked with blood stains as the creatures bit her and scratched with their tendrils.

More people began to panic, and a few started to shoot at the ground as more of these tiny monsters appeared. They hissed and chittered as their numbers grew. Sylvia ran forward and squashed and slashed any that got close to her. Lady Therese waded into the swarm to help people pull back. The swarm hissed angrily and broke around her as they advanced.

"Grenade out." Someone shouted. The bang went off after a few seconds and sent tiny body parts and screeching monsters flying through the cave. A few more grenades thinned out the disgusting monsters.

Jonas still stared down his sights intently watching something in the thinning gas beyond the wall of wind. He tugged his goggles down; I noticed a smirk creep across his lips.

"More coming." He shouted and fired his rifle. It let out a bang that caused my ears to ring. He pivoted the barrel and pushed a paper-wrapped packet from his palm into the just-fired barrel, then pulled the flintlock back in a practiced smooth movement.

Twisted human forms launched themselves through the wall of wind running on all fours after the orderlies. These were dressed in civilian clothes in varying states of disarray. Sylvia and Lady Therese ran to meet the charge and made short work of any creatures that got too close. Several took to attacking the crystals, punched and biting at them or caving their own heads in trying to head butt them.

Jonas sat back behind the barricade with the rifle pointed straight up. The sneer on his face turned into a wide toothy excited grin.

"Watch this," he said and fired again. This time I got my hands over my ears but still felt the blast in my chest. The bullet caught two creatures clawing at a crystal and splattered their brains to the stone wall. Another shot and this time three dropped. Jonas reloaded just as fast as he fired and continued to shoot from cover and increase the enemy's body count.

I pulled my gun out and aimed over the barricade to provide what cover I could. Pop shots at creatures that were coming through the barrier and neared Lady Therese as she bashed in skulls.

"Bout time you grew a pair." Jonas remarked and gave me a jab in the ribs, "There's hope for you yet Dodger." He chuckled and peeked over the edge of the barricade for a second. "There you are." He lined his rifle up taking careful aim.

I followed his rifle to a figure standing in the thinning gas. Dressed in a long black coat and a black turtleneck, with a black gas mask I couldn't tell if the glass was tinted red, or the colouring came from within. It looked human and stood still with its hands behind its back, observing instead of charging like the others, hands held behind its back only its head shifted from side to side. Looking between Sylvia and Lady Therese as they battled with the others against the dwindling number of monsters.

Jonas smirked and pulled the trigger. The shot was quieter, or I'd lost my hearing. But I saw the round pierce the wind barrier headed right for the figure's head. I blinked to avoid seeing the gore of his brain matter splashing through the air. In that brief flash, the observer had moved. He stood in the same place and though his head didn't shift back and forth anymore. His hand gripped the air before him.

"No, fucking way." Jonas said with wide eyes and a slack jaw. The observer dropped a metal marble to the floor soaked in toxic blood. Jonas panic'd to reload. "Son of a bi-" He froze with a grunt in the middle of pulling the hammer back. His body trembled, his eyes transfixed on the observer.

The observer's glasses shown yellow in the fading green mist. I looked back and saw Jonas's face turning red. He wasn't breathing. My feet moved before I even thought about what to do next.

I ran. Straight for the observer. I levelled my pistol and shot at him in a panic. I had to stop him somehow. Most of my shots went wide, but a few hit his chest and legs.

He didn't even flinch. I saw the rounds fall off him and bounce on the ground. Regular bullets weren't good enough. I looked around and saw an orderlies rifle on the ground. I scooped it up and took aim. Center mass. I reminded myself. I pulled the trigger and a blast of light came from the barrel. It shot through the barrier and missed where I was aiming. It hit the observers mask and shattered the glass.

He lurched back and held his face. I heard Jonas gasp for air behind me and he finished cocking his hammer.

I did something. I marvelled at myself for a moment. I actually did something right. My chest swelled as I took a few deep breaths. A possessed woman screeched and lunged at me. I roared back and thrust the rifle's bayonet into her chest and pinned her to the ground. She slashed at me with sharp boney fingertips and struggled while I pulled the bolt back and reloaded. Another flash of light and she fell silent. A wispy shadow faded from her body.

I looked at the observer who had gathered himself and was glaring at me. His yellow eye had a vertical iris in it and blood poured around it. I pulled the rifle out of my kill and levelled it at him. He lept back as the bright round sailed past him.

Jonas took a shot from behind cover and the Observer swatted it away. He retreated to the elevator. I shot at another possessed by Sylvia and found myself out of ammo. She gave me a smile and nod of thanks before piercing the heart of another.

The creatures' numbers had dwindled to a mere handful that were busy chewing on the bodies of the dead, their own as much as ours. Those that were still able too, quickly cleaned up the few with execution shots.

I let out a sigh of relief and sat back against a barricade my knees shook almost as much as my hands. I felt my heartbeat pounding in my neck.

The distinct clop of horseshoes echoed in the now quiet bunker. I looked towards the gas-filled area to see a much larger shadow than the observer looming in our direction. It was a horse and a rider. It drew closer, and I realized the rider had no head, the horse was black as coal and snorted steam.

"Get back." Lady Therese yelled as the rider strode casually past the wall of wind and stopped. The people closest to the monster froze. I worried that it was the same as Jonas and scrambled to find another mag or gun with blessed rounds. But they just dropped their weapons and fell to the ground. Like something inside of them had just turned off.

A shadowy mist lifted from their bodies towards the rider who had a head tied to his hip by its hair. It's grimacing mouth chattered, and it consumed the mists. Its eyes opened and darted around like mad. They would freeze on someone and they too would drop to the ground.

I ran at the monster. Bloody bayonet bared ready to impale the rider or the horse. I couldn't let it have its way and take lives. The eyes set on me and I stumbled to a stop; it felt like it was dragging something out of me. Every muscle in my body flexed and spasmed as I strained against the pull. Its grip tightened, and it felt like it was pulling everything about me out. My memories, my life, my very soul. It hungered for them.

Sylvia leapt at the rider from the other side. It pulled out a whip made of bones that latched around the invisible blade. With a flick, the rider pulled it free from Sylvia and kicked her back as Lady Therese came to my rescue.

"Hold on to your soul Pepper. Fight it with everything you've got." She shook me hard, but I barely swayed. The monster turned to her. When my focus shifted to her, I felt the pull lose its grip.

"L-look out," I said and tried to shove her back, but she wrapped a strong arm around me. I gripped the shield and tried to push it to help her. She overpowered me and kept it around me, I almost felt safe. Then she screamed out as the whip cracked overhead.

She lurched to the side and fell to the ground. She shoved the shield from her arm and reached for her face. I couldn't see what had happened. Only that blood now trickled from under her hands.

The monster's whip recoiled and circled ready for another deadly strike. I looked around. Sylvia was getting to her feet, eyes on Lady Therese. The orderlies were retreating into the other rooms and hallways and I couldn't see Jonas. Lady Therese and I were the monster's next victims. The horse whinnied and reared back. Its huge black hooves with spiked shoes were ready to stomp us to death even as the whip arched down.

I grabbed the shield and prayed it'd work. Not for me. But for Lady Therese, and the orderlies that desperately needed it. For those like Sylvia that were still alive and needed time to recover. Even for those who were working on something to help, like Jonas.

I braced for the impact of the hooves and saw the whip arching around my shield. With eyes closed, I clenched my jaw and prepared for the sting. I hoped that my sacrifice would buy the needed time.

The whip slapped my face but felt like a feather caressing my cheek. The hooves slammed the shield and I heard a snap. The horse whinnied and limped back a step before it collapsed to the ground and pinned the rider.

The boom of Jonas rifle followed and the horse and rider burst into a blue, purple flame. They both flailed as the face took on a silent scream.

I stood and watched in horror as the monster burned. Despite everything, it felt wrong that it should suffer. I turned to Jonas as Sylvia ran to Lady Therese.

"Hit it again." I told him.

"What? It's gonna die anyway why waste the ammo."

"Just DO IT!" I yelled with a fury that made him lean back. I could see him forming an argument in his eyes. One I didn't want to hear; I prepared to yell again.

"Do it, Jonas." Lady Therese's voice trembled. "End this, please."

Jonas straightened up and aimed his rifle skyward before firing it off. The round slammed into the head and it shattered like glass. The rider and horse went still as the flames turned them into a pile of ash.

Jonas and I glared at each other for a long moment. His gaze shifted behind me and I turned, shield at the ready and reached for my gun. I'd forgotten I'd dropped it when I picked up the rifle that now lay a few strides away.

In the mist of gas stood the observer. Dozens of new possessed people coughed and sputtered around him. We didn't have the numbers to fight this again. Sylvia helped Lady Therese up and headed back towards the escape tunnel.

"Head's up," Jonas shouted and fired the Rifle at the observer. The round was bright like a blessed round but blue and I felt the heat as it passed. It shot through the wind barrier and into the gas that flashed white before exploding with enough force to shatter the crystals and shake the cave. I worried that Rome would be brought down on our heads, but held my ground.

Chunks of stone fell around me as smoke wafted past me. After a long minute, I looked up to see scorch marks along the walls and ceilings all the way back to the elevator. But it stopped just short of my feet. A distinct line of debris and destruction divided the bunker. I couldn't understand what happened, I had felt no impact on the shield.

Chapter 12
Safe

The now scorched side of the bunker sat in ruin, what hadn't blown apart smouldered with small fires. Large chunks of stone and steel shifted and settled. The sting of burnt chemicals almost masked the acrid smell of seared flesh. Strewn about were body parts that sizzled and crackled on fire. I could identify only a handful of the bodies as formerly human.

"What..." I tried to get a thought out, any thought. But I couldn't process the carnage before me. Movement in the smoke caught my attention, it was the Observer, somehow he'd survived. His form smouldered as he crawled towards the elevator on the blackened ground. A trail of blood led from the stub of his leg to a slab of stone where the rest sat pinned.

I clenched my teeth and grabbed a nearby rifle to run after to him. He caused this. He brought this upon us and after all this he would not escape. I stepped in front of him and pushed the bloody bayonet of the rifle under his chin. He stopped crawling and looked up at me with a sneer and gnashed sharp teeth at me.

He spit on my boot and spoke, but not a language I knew. I imagined he cursed me, my family, all I cared for, threatened them all. Or maybe he was begging for his life? Tears formed in the eye I could see as he sputtered.

I pulled back the bolt to reload the rifle; he didn't wince. I shouldered and aimed down the sights for his head; I wasn't likely to miss this shot. One trigger pull and it was over. But part of me knew it wouldn't be. Sure I'd end his life, but what did that do? He was un-armed and injured. Was this right? I hesitated and lowered the rifle.

The observer grabbed the barrel; I tensed until he aimed the rifle for his head. He made sure I couldn't miss even if I tried. Did he want to die, why? Was he more useful alive and knew it? Was he chal-lenging me? Did he think I couldn't do it? A bloody smirk grew on his lips as he glared up at me, a sound came out of him like a snakes laughter.

I took a deep breath and tensed up as my finger closed around the trigger. I hesitated again, is this right?

His eyes went wide and his grip faltered on my rifle before he coughed up blood. I tore my gaze off him to Sylvia who twisted her blade in his back and pulled it free. The blood fell from her blade onto his back and turned to ash. He sputtered a few more words that felt old, older than humans will ever remember. The rest of him turned to ash before my eyes.

I hadn't been able to do it, and he knew It. I dropped the rifle and stumbled back to a wall my legs buckled under my weight and I slumped to the floor. The full scale of the destruction hit me. The car-nage, the loss of life. This wasn't supposed to happen here. This was Rome, far from the front lines. Yet it looked every bit as horrifying as the worst days of my life.

"Come on Pepper." Sylvia held a hand out. "We are getting out of here."

"You're better without me," I said and pulled my knees to my chest and wrapped my arms so tight around them I couldn't tell if I was short of breath because of them or the horrors before me.

"Come now, you can't be serious?" She said and took a knee try-ing to catch my gaze but I turned away.

"I've been useless from the start. I should have died in the trench-es on my first day." I fought to keep the tears back.

She caught my chin and pulled me to look at her. Her soft sad eyes stared so deep into my soul. Did she learn that from Lady Therese? No, her stare bore in deeper. I didn't think I could hide anything from her if I tried. Nor could I bring myself to pull away.

"You saved lives today, whether or not you see it." She pointed to the escape tunnel. "Now come on, this isn't the place we should linger." She stood, hand still out for me. I stared at it for a moment before I looked up at her soft forest green eyes. It wasn't sadness I saw in them. It was compassion, empathy and concern. She cared, though I didn't know why. I took her hand, and she helped me stand. We walked carefully through the bloodshed to the tunnel everyone else had retreated down.

As she led me I noticed her hand was slender yet strong, a little rough, and it felt cool in my palm. I tightened my grip when it felt like she was about to slip away and hurried to keep pace. She smiled and pulled me to walk beside her when the tunnel allowed.

The crystal lantern we walked by gave her an almost celestial glow that threatened to take my breath away if I stared for too long. I missed the smear of crimson across the side of her neck until we made it to another large bunker like cave. Floodlights glinted off the smear before they blinded us both. The sounds of a dozen rifles being cocked made me freeze.

"It's just us. No followers." Sylvia said and let go of my hand to hold hers up, one moved to shield her eyes from the bright lights. I did the same and remembered I still had the shield on my arm. It felt so natural and light that I'd forgotten it was there. I saw a line of hastily configured crates with a line of young men in dark robes and crosses around their necks.

"Collapse the Tunnel." Lady Therese said from a seat behind the crates. An attendant wrapped gauze around her head a few times. A distant thump came from the tunnel followed by crumbling and a wave of dust.

We made our way over to her and I saw that the several dozen orderlies that had been running around before were down to less than a dozen or two active bodies. A dozen others limped around or were being tended to as others brought stretchers to carry them off to another part of the cave.

Sylvia motioned me over to Lady Therese. Jonas stood behind her and eyed me up as we approached.

"Here is your shield back Lady Therese." I held it out for her.

She tilted her head in my direction and cocked it to the side. "It is no longer mine, Pepper."

"What... what do you mean?" I asked and looked between Jonas and Sylvia.

"The shield has chosen you." Lady Therese continued. "You wield its power far better than I ever could."

"But, I don't know what I was doing," I replied.

"And yet, you still did. You acted intuitively." She sighed. "It took me a decade to tap into the shield's powers automatically. But It was never as good as I'd seen it before." She reached a hand to her face. "I guess I never will see it again." She smiled the most heart wrenching smile I've ever seen.

My eyes widened, and I looked to the others, this time to refute my fears. Jonas looked away and inspected some dust on his sleeve, Sylvia choked back tears for about two seconds before she turned away too.

"Then... what about the war?" I asked.

"I... I don't know." She sighed. "That will be something for later. I have much to discuss." She reached out and pushed the shield back to me. "For now, be around the others." She smiled past me and I nodded.

"Yes, Sir." I straightened up and swallowed the lump in my throat.

Lady Therese corrected her smile. "Jonas, can you be my guide," she asked and held her other hand up. "I need to speak with Stephan."

"Yes, Lady Therese" Jonas sounded reserved. He took her arm and helped her to a nearby door and closed it behind them.

Sylvia put her hand on my shoulder.

"This is too much," I said and shook my head and looked to her for a moment, then past to the guards that still watched the collapsed tunnel. They looked more like priests dressed in black, a few held rosaries, most had more than one cross on their robes, and around their necks.

"I understand. This is the worst I've ever seen." She sighed and wiped tears from her eyes and followed my gaze. "I always thought of Rome as a safe place. Now I wonder if there is such a thing."

I took her hand and gave it a squeeze. "I'm sure we will find a place that is safe." I did my best to sound confident and smile, but I was just as worried as she was. She smiled through a sniffle and I almost believed myself.

Chapter 13
Dancing

It was several days before things began to get back to normal. Or that's what Sylvia told me, It all felt as foreign to me as the language the locals spoke. At least in the trenches, you could usually understand your neighbour.

They held a vote for new councilmen with Lady Therese getting the head councilman seat. They also elected a half dozen of the surviving orderlies to some other roles. Lady Therese smiled when people congratulated her, but it felt hollow to me. The bandage over her eyes helped hide her intentions but I don't think she wanted the seat.

We set up in a three-storey apartment just outside the Vatican. It looked like any other except for the two armed guards stationed at the entrance that inspected everyone who showed up. Even Stephan who came by a few times a day to speak with Lady Therese.

I could tell by the way he stomped across the blue and turquoise carpet of the foyer today he was losing his patience with the men who poked through his medical bag each time.

"Is there a problem Stephan?" I asked and set my book down. It was boring, but it was better than doing nothing.

"I know those oafs are just doing their job, but every time they disorganize my bag." He grumbled and shuffled things in the black bag back to how he preferred it. "Is Therese in her room?" he asked.

I shook my head. "No, she's been in her office with the other council members since lunch."

He sighed. "I don't care if she's in charge, I'll drag her out by her ear if I have to," he grumbled and closed his bag. "There has been correspondence from the front. You might want to get Jonas and Sylvia and meet us in the office."

"Yes, sir." I nodded and headed upstairs for Sylvia first. I knocked on the door to her apartment and was greeted by her bright smile and the rare sight of her out of uniform. She was in an ocean blue dress and matching frock with her hair down around her shoulders in dark waves. Her soft lips a shade of red that caught the eye and held them.

She didn't look like the tough military woman I knew. Aside from the grey beret with a snowy owl brooch, she looked like a regular girl going out on the town. I was gobsmacked, mouth hung open and eyes moved over her, drinking her in like a man that had survived the desert.

"What is it Pepper?" she asked, a flush came to her cheeks. It somehow made her more beautiful, and I felt my own face burn before I realized I was staring.

"Oh," I looked away. "Stephan asked me to get you and Jonas. We got some news from the front." I willed my heart to stop pounding so hard against my ribs, I was sure she could hear.

"Fuck." I blinked hearing such a crude word coming from such elegant lips. "This better not be what I think it is. I'm supposed to meet with my family today." She sighed and stepped back to grab her Sword from her room.

"What do you think it is?"

"They are going to call us back to the front today. Some kind of emergency, at least it better be." She grumbled and tied the belt around her waist. The weapon was a stark contrast to the otherwise well done outfit she had on.

"I'm not sure," I shrugged. She closed the door and we headed to the second floor where the council's new office was.

"Jonas was talking to the council an hour ago. He's likely pushing for us to go back anyway," she said.

It felt far less grand than it should. A couple of long tables pushed together for the seven council members to sit at. A few extra chairs sat against the far wall and a stool sat between them for anyone who addressed the council.

When we walked in Jonas sat on the stool and tapped his foot on the floor while Stephan leaned on the table in front of Lady Therese.

"I don't care, you need to rest if the spell is to work. It could kill you otherwise." He said to Therese. Sylvia and I skirted the room to a pair of empty chairs.

"That is a private matter that we can discuss-"

"Later? You keep saying that but never follow through. Now with this letter," he held up the envelope. "Calling you back to the front." He tossed it to the table. "And you've lost more than your sight if you think I'll let you go in your current condition." He crossed his arms over his chest.

Sylvia tensed hearing the news about the letter. I stole a glance at her and hesitated to put a hand on her knee, that would be too bold in front of everyone. She forced a smile but didn't look my way.

Lady Therese sighed and reached for the envelope patting the table a few times before she found it. "Is that true?" She asked and handed it to the councilwoman beside her.

"Well, it's not going to be a fucking love letter from the GHQ." He turned and scowled at Jonas. "Looks like Christmas came early for you."

Jonas straightened up, I imagined he was trying to hide his smile, if only just barely.

"It seems the Russians have taken Somme back." The councilwoman said after a moment of silent reading.

"Again?" Jonas asked. "How many times must we fight over the same patch of land?" he mumbled just loud enough I could hear him.

Lady Therese sighed. "And they want our help to take it back. I've told them we aren't an offensive force." She rubbed her head.

"It's still a call to aid and we've yet to re-negotiate," Sylvia said nervously as the woman said as she passed the letter around.

"This recent attack proves, once again, that we've been mismanaging our resources." A man near the other end of the table said. He was young but had a bandage over part of his face obscuring one of his eyes.

"This is something we will have to discuss... later," Lady Therese said and tilted her head to Stephan with a soft smile. I held in a chuckle as I smirked. "For now, we answer the call. You three leave tomorrow evening. Jonas, Sylvia. We will promote you to Knights."

"What." A few council members said in unison. "Preposterous. We've yet to address that." A few others raised concerns but Lady Therese continued on above them.

"Jonas go to the station and get the tickets. Sylvia say hello to your mother for me and take Pepper. He needs to get out." She said with a wave of her hand.

"Yes, Sir." The two stood and saluted with their hands over their hearts I mimic'd their motions with a short delay.

"Come on," Sylvia said and took my hand again. I gave hers a squeeze as she led me out of the room.

"Mind if I clean you up first?" Sylvia asked as we walked back up to her room on the third floor.

"Um, I guess not. Do I need to be cleaned up?" I asked and ran my hand over my cheek. I shaved this morning and should be good for another day or so. She smirked and stopped an orderly to whisper something to her. The orderly nodded and headed downstairs.

"Just a final polish is all." She smirked and opened the door to her suite, then guided me to her bedroom. She motioned to the seat in front of the vanity dresser while she moved over to hang her sword on a bedpost.

I took a seat and looked at myself. "Yeah, I guess I could use it." I caught her eyes in the mirror when she stepped behind me. She smirked, it made me smile. I smelled the perfume she was wearing or had left on the table, it tickled with vanillas and the scent of flowers I'd never known.

"Truthfully, you could use a haircut." She said and ran her fingers through my hair. "But we don't have time for that. Though mama may try to do it after supper." She said and plucked a comb from her dresser to work through my hair. She got a dollop of pomade into my dark locks. A slick, stylish shine worked its way across my hair as she worked the comb to a side part. It was simple, but it made me look professional.

"So your mother is a hairdresser?" I asked trying to make conversation and distract from the tingle in my gut.

"She was before she met my father. Still does my sibling's hair and a few friends of the family. You'll get to meet them all tonight."

"What's the occasion?" I chuckled.

"It's Sunday." She smiled and stepped back. "We have a big family meal every Sunday, and it's also All Saints day. So more family and neighbours." She leaned in closer, her breath against my ear. "My advice, don't fill your plate up," she giggled. "And leave it half full if you are done eating. Or Mama will feed you till you burst." She looked me over in the mirror and patted my shoulder. "Looking good Pepper, very spicy," she snickered. I rolled my eyes.

"Haha, so very original." I shook my head but couldn't stop smiling. A knock at the door made us both look.

"Do you still prefer to go as Pepper?" she asked while she made her way to the door.

I shrugged. "Pepper, Pip, I went as Pearson for a while."

She cringed before opening the door. "You are not a Pearson."

The orderly from before stood with a grey pinstriped suit in one arm and a blue suit in the other.

"This one will do," Sylvia said and picked up the pinstriped suit. The woman said something in Italian and Sylvia shook her head then replied in Italian while motioning at me. The orderly's eyebrows raised, she nodded and left.

"What'd she say?" I asked, eyeing the pinstripe suit.

"That we'd match better with the blue suit." She hooked the suit up in the bathroom.

"Is there something wrong with matching?" I asked because I thought it was usually a good thing.

"Knights aren't supposed to be toge-... aren't supposed to be too friendly with each other."

"Why not? You all seem rather close already." I realized what she meant after I spoke, and how clueless I sounded.

"Old rules to prevent favouritism, or a power imbalance. We can be friendly but not too friendly," she looked me over and just as I was about to inquire why she spoke again "How about Peter? Or Peet?" She asked.

"What? Oh, Uh Peter sounds better I think. Why?"

"Well, do you want everyone asking about your name tonight?" She asked motioning to the bathroom "It should fit you well."

I considered her question and got to my feet. "You have a point." I had wanted to change my name for most of my life. But now, when I had the chance, something about it didn't sit right with me. I stepped into the bathroom and turned the light on to look at the suit. It was made of nice fabrics and looked crisp. The stripes glimmered like silver and it had a silk handkerchief tucked in the front pocket. I figured it cost more than every piece of clothing I'd ever worn.

I stripped out of my uniform and put on the pants and shirt on. It settled about me in an unsettling way, soft and light on the skin, not how I was used to clothes feeling. I was really wearing it above my station right now. I pulled the suspenders over my shoulders and slipped the jacket on.

I looked in the bathroom mirror shocked to see a man staring back at me. Framed by the light of the window. I'd only been able to dodge the draft because of my boyish looks.

I could tell something changed. It was more than the hair style and suit. It was something in my eyes. I didn't want to believe the war changed me that much.

A soft rap came at the door.

"Pepper, Lucia brought a few ties for you to choose when you are ready," Sylvia said.

"Okay," I replied and looked myself over once again. The soft boyish face stared back at me. Maybe I imagined it?

I stepped out of the bathroom and Sylvia gave me a once over.

"H-How do I look?" I gulped the lump in my throat down hoping it wasn't loud enough for her to hear.

"Not bad. You clean up nice Mr. Gregor." She smiled with a glint in her eyes.

"Thanks." I tried to fight the flush that crept across my face.

"If you need help with how to tie a tie, I think you'll have to ask Jonas." She said and reapplied her lipstick in the mirror.

"I got it," I said and picked the light blue tie off out of the briefcase of ties that sat on her bed. I slung it around my neck and worked the silky fabric around a few times until It was the way I wanted.

"I've never seen a tie like that," Sylvia said with a raised eyebrow.

"It's a Trinity knot. My father taught it to me. He liked things being just a touch different."

"Trinity knot? Thought you said you weren't catholic."

"It's Celtic actually." I smiled.

"Really? Well, I think it looks good on you." She smiled and picked up her blue purse from the table. "We best hurry or we'll be late."

"What time is supper?"

"Eight, eight thirty"

"It's barely six. How far do we have to travel?" I asked with a tilt of my head.

"About an hour's walk. But we have to stop along the way." She said and headed for the door. "And I have catching up to do."

I smirked and chuckled. "And introductions to do. If you wander off I'm leaving you behind."

She laughed out loud. "Think you could find your way back here without me?" she smirked and raised her eyebrow.

"Eventually, though Jonas may have to come to find me." I chuckled, and we headed downstairs.

We walked along the streets with glowing crystals suspended above wooden posts; they reflected the light of the day they absorbed, dotting the streets of Rome. We talked and joked as our feet tapped along the stone streets, we made our way around one corner then another and another. I was quite lost and totally at the mercy of my companion. Yet I couldn't think of anywhere else I would rather be.

We ducked into a small grocery store that didn't have much on the shelves. The war was taxing every country that took part in it. The essentials flour, vegetables, and dairy made up most of the shelf space with the odd container of spices, canned meat, and a single box of sweets dotted the store. Though I peeked inside and found several of the spice containers empty.

Sylvia spoke to the storekeeper and got a sack and a bottle of wine. She tried to return the wine but the store owner wouldn't have it. It was the only bottle of wine in the store it seemed.

"Grazie senior." She said and tucked the bottle of wine under her arm. "Can you carry this Pepper?" She asked and pointed to the repurposed floral patterned sack.

"Sure." I sauntered over and grabbed the bag. It was heavier than it looked but I wrapped it around my hand and we headed out of the store on our way.

"So..." Sylvia said slowing down her pace a few blocks away. "I need you to help keep a secret for me." She kicked at a small stone with her boot.

"What would that be?" I said I put the sack down for a moment, thankful for the break.

"My family doesn't know about the Knights. They know I've been helping the Order. But they don't... *know*, you know?" She stopped and locked her eyes on mine.

"Know you're Blessed?" I asked.

"Or that I serve on the front lines, fight monsters or anything else. They think I travel as a secretary."

My eyes widened. "Really? Jesus Sylvia."

She gave a sheepish nod. "So if you could play along with that. It would make the night go a lot smoother." She smiled warmly.

I wanted to tell her no, and that she needed to be honest with her family. It was the right thing to do after all. But that smile. It melted any resolve I had. I groaned.

"You know you should tell them, right?" I said and stepped closer to keep the conversation private as someone walked by.

"I will... after the war is over," she explained.

"That day may never come," I replied and rubbed at the back of my neck. "Yeah, okay. I'll keep quiet about it. But what am I supposed to say?"

"Thank you." Her smile grew and so did my heart. "You can say you are an accountant. You keep track of travel expenditures and such. Should be boring enough no one will bother with more questions."

"Oh? Just a boring man you brought home."

"With a stable, safe job." She added. "Served his time on the front. Should keep you in everyone's good graces."

"But I haven't served my time." I reminded her.

"A white lie won't hurt anyone." She motioned me to follow as she started walking again.

"This is a new side to you." I slung the sack over my shoulder.

"No, this is my normal side. You are just lucky enough to see it. We all have our secrets Peter," she said when I caught up to her.

"I hope it's not too much further," I said after a few more blocks. The sack felt like it was full of rocks by now.

"Nope, I can hear my uncle now." She said, and we slipped between two buildings. The distinct sound of bellowing laughter grew louder, as did the smell of fresh bread and other delicious foods. We moved through an archway into a courtyard that had a few tables set up. People were setting up chairs along both sides of them.

It took a moment for people to notice us, but the greetings were quite warm once they did. Though I got plenty of suspicious glances even as Sylvia introduced me. Handshakes that threatened to crush my hand came with strong slaps to my shoulder. I wasn't sure if they were being friendly or testing me. A loud cry filled the courtyard and everyone's head snapped to the woman with gray streaks in her hair. She rushed through the crowd and wrapped her arms around Sylvia.

"La mia bambina." The woman cried.

"Mama." Sylvia hugged back but winced as the woman squeezed tighter. The woman kissed Sylvia's lips and her cheeks repeatedly. Before she started speaking to her in, I assumed Italian.

"I didn't know I would be here this long Mama." She replied. "This is Peter, he's an associate of mine. He had no plans. So I invited him to dinner." Sylvia explained with a smile. Sylvia's mom gave me a hesitant once over, but smiled and gave me a warm hug. The other's suspicious glances softened to friendly smiles and handshakes became tight hugs, claps on the back became awkward kisses. Thankfully, only on the cheek.

Sylvia said something to an older man, and he took the heavy sack from me. He patted my shoulder before following Sylvia and her mother back inside the house. A few of them asked me questions, and I just stared fish-eyed at Sylvia. "He only speaks English." She shouted back as her mother guided her off.

"Ah, Peter. You must forgive us. We don't get many English here." A man a few years older than me said in a gruff voice I learned this was Sylvia's older brother. "Come, come. Make yourself at home." He wrapped his arm around my shoulder and pulled me towards the tables.

There was a cheer from the kitchen as Sylvia's brother poured me a glass of wine. I sipped it and found it notably watered down, which didn't bother me at all. Though I saw the twisted faces of the other men at the table, to their credit, no one complained. I made small talk with them and did my best to avoid questions about the war or my work with Sylvia. Saying it was boring numbers that dissuaded most of them. Though Toby, Sylvia's eldest brother pressed a bit.

It was hard to hold a conversation with him since he was missing his right arm from the shoulder. He blew it off as a war injury, but I found it hard not to steal a glance at the folded sleeve when I thought he wasn't looking.

Someone pushed their radio near a window and turned it up before the women of the family brought supper out. Sylvia sat beside me while we enjoyed the feast of grilled veggies, chicken and pasta like I'd never had before. It's true what they say, you haven't had real pasta until you've had Italian pasta. The red sauce had a hint of garlic in it and a crunch of crisp onions. The bread was warm and soaked up the sauce well.

I ate my fill of it and then half of another plate, remembering Sylvia's warning. Her mother seemed intent on me not being able to move from the table.

"He's much too skinny, he needs to put some meat on." She said more than once. Sylvia came to my defence a time or two.

"Mama, he doesn't need to get fat off your home cooking like Papa." She'd motion to the old man who took the bag from me earlier. The stout man laughed and gave a slap to his stomach.

She wasn't wrong though. Most of the other men at the table dwarfed me. Some from their guts, others from their height. Apart from the children, I seemed to be the shortest male at the gathering.

Once Sylvia's mother accepted that I couldn't eat another bite, after I'd taken one last bite. The tables were cleared and pushed to one side. They turned the radio up and people began to dance. I helped put the chairs away and came back to watch as couples paired off. Sylvia danced with a cousin's child in her arms and It made me smile.

She was perfectly happy here, dancing and laughing, surrounded by loved ones. Not with the Knights, or on the front, fighting for her life. It was such a contrast to the other day, when we were fighting for our lives. I pushed the memory of the recent battle further back in my mind

Sylvia's father stepped up beside me as the song was winding down. I looked at him with a smile. He was a little taller than I was with many laugh lines and salt and pepper hair. He had a sturdy build from years of hard work and good food.

He held out two glasses of wine and motioned toward Sylvia. She handed the baby back to its mother and laughed as the baby cried and reached out for her. She pressed a finger to its nose and made a face I couldn't see. The baby laughed and leaned against its mother.

"She smiles brighter with you around." His words reminded me that he stood beside me.

"W-what?" I asked, taken aback by his words.

"You like her, yes?" He said with a knowing smile.

"Well, uh... she is a beautiful and smart woman. But workplace relationshi-" He cut me off with a strong pat on the back as he smiled.

"Be good for her Peter." He gave my neck a squeeze and pulled me closer. "We have connections." He said softly and shook a finger near my face. I gulped, unable to tell if he was joking or serious. The stories I'd heard of the mafia back home made me smile nervously.

"Papa," Sylvia said. "You aren't trying to get Peter to join the factory are you?" She stood with her hands on her hips and an adorable glare on her face. We both chuckled, he gave my back a pat hard enough to force me forward.

I moved with the momentum and walked over to give Sylvia a glass of wine.

"Thanks." She said, taking the glass. "I should have warned you. He doesn't talk much but he'll try to get you to work for the factory. Sometimes I swear he's just trying to take it over." She laughed. That sweet laugh that made me smile.

"Ah, no he had nothing to say about the factory," I said and lifted my glass. "Cheers?"

"Cheers." She replied and clinked her glass against mine and we took a sip of genuine wine, which I was not prepared for. I coughed a bit and looked almost as surprised as Sylvia.

"Mama!" She threw her hand in the air at the glass. "I got that for you and Papa."

Her mother replied in Italian. Sylvia's eyes went wide and her face flushed. They had a brief back and forth before Sylvia huffed. She turned and crossed her arms before she took another gulp of wine.

"Uh... do I get filled in on what was said?" I asked.

"No." She pouted.

I looked back at her parents who had started to dance to the newest tune. It was slow and though I couldn't understand the words, it felt passionate. Her mother waved me forward with a smile and I got the jist of their conversation.

"Care to dance?" I asked after another sip of my glass.

"You know how to dance?" Sylvia asked with a raised eyebrow. She glanced at me with a slow turn of her head. Her eyes looked me over, assessing the validity of my claim.

"Yeah. Is that really so surprising?" I held my hand out to her with a playful smile. She held my gaze for a few seconds and then finished the rest of her wine.

"Yes, it is." She plucked my glass and finished it as well before placing them on a near-by table. She walked back brushing the skirt of her dress. "All right Mr. Gregor," She placed her hand in mine. "One dance shouldn't be too scandalous."

I pulled her closer and moved my hand to her back the other out before us. Her hand held my shoulder, and I took the lead with a slow step and another. Then two quick steps to the side. She kept pace, and I watched her eyebrows raise in surprise.

"A foxtrot?" She asked with a smirk. We continued across the stone courtyard turning slowly with the tempo of the song. "Self-taught?"

I shook my head. "My mother was a dancer when she was younger. Dancing was the only time she smiled." I said with a shrug and turned her more. "How does a squire learn to foxtrot?" I asked. She took the lead for a moment and spun us a few times and pressed herself closer

"You know how." She smirked, and we continued. I wondered just how much of what she knew was hers and how much she gained from others.

We danced through the next three songs, picking up the pace and eventually slowing down until she could rest her head on my shoulder. Her breath brushed my neck as her soft perfume tickled the edges of my nose. I wanted to breathe it in, but couldn't figure out how to do that without looking like a creep.

"You ever think of running away Pepper?" She spoke so softly I almost didn't hear her.

"Hmm?" I wasn't sure I heard her right.

"Take off. Forget about everything and find a quiet island or secluded area to escape too."

"Like escape the war?" I chuckled. "Yeah, the second they drafted me." I smiled. She leaned back and looked me in the eyes with a solemn expression.

"You're serious?" I asked and stopped swaying and I held her gaze for a moment. "To where?"

"Someplace safe," she said with a shrug before she pulled away. A tear threatened the edges of her eye. She walked off the makeshift dance floor, down the alley we'd come from.

Stunned, I stood alone for a long moment. Was there somewhere safe? Could she have a plan? What about the order? I thought she was loyal to Lady Therese.

A napkin bounced off my head and I turned to see Sylvia's father motioning for me to go after her.

I headed out of the lantern-lit courtyard and found Sylvia in the dark alley between the two apartments. War bond posters plastered across from the garbage bin. Her back turned to me and her shoulders shuddered. I took a tentative step closer and brushed a hand over her back.

She gasped and spun on her heels to clutch the front of my jacket with her other hand clenched. I held my hands up and my heart broke when I saw her tear-streaked face glare at me. It melted away when she realized who I was.

"Oh, Peter." She released me and turned away again. "Sorry, I thought you were a vagrant or worse." She sniffled and tried to wipe the tears from her eyes.

"If you need a minute alone. I understand." I said with a step back.

She shook her head. "No, It's..." She sighed. "It's not me. You are the only one who will get it." She wiped a few more tears away.

I didn't know what to do. I understood but didn't know how to help. What had set off whoever this was? Was there a way to appease them? I patted my pockets. Or did we just have to wait till it was over? My hand patted over my chest and I plucked the handkerchief free.

"I get it," I said and stepped closer to hand it to her. "But I dunno how I can help. This doesn't seem like Daniel, so I doubt bringing you to the kitchen will do anything."

She laughed and took the cloth to dab at her eyes. "No, it's someone else. I thought they'd moved on." She took a few deep breaths and leaned against the brick wall.

I stepped up beside her and straightened my jacket and tie. "Were you really going to clock me?" I asked.

"Had you not been you? Likely." She laughed and smiled.

"Careful, I'm fragile," I added. She laughed louder and shook her head.

"I've seen what you can do Peter. You're far from fragile."

"Maybe with the shield. But without it I'm just a boy from Chicago." I replied and looked to her eyes. Those glistening pools of emerald.

"And with it, you become a paragon of peace." She leaned closer. Our shoulders touched. "A beacon of security," she added. Her hand found mine, I gave it a squeeze. She smiled again. The tears all but gone, her cheeks were rosy. I wanted to reach out and touch them, but hesitated. Instead, I clenched my fist and cleared my throat.

I was about to say something when she moved and pressed her lips to mine. A shock burst through my body and fried my brain for a moment. She stepped back and smiled.

"Thank you." She said and handed my handkerchief back.

"For what?" I said, though I wasn't sure it came outright. I stared at the handkerchief for a moment trying to process what it was and where it came from.

"For being here." She said and blushed. I took the cloth after a moment, still dumbstruck. "Come now, Peter. It was just a kiss," she said.

"The best kiss," I added. She rolled her eyes and her cheeks flushed more.

"Come on. Don't try that mushy stuff on me." She took my hand. "We best get back."

We returned to the courtyard as another upbeat song started and a couple of people started to swing dance. Sylvia pulled me back to the dance floor, and we spent the rest of the night dancing, laughing and being part of a new family. One of the most memorable nights of my life.

Chapter 14
Burden

We arrived back at the apartment after midnight. The streets were quiet and mostly empty except for a few people making their way home. It was a bit unsettling outside of the street lights, but I could ignore it easily with Sylvia at my side. We did our best to be quiet as we made our way upstairs, but a few people peaked out of their rooms when Sylvia bumped into a table and knocked over a vase. To be fair, who puts a vase on the staircase landing?

We straightened up and continued on our way to the third floor. The rush of the night gave me a buzz only matched by the wine. Or maybe it was the other way around.

"Shhhh, Peter," Sylvia said louder than I'm sure she meant to. She'd had more to drink than I had and we'd gotten lost a time or two on the way back. We might have walked past the building had I not recognized the guard at the door.

I helped her down the hall to her room and was about to bid her good night when she threw her arms around my neck.

"Don't leave yet." She whispered in my ear. It would have been sweet were it not for the sour alcohol on her breath.

I wanted to say yes, stay the night at her side. Even if it was just to hold back her hair if she got sick. See her emerald eyes first thing in the morning. But a throat clearing behind me made us both stiffen. We were caught in the act, was it too intimate of an embrace?

"Have a fun night?" Lady Therese asked from a chair in her suite across the hall. It sat near the window, the light of the moon that had helped light our way home now looked eerie on her pale skin and light night robes.

"Y-yes, sir." Sylvia straightened up. She cleared her throat and her smile faded to the stern, serious expression she normally wore.

"Pepper?" Lady Sylvia asked with a tilt of her head.

"Yes, Sir." I straightened up too.

"Good. Jonas got your tickets for tomorrow evening. I suggest you both get a restful sleep." She stood up and used a stick to sweep the floor as she walked forward.

"Yes, sir," Sylvia said. Without a glance in my direction, she went into her suite and closed the door.

My chest deflated as she left me in the hallway. I'd hoped for at least a final good night.

"Pepper." Lady Therese called for my attention.

"Yes, sir?" I asked as my eyes lingered on Sylvia's door.

"This way Pepper."

How did she know where I was looking? I turned to face her. She stood in the doorway of her suite. Fresh bandages wrapped over her golden hair framed face.

"Thank you." She said with a knowing smile.

"For what?" I asked.

"For many things, but right now. Thank you for taking care of Sylvia."

"I don't know what you me-"

She held a hand up to cut me off. "Please continue to do so in a more discreet manner. The rules have yet to be corrected." She smiled and closed her door.

Once I made it to my suite I undressed leaving my new suit jacket on the small kitchen table. I headed to the bedroom and flopped down onto my bed in the dark. I groaned as something hard dug into my stomach. I rolled free of the brick-like object and flicked the bedside lamp on and held it up to find a book with a note on it.

It was an old book with worn edges and a few stains. I picked the note up.

"Time for you to learn something Dodger."

"Gee. Thanks, Jonas." I sighed and crumpled the paper and tossed it into the trash. The book was a foot wide and wrapped in dark worn leather. The lettering on the front was hard to read. I debated shoving the book off my bed and dealing with it in the morning. But curiosity urged me on.

I opened the book and read. "The Relics of the Volatile Blessed." A page was bookmarked with a silk strip. I ignored it and looked over the table of context.

The Relics were all listed, including one crossed out, The Lantern.

I was too tired to do much reading, but I opened the book to the marked page.

It had elegant lettering that spelt out "The Shield" in large sweeping green letters. The whole book was composed by hand and must have taken the craftsman years.

I pulled the book to my lap and sat reading about the Relic that leaned against the foot of my bed. It was hard to read, but I worked it out after a moment. I read about the year they made it, the person who created it and used it in battle. The tests they ran on it, how it could stop cannon fire and those near the shield weren't bothered by arrows and protected from sword strikes.

It was an extremely clinical read. I yawned and rubbed at my eye. Just before I decided to close the book and forget about it. One word caught my attention.

Burden. Written in red ink with a different style than the other words.

"The chosen user will find people seek his company in a friendly or romantic nature. But the truth of the matter is that they care not for the user but the safe nature the shield gives off. It is strongest when the chosen is in contact with the shield. But others can feel the effects for days after. Future users are warned to keep others at arm's length until they can verify their authenticity. The Chosen for the hammer, spear, gauntlet, sword and rifle seem to be exceptionally susceptible and prone to violence over the attention of the shields chosen. Exercise extreme caution and keep these users from consorting for the protection of their own lives!"

They underlined the last word three times.

My shoulders dropped and my eyes drifted off the page. I was a danger to Sylvia? Or was she a danger to me? She said she felt safe around me; I didn't get why but now... I wish I hadn't found out. I slapped the book shut and dropped it off the bed.

"What does it know?" I grumbled and clicked the lamp off. What we felt was real... wasn't it?

The question tore at me all night. It dogged me in my sleep with nightmares and when I woke to roll over; it was there laughing in my ear. Even as the sun came up, and I heard others milling about in the hallway. I stared angrily at the ceiling like it was the reason for such a horrid night.

I swung my feet from the bed and stepped onto the book. The real source of my aching chest and strained nerves. I ignored it getting dressed in my spare uniform with a glare for the tired man in the mirror. I went to leave my suite but glanced over at the book. It disgusted me and I didn't want to come back to it. So I picked it up and brought it down to breakfast with me.

Jonas and Lady Therese sat eating. Jonas had a newspaper out and the rifle leant against his chair. I dropped the book on the table beside him. It rattled the dishes and made them both jump.

"Thanks for this," I grumbled and glared Jonas right in the eyes when he lowered his newspaper.

"You didn't have to stay up reading it all" Jonas said with a light-hearted chuckle. I clenched my jaw, I wanted to punch him. He knew what he had done.

"Read all of what?" Lady Therese asked and reached for her teacup on the table.

"I figured Dodger could read up on the Relics since he has one now. So I left the Volatile Blessed on his bed last evening."

"Oh, how did you find it, Pepper?" Lady Therese asked and took a sip from her cup.

"It was dry," I said plainly and moved to an empty seat. Orderlies came out with a tray of breakfast options. "Coffee, black." I sighed and rubbed at my forehead. The words still whispered in my ear. "For the protection of their own lives!"

"It is dry and dated. Some 'commandments' have long since been abandoned. Like, having a family and children. We encourage people to have a life beyond the order now."

"But still expect them to show up when called," Jonas added.

"Yes, well prior to the war it wasn't an issue to call three or four knights in to tend to a job."

"A job doing what?" I asked.

Jonas looked up from his newspaper again, Lady Therese tilted her head.

"Oh, my... no one has told you?" She asked and looked to Jonas. "I thought you filled him in on patrol that first night?"

"I thought Sylvia explained it when she transferred him," Jonas explained with a dismissive shrug.

"Explain what?" Sylvia asked as she stepped into the dining room.

"No one has told Pepper who we are and what we do." Lady Therese replied.

"I thought Jonas would do it on patrol," Sylvia said and moved behind me, her hand brushed over my shoulders, I stiffened as the warning rang a little louder.

She took a seat two away from mine beside Lady Therese. Jonas tossed his hands up.

"Why do you both put it on me to explain things? You've both been in the order longer than I. He folded his paper and tossed it on the table and leant forward to look me in the eyes.

"Normally, this is hard to explain, but after the other day it won't take much to convince you they established the order to hunt monsters." He said straight faced. Even though I'd seen monsters it was still hard to process.

"Hunt? Then what was that attack about?" I asked. My stomach tightened and grumbled some. I thought about a piece of toast to calm it but I didn't want to miss out on the information.

"Some feel it's proof that we've been too focused on the war instead of our regular job." Lady Therese added.

"But we have a duty to answer the call to the front." Sylvia insisted.

Jonas shrugged. "Do we? Dodger?" He held my gaze and I could tell he was trying to get a reaction. I wouldn't give it to him. I shrugged and reached for some toast and jam.

"That's not my call," I said and took a bite, raspberry jam? I thought it was strawberry, not that I cared both were great options.

The rest of breakfast was quiet. I left the table shortly after Sylvia took her leave and followed her back up to her room. With a quick knock on the door, I took a step back and waited.

She opened the door with a smile. "Oh good. I was hoping it was you." She said and stepped out of her suite with her warm smile.

"I uh, I just came to grab my uniform," I said fighting back my own smile.

"Certainly," she said and pulled it out of the closet by the door and handed it to me. "Hey Peter," she added when I took the hanger from her. "Would you like to get lunch with me? There is a nice cafe a few blocks from the train station." Her eyes urged me to comply, and I almost did, but the warning was too fresh.

"Thanks, but I think it's best that we avoid that," I said with a heavy heart, her smile faded. "I didn't sleep well last night. I think it's better that I skip lunch and try to get some more sleep." I half lied which didn't sting nearly as much as the look in her eyes. Oh, how I hated that book and Jonas for putting it on my bed for me.

"Oh," She brushed her hair back behind her ear. "I hope it wasn't anything you ate?"

"No, no, the food was great. I just... had a lot on my mind after last night." I explained.

"Oh," She said again and rubbed her thumb across the other thumbnail. "I'm sorry about that." She stepped back to her suit and the warmth I'd felt before became a cold emptiness between us. It reminded me of my mother's passing.

I wanted to take it all back, go with her to the cafe, hold her hand, and kiss her lips again. To feel the spark that could keep me awake no matter how tired I was.

"I hope you feel better." She said without looking at me then closed the door.

I clenched my fist and stood there for a long moment trying to think of a way to undo what I'd done. But it always boiled down to 'it's for her own safety.'

"Fuck." I cursed quietly and made my way back to my suite. The warning rang in my ear again as I laid down on the bed. Too tired to get out of my uniform, or maybe I didn't think I deserved to be comfy. I banged the back of my head on the wall a few times before I rolled onto my side.

Eventually, sleep took hold, and I slept until the lunch bell rang. I groaned and got to my feet. A few hours before our train was due to depart. I packed my duffle bag with my extra uniform, heavy jacket, the new pair of boots I got from the armoury. They came with instructions but I was distracted by Sylvia's playfulness. I only remember that they would be the best pair of boots I ever wore.

I grabbed the shield and headed downstairs. Lady Therese was just sitting down to a meal of soup and bread.

"Take a seat Pepper." Lady Therese motioned to the seat by her. I looked at the clock on the wall. "You have time to eat before you leave." She assured.

I stared at her while she sampled the soup. "How do you do that?"

She smirked and took another spoonful but never answered. I decided the soup smelled wonderful, so I took a seat and set my bag aside.

We enjoyed our meal of beef and barley soup with very little beef or barley. My mind kept shifting between the warning about the rifle and sword and Sylvia's serious expression when she closed the door. I could tell she was hiding something but was it to save my feelings? Or not show how hurt she was? I absently knocked my glass to the table. It bounced and splashed across the tablecloth.

"Shit. Sorry about that." I said and used my napkin to prevent it from ending up in Lady Therese's lap. An orderly came over to help with a towel and I sat back in my seat with a frustrated sigh.

"Something bothering you Pepper?" Lady Therese asked with a sip of her tea.

"It's nothing," I said and swirled my spoon through lunch.

"Sounds like a heavy nothing."

I looked at her and narrowed my eyes. Could she be reading my mind? If you can read my mind raise your hand, I thought.

"But I will not press if you don't wish to share." She continued. She was probably the best person to talk to about my issue and this might be the last time I saw her for a while.

"Do you think it's a good idea to send me to the front with them?" I got out.

"The shield is necessary on the front." Lady Therese said. "It may scare you Pepper, but I believe in you." She set her cup down and reached out to pat my arm.

"What about the burden?"

There was a moment's pause before she spoke "Sylvia has hers under control. Jonas has his moments, but don't let him get too carried away with being in command."

"What about the shields?"

"The shields burden?" She cocked her head. "Oh, that- oooooh." She snickered. "You worry about Sylvia." A knowing smile crept across her lips and a flush burst over my cheeks.

"Of course I worry about her. I worry about her going to the front. I worry that I'll be putting her in danger. I worry that what we feel isn't real." I finally admitted the part that really tore at me.

"Does it matter if it's real?"

"Of course it does," I said, aghast that she would even suggest such a thing. "If it's not real, then what's the point?"

"Who's to say it's real or not? If you feel it and she feels it. Is that not love?" The word caught me by surprise, was it really love we felt? Or was it merely childish infatuation? Would something so fleeting feel so powerful?

I tried to fire back a retort but found my mouth hung open as her words took root in my mind. That's what love was, wasn't it? I'd never let myself hope for something so wonderful. It just seemed like something other people got and I watched from afar or read about in fairy tales.

"Someone else doesn't get to decide how you feel. Some people think Stephan and Rheiners love is not only fake but a very real and condemnable sin. But those two have the most passionate embraces I've ever witnessed."

"Stephan and... oh. I had no idea that they were-"

"They keep it a secret. I trust you will afford them the same confidentiality I have given to you and Sylvia."

"But, what about her safety? I read that It could cost her life."

"Every Relic has that warning. Yes, Relics are dangerous and getting too involved and heated can lead to in-fighting. But you both are level-headed enough that it shouldn't be an issue." Lady Therese chuckled. "Your fretting over her is admirable, I dare say adorable. But misguided. Two chosen in love is a beautiful thing. Something the world needs more of. Stop being silly. Go be her shield, let her be your sword. Keep each other safe."

She was right; I was being stupid. If she felt the same as I did then it didn't matter what a book said. I shot up out of my seat. "I need to make things right with Sylvia." I grabbed my bag and hurried to leave.

"Stop by a flower shop on your way" Lady Therese shouted.

Chapter 15

Heavy Moniker

I jogged most of the way to the station, only stopping to catch my breath twice. Once when I stopped at a flower shop. There weren't many options, and I didn't know what to get. So I settled for a rose.

I got to the train station as the train pulled up. It took me a moment to find the pale grey uniforms of the orderlies who were joining us on the front. I scanned them quickly but didn't see Sylvia.

"Has Sylvia shown up?" I asked the nearest Orderly.

"Sir, no she hasn't. Sir." The man that was at least ten years my senior with a full mustache and dark hair stiffened and saluted.

"Oh, uh no need to be so formal," I said and brushed the back of my head.

"Yes, sir." The man widened his stance and moved his hands behind his back.

"Uh, as you were." I gave him a casual salute and put my pack with the others.

"There you are Dodger," Jonas said walking back from the ticket office. "I was beginning to think you were trying to dodge again."

I did my best to ignore his raz. He smirked and handed out the tickets. Two were left in his hands when he got to me.

"I can take Sylvias," I said and held my hand out.

Jonas looked at my hand and then into my eyes. He sighed and motioned me to follow as he stepped away from the group. I followed him several steps; he put his arm over my shoulder to pull me closer. "I know Therese is overlooking you two. But when we are on the front, you need to keep it in your pants. Got it?" He ordered with a finger in my face. "Orders come first. I can't have you going rogue for a woman."

"She's a Knight. Just like you." I replied and lifted his arm off my shoulder.

"No, she's not," Jonas said and glanced at the flower in my hand. "The council said she's still too unstable to be a knight. You are both still squires." He shoved the tickets against my chest. "And you'll both follow the orders I give you."

I wanted to punch him, again. He could probably tell and smirked as he glared back, daring me to take the swing.

"Understand?" He snorted.

"Yes." I took the tickets.

"Yes?" He pressed.

"Yes, sir," I said through clenched teeth. My fist clenched around the stem of the rose.

"Good boy Dodger," he said with a condescending pat to my cheek. I jerked away from his hand. "I'll make a proper man of you yet." He chuckled and walked back to the group as they began to climb aboard.

The hard leather case carrying his rifle toppled to the ground and Jonas began to yell. I wondered how he'd react if I were to toss it off the train. I took a deep breath and realized a thorn dug into my palm painfully.

I switched the rose to my other hand and flexed the pain free. I looked around and saw Sylvia coming across the street to the platform. My stomach fluttered, I tried to think of a way to explain my behaviour. The truth felt too weird, but I had to come up with something.

I tucked both hands behind my back as she walked closer. The crowd gave her a wide berth and some weird looks. Her hand rested on the handle of her sword and the other carried her suitcase. She either didn't notice the stares or didn't care about them. Her pale grey uniform was sharp as ever but the long dress bottom seemed out of place. I'd always seen her in pants which seemed weird at first, but now the dress felt more out of character.

She walked past me without so much as a nod. A little cold, but I suppose I deserved that.

"I have your ticket here," I said and turned to hold it out along with the rose.

She turned with a scowl and looked like she was about to tell me where to put the ticket. But the rose gave her pause. She looked at it and narrowed her eyes at me.

"What's this?" She asked.

"A rose," I replied. She rolled her eyes and put her case down and pursed her lips.

"I mean, why do you have a rose?" She asked and crossed her arms.

"Because..." I hadn't thought of that. "Lady Therese suggested I make up for this morning."

She took the rose after a moment and rolled it between her finger and thumb while she examined it.

"I shouldn't have been so distant," I continued. "I hadn't slept well and wasn't thinking right." Her eyes lifted from the rose to match mine. "I hurt you and that wasn't fair. But I want you to know It won't happen again."

She lifted the rose to her nose for a long moment. The longest moment of my life. My heart pounded in my ears and my throat tightened more with each second. "Did Lady Therese tell you these are my favourite?" She asked.

I let out the breath I held in and shook my head "No? Lucky guess?" I chuckled with a shrug and a smile.

She rolled her eyes again. "We all have our bad days Peter," she said with a smile. "No need to be so apologetic. You've seen me at much worse." She held her arm out and motioned for me to join.

I stepped forward and picked up her suitcase before I looped my arm in hers. We walked towards the train car the orderlies climbed into.

Jonas stepped out to meet us. He stepped up to Sylvia shaking a finger in her face.

"I'll tell you the same thing I told your boyfriend. You will follow orders out there no matter the situation." He growled.

"Jonas," Sylvia said calmly. "You may be older than me and have rank on me, now." Her arm pulled from mine, and her hand came to rest on her Relics handle. "But don't think for a second I won't flay you open for the crows if you try to lord over any of us."

The heat from their combined fury forced me to take a step back. I thought about reaching for the shield, but I didn't want to use it to hold power over any of them. If it really did what the book said. I should have read more. I scolded myself.

"I've been on the line longer than you. Rheiner knows me, not you. You will be in command, but Lady Therese will have the final say and I will report directly to her."

Jonas clenched his jaw and fists. I thought he would a swing this time. It wouldn't end well for him though.

"I'll follow orders until you give ones that get people needlessly killed." Sylvia finished.

Jonas ran his tongue under his lip and he glared at Sylvia.

"Fine, but I best not see or hear of any grab ass between you two. The rules haven't changed, yet, and I will send one of you back. Keep it professional." He said with one more finger shake at us both.

We each gave a nod but Sylvia rolled her eyes when he stepped back into the train car.

"Have I told you how terrifying you can be?" I asked once Jonas was out of earshot.

"Oh, that? I was just reminding him he doesn't have seniority." She said with a smirk. "He has about six months more seniority than you."

"Oh? I thought he'd been with you for years?"

She shook her head. "He'd been in the trenches for about two years before we crossed paths. Lady Therese found him the same way she found you. He picked up the shield." She climbed up into the train car.

"Is it really that heavy? I almost forget I'm carrying it." I said while we made our way to our seats.

"To a blessed, it's almost nothing. But to a regular person, it's impossible to lift." She said once seated. "Some have called it Grave marker. Because until another blessed picks it up. It marks where the chosen fell."

"That's..." I searched for the word

"Morbid?"

"Creepy," I said and looked at the shield stored in the overhead compartment with my duffle bag.

"Perhaps," Sylvia said and brought the rose to her nose again. "You seriously had no idea?" She looked from the flower to me with a smile.

"None. It was pure luck." I smiled back.

"Well, hopefully some of your luck can rub off on the rest of us."

We were inseparable for the rest of the trip. We stayed up late talking, played cards and took advantage of someones Chess set. We went to meals together and even slept side by side when Jonas was on watch. As well as anyone can sleep sitting in a train booth.

One cool morning I awoke with her head resting on my shoulder, the soft sound of her breathing tickled my ear. She hugged my arm close to her and although I knew what we were headed for, that

moment made it all seem like a distant nightmare. Like it was someone else headed for the muck and murder of the front lines.

Sadly, the moment was short-lived. A few days, four trains and
one long truck ride later, we were back on the front lines. They felt
just as oppressive as the first time I saw them. It was a sunny evening
but the trenches had a looming shadow over them. Lifeless despite
the many people milling about, training, moving supplies and gear
around. Maybe it was the snow that now coated the ground and
turned the muddy paths to ice.

"I'll report to Command and see what the situation is," Jonas
said. He slung his Rifle over his shoulder. "You two head to camp and
get ready for a patrol tonight." He marched off towards the tents set
up far enough away from combat for the Commanders to feel safe.

I picked up my bag and followed Sylvia who lead the orderlies
to the grove where our tents still sat. There was a brief exchange between the original Orderlies and the ones that accompanied us before they headed back. I went off to my tent, and I stumbled when
my foot broke through a frozen puddle. I winced as cold muddy water filled my new shoes. Could I not get one day with warm feet out
here?

"Fuck." I groaned and shook off what I could before I continued.
A new stove sat in the middle of my tent and a stack of logs sat near
the foot of the bed. It was warm enough inside that I shrugged my
jacket off and took my shoes off. I grimaced at the tarnish across
the brand new custom fit leather. I'd been so happy to get them and
swore to take the utmost care where I stepped with them.

With a sigh, I opened my bag to pull out my boots and spare
socks out. I laid them on the bed and also took out my spare uniform
to hang it in the armoire. Along with the other fresh fitted clothes
I got. It was a strange experience, for a boy that grew up dreaming
about hand-me-downs, to not only have new clothes but custom tai-

lored ones. New leather boots that gleamed in the candlelight, and a few pieces of magical gear.

I curled the thick belt up and set it on a shelf beside the boots and a scarf. I searched my bag for the instruction papers they gave me, to no avail. I remember the belt was Lady Therese's but I couldn't remember what it did.

The scarf was something to do with gas? There were talks of outlawing it, but the Russians still used it from time to time. They weren't as effective as when the Germans first used them. But the idea of being caught out in the open without a mask was something everyone dreaded.

I'd heard the horror stories from the older soldiers who survived the attacks. They carried friends away only to watch them die slowly over days while others coughed their literal lungs out in the field. I wasn't sure what was worse until I saw my first shell hole with a bunch of boys gassed dead in the bottom. Claw marks on their throats, black blood caked their uniforms eyes bulged out beyond what I thought was humanly possible, foam dripped from their lips. It made me scared to jump into shells for days after.

The boots were Imped-treads, I only remembered that because they were exactly like the ones Sylvia and Jonas wore. But I couldn't remember what they did either. Magical clothing wasn't uncommon, but it also wasn't cheap. Each item was likely a years' pay at a factory to afford. I glanced at the shield still tied to my pack. I had refused to pick it up while we were on the train. It was impossible to put a price on that.

I shaved and got ready for patrol. The standard moustache most men could grow still avoided me. Though mine had started to show up, after several months on the front.

"Peter?" Sylvia called from outside my tent. "Are you decent?"

"Yeah," I said while I tied the new boots and reminded myself to watch out for that puddle when we left.

She came into the tent back in her full gear. Sword at her side her metal gloved hand resting on the handle. Her eyes looked me over as I stood and puffed my chest out a bit.

"You look good in a fitted uniform." She said in a hushed tone.

"So do you," I smirked, she rolled her eyes. "Don't forget the scarf and belt. You never know when they'll come in handy."

"It is cold out isn't it," I said and grabbed the scarf and my new jacket. It was so clean and I dreaded what the trenches would do to it. I holster my gun and patted the jacket to double-checked for extra mags before I followed her out of the tent.

"Grab the shield." She said with a laugh as she shook her head.

"Right," I ducked back and reached for the shield but hesitated. Lady Therese's words rang in my ear.

Does it really matter? I thought about it often this past week and how close we grew without the shield.

It doesn't. I slipped my arm into the strap and folded the wooden handle up. I gripped it tight and flexed my arm. If it wasn't for the strap and handle, I'd not know it was there. There was no weight to it. Had I not seen its power first hand I'd doubt this could stop a stiff breeze.

I stepped out of the tent "Honestly Peter," Sylvia said. "I worry you'd forget your head if it wasn't attached." She continued with a shake of her head. Her hair was just long enough to sway with the motion.

"Sorry about that." I rubbed the back of my head. She stepped closer and slipped something into my pocket. I looked at her with a raised eyebrow.

"Just in case," She said. I gave a pat over the pocket when she stepped back. It was a pocket pistol.

"But I have my sidearm." I pointed to the holster at my hip.

She shrugged. "Like I said, just in case." She turned and headed through the camp.

I looked around the dark camp lit by a few crystal torches and two fire pits with pots that sizzled with snow melting for canteens. "Where's Jonas?"

"He hasn't shown up yet. He might still be talking with Command." Sylvia said with a shrug.

"Must be something serious they called us back for."

"Or he's being an ass."

"You don't like him do you?"

"It's not that I don't like him. I don't like his attitude," she said. "He's entitled and doesn't understand the dangers of using a Relic."

"So all the Relics have burdens?" I asked while we walked through camp.

"Yes," Sylvia said after a moment. "But the rifle's burden is different. Most will compound. But the Rifles require that the burden already exists."

"What kind of burden?" I asked and remembered to watch out for the puddle. I scanned the ground ahead but didn't see it. I turned to see we had just walked over it. I looked at my boots, perfectly dry. Sylvia's were the same.

"The books say something about a dark intent to..." She cocked her head. "What are you looking for?"

"That... that puddle. I ruined my shoes coming into camp. Did we both miss it walking back?" I asked.

Sylvia shook her head. "You weren't paying attention to the Quartermaster when they issued your gear were you?"

"In my defence," I tried to explain. "I was distracted."

"You can't keep using me as an excuse," Sylvia said with a straight face for about a second. The right side of her mouth curled as she fought a smile.

"I can while it's true." I replied and watched her walk back to the puddle.

"They are Imped-treads." She stepped down but didn't sink below the surface of the puddle. "Things like mud, snow, soft soil, puddles, and even quicksand won't impede you." She jumped on the puddle and made a small ripple.

"Quicksand?" I cocked my head. "What's that?"

"Something that is a common occurrence." She continued. "Did you pay attention to your other gear?" She asked as we made our way to the edge of the camp.

"Umm."

"Peter," she scolded and shook her head. "This is serious life-saving gear." She tugged her scarf from a pocket on the front of her jacket.

"It's a Gas Scarf if there is a gas attack wrap it around your face to breathe and keep the gas from your eyes." She returned it to the pocket. "The belt is a Lifters belt. It makes you stronger, able to lift heavy things."

"Oh," I said. "Anything special to activate it? Cause I don't feel stronger."

"Grab here." She motioned to her belt. I took hold. "Now lift me up."

"What? With one hand? I couldn't do-" She cuffed me up the side of the head.

"Just do it." She said with an unimpressed pout. I realized the mistake in what I said and gave a nod. I bent my knees and heaved with a grunt.

She shot off her feet into the air, I almost lost my grip on her belt. She caught my arm and I held her with one arm over my head. My eyes wide with amazement as she laughed, her feet dangled free from the snow. She was as light as a child and I felt like I could carry her like this back to the camp if I wanted.

"See, stronger." She added and held onto my arm. "You can put me down now."

I lowered her but stopped a few inches from the ground. I looked around and seeing no one was around I pulled her closer.

"Not before I get a kiss." I smirked.

"You are incorrigible." She rolled her eyes and wiggled her feet to get back to the ground. I lifted her higher just encase she could reach with her toes. She huffed and pouted with her cheeks before she leaned in closer.

I pressed my lips to hers and held them for a long moment. I let the sparks course through me and fill me with life. My heart thumped as I lowered her down, only breaking the kiss when her feet were flat on the ground again.

"We can't do this too often." She said. Her hand brushed over my chest in the darkness of the forest.

"That just makes the times we can do it more precious." I said and leaned in to kiss her again. She brought her hand up to stop me. The sounds of crunching snow caught my ear, and I cursed it.

I stepped back and released her belt to face a pudgy older man with grey hair, a fake leg and one sleeve folded and pinned up. He walked with a limp and a cane in his hand.

"Ah, there you are. Good. Saves me walking the whole way." The man said. "Knight Fraser has requested his squires join him on the front." The old man spoke with a mechanical voice that vibrated and hummed through each of his words.

"Thank you, Captain Lopez." Sylvia said. "We are headed there. Do you know where he is waiting?"

"Hmm somewhere between Rue de la Grotto and Greensfield Ave." He replied.

"Thank you," I said and Sylvia gave him a pat on his shoulder as we passed.

THE TRENCHES WEREN'T as bad as I remembered. Maybe it was because the mud was frozen and didn't stick to our boots with every step. Or it was the small stoves posted around that gave more warmth when they'd been so sparse before. The smell of burning wood wasn't unpleasant either. Or maybe it was the fresh faces on the front line. No. That was what made it terrifying. So many young boys and girls, some not old enough to drink. Yet, they were expected to fight, and kill. Most of them wouldn't make it through the winter.

I gripped the handle of my shield tighter at the thought. One woman knelt before Sylvia and clutched a cross in her hand as she muttered. Sylvia didn't acknowledge her as we passed. I couldn't be that cold so I gave her a smile. A few others recognized and offered prayers but most just gave suspicious glares. None were hostile, they likely wanted to know who we were and why we were so clean. Or what we were doing with a sword and shield on a battlefield of bullets and bombs.

A loud shot rang out ahead of us and everyone jumped, myself included. Most for their guns but a couple ducked behind cover. Those are the ones that would survive, I thought. Sylvia didn't miss a beat, so I straightened my back and followed.

We rounded a corner with a sign "Greensfield Ave" with the green scratched out and "Rats" written over it in large charcoal letters. Jonas was halfway down the curve of the trench talking with a few men. As we got closer, I could tell they were marvelling over his gun and he was drinking it in.

"Quiet the pretentious ass that one." An older man in a group of others said as we passed. "Has a magic gun and shows it off like it's his god earned talent."

"He's not wrong." Sylvia muttered a few steps away, I smirked. Jonas turned to us and I swallowed my smile.

"Bought time you two got here. It's been dark for well over an hour." He said looking at his watch.

"You didn't give us a time to meet." Sylvia replied.

"We always met at the trenches when it was dark." Jonas replied. He slung his rifle over his shoulder and stepped forward.

"The boys say there is a Russian commander a dozen yards or so away. He might have some intel on him. Dodger. I want you to go out there and check."

"Me?" I gulped. My veins turned to ice at the thought of going over the edge again. Memories swam around in my mind of the first time. The explosions, screams, machine gunfire. It rattled in my head and I struggled to think through it, a voice squeaked through and urged me to tell Jonas off.

"Yes, you. You have the shield." He replied and crossed his arms.

"Uh, I'm not so sure about that." I stammered.

"I'll go with him," Sylvia said.

"What?" Jonas and I said in unison.

Sylvia grabbed a ladder. "I said, I'll go with him," she repeated. "Unless you need me to watch your back," she said louder as she set the latter on the sandbags. A few men in the group behind Jonas snickered, he glared at her.

"Fine, but only because Dodger doesn't know what to look for." He said, and wasn't wrong. "And make it quick. We've got reports of gremlins command wants us to take care of."

"Really? They called us back for that?" Sylvia asked.

"No, it's just something extra they've requested." Jonas replied.

"Gremlins are real? I thought they were a myth." I asked. A few others around me nodded.

"Oh dear God, Dodger." Jonas rubbed his head. "You have so much to learn," he shook his head. "We'll fill you in later. Go check for intel, I'll cover you." He said and slid his goggles down, he hopped to peak over the sandbags quickly. "You're clear." He said once he landed.

I looked to Sylvia who gave me a soft nod and held the side of the ladder. With a deep breath, I gripped the rails and cursed under my breath with each step. A scene of men running to their deaths through gunfire and shells flashed before me when I peeked over the bags for a second, before the stillness of reality settled. It was dark and shadows played on my eyes. I thought I saw movement everywhere. With a deep breath, I kept low and stepped off the ladder waiting for Sylvia to join me.

"Stand tall." She whispered once we were both on the fringe of no-man's-land.

"Are you insane?" I whispered back.

"Do you remember Lady Therese's moniker?" She looked to me. It was hard to see in the dark since she was a few feet away, but her eyes found mine.

I nodded and replied. "Lady Unbroken."

"She was a symbol, now that you have the shield you must be that symbol too. Stand tall, proud and unafraid."

"But I am afraid," I replied. She smiled and shuffled closer to grip my arm.

"So was she," she replied. "Every day, even now she's scared for us. It's not fair, but out here we have to be that symbol."

The realization hit me like a boulder and that light piece of magical metal suddenly felt heavier than a train. I understood Lady Therese's words and her anger when I walked into the tent. 'It's a moniker, one that must remain.' I pressed my fist to my forehead, I'm so naïve.

"It really isn't fair," I said with a sigh and gripped the handle of the shield tighter. My arm trembled under the crushing responsibility it carried. The promise it had proven to be time and time again. One that now rested squarely on my shoulders, salvation. Salvation didn't hide or skulk through the night.

I took a breath and forced my legs and back to straighten. I stared out over the dark, desolate field. The glow of fires from the trenches in the distance were the only light in the cloudy night. The first step complete, now I had to convince myself to walk. Though my legs were like ice and they refused to move forward. Tears formed in my eyes and I lifted my foot from the ground, my leg moved forward, ice broke free from my muscles until I'd taken a step into no-mans-land. I let myself breathe and tried to relax, hoping this wasn't my last moments.

"Hurry the fuck up before some harvesters get to the body," Jonas shouted from the trench.

I clenched my teeth and resisted the urge to tell him off.

"For god's sake Jonas, fuck off or come up here yourself you cock-alorum." Sylvia spat in my place before she stood beside me. Her hand found mine and the ice in my legs melted away, I dared a glance at her. She didn't look my way but smiled. I smiled and took another step forward just as I saw a flash and something hit my chest.

Chapter 16
Failed Test

I took a step back to stabilize myself and I stared in awe as a bullet fell into the snow. It disappeared under the powder and I clutched where the bullet had hit and looked at a clean glove. I rubbed my fingers against a hole through my jacket to double check, again no blood.

The loud blast I associated with Jonas rifle rang out and I watched a red line zigzag through the air. It dropped right on top of where the first muzzle flashed.

"Got you covered Pepper," Jonas shouted from the trench.

"Cover comes before you get shot, Jonas!" Sylvia snapped back and checked the wound. "God, are you okay?"

"Yeah... I barely felt it." I triple checked. Had I died and just didn't know it yet?

Sylvia sighed once she was sure I was okay. "Try to keep the bullets on your shield." She joked.

"I'll try." I said and tried to shake the trembling from my fingers. "Not every day you survive getting shot." I joked back.

She let out a snort of laughter and smirked. "I have a feeling that will be more common than you realize. Care to take the lead?" She asked and motioned with her gloved hand.

"Uh, sure." I said and led our way into no-man's-land. Sylvia kept a hand on my back as we made it to the fallen tree that held the pinned corpse of the Russian commander.

"I'll lift, you search?" I suggested and put the shield down beside the tree, I put my boot on a corner as I searched for a place to grab.

"Lady Therese taught you well," Sylvia said as she knelt beside the body.

I found a handhold with a thick branch and a couple of bullet holes and heaved the tree up a few feet. It was much heavier than Sylvia and took some focus to keep up.

"What?" I grunted as she struggled to free the body.

"Your foot, it's on the shield." She replied with a few grunts as she tugged on the body. "Damn. He's frozen to the ground. Can you hold it?"

"Yeah, sure," I replied with a grunt. The strain on my muscles had only just reared its ugly head. I could hold for another minute I figured. "I saw her do it on the train," I replied between breaths.

Sylvia searched the man's pockets pulling out a crushed pocket watch, a ruined packet of smokes and matches, a handful of papers she stuffed those into her jacket along with his ring and a locket that somehow survived around his chest.

"Okay, clear." She said and I let the trunk down slowly.

"Did you need his ring and locket?" I asked.

"More than he did." She replied and tucked them into a pouch. "Come on, let's get back."

I bent down to pick up the shield, and an arrow struck the wood inches from my face.

"Gah." I stumbled back with the shield lifted. I scanned the darkness for where the arrow had come from but couldn't see anyone.

"Relax," Sylvia said and waved her hand high. "If she wanted to hit you she'd have done so," she said. "Looks like Rheiner has a message for us." I pulled the arrow free with some effort and grabbed the piece of paper wrapped around the shaft.

"We can read it when we get back to camp. There are a few there who read german." Sylvia said and started back. I opened the paper and looked it over in the dark.

"He's requesting a meeting," I said. "Things have taken a turn. Russian command fears a revolt and has scattered the Blessed." I squinted to examine the letters better It had been so long since I read letters to my mother. "And executed some commanders Lady Therese was in touch with. He thinks Zakeem had something to do with it." my brows furrowed as I looked up. Sylvia's eyes narrowed suspiciously at me and I realized my mistake.

"How do you know that?" She asked and took a cautious step back.

"Uh," I racked my brain for an excuse. Lucky guess? No, it's all written in german. I must admit to the truth that got me beaten up as a child, lost me jobs and almost got me killed back in America. My shoulders sagged as I sighed. "I am fluent in german. My parents were German."

"Are you a spy?" Sylvia asked and took another step back as she glared at me. That glare stung more than any beating I'd ever received, more than being called a Kraut or a Jerry or any of the other words people slung.

"No. I've never even spoken to a German soldier," I admitted the sting burned inside and boiled over.

"What about the Russians?"

"Nor them! I've only ever been part of the US army. I was born on US soil and with my mother dead I have no ties to Germany. They are my enemy!" I said in frustration and pointed at the German trench "Look, I get it. You've no reason to believe me. We've known each other for a few weeks. If you don't believe me tie me up and bring me to the Honesty seat. I'll tell you the same thing over again."

Sylvia's glare softened, she took a few steps to close the gap between us, suddenly she was too close. She pressed to my chest and leaned in until our noses almost touched. Her eyes bore into mine and I wanted to take a step back but her gaze held me in place.

"Who's your enemy?" She asked pointedly.

"The Germans."

"Why do you know their language?"

"Because of my mother. I just told-" She held a hand up to stop me and continued.

"What would you do if a german attacked you?"

"Kill him."

"What if he came after me?"

"Destroy him."

She smirked and took a step back. "Okay, I believe you." She said.

"That's it? A couple of questions?" I asked trying to piece together her train of thought.

"Yep. You answered without hesitation. I believe you. Jonas might not though." She said with a shrug.

"Do we have to tell him?" I asked.

"Better we be forthcoming earlier than hide it and have him find out say in the middle of no-man's-land." She said and took the note. I gave a nod. "We can wait till we get back to the grove. Easier to sit you on the Honesty seat."

"That's fair, just don't ask embarrassing questions please," I asked as we started back to the trench.

"I hadn't planned on it. But now, I make no promises." She teased with a smirk.

We followed our footprints back and gave Jonas the pack of maps and info from the captain which he handed over to the Allied Command. We waited until we got to the barn with the gremlins to tell Jonas about the note from Rheiner. I didn't mention the rings and Sylvia didn't mention my German genealogy.

He told us we'd deal with it when we got back to the grove. So we spent the rest of the night hunting gremlins. Which sounds much easier than it is in practice. Normally something like this was mages work. But those were in short supply these days. The few the army could get their hands on were used to counter scrying or crafting magical defences.

The foul furry little bastards are agile, more cunning than a toddler and screech twice as loud. Which doesn't sound bad until there are fifty toddlers the size of a New York rat running through ammo and food stocks? They're ugly, smell worse than a communal toilet and though their teeth couldn't puncture a leather glove at first bite, they'd grind their teeth back and forth and tear holes in just about anything before too long.

We did our best to not blow the barn sky high and thankfully the few times Sylvia missed it never caused a spark. By morning's light, we were exhausted but had a barrel full of gremlin corpses. This was more work than taking care of the rats in the trenches, at least there you celebrated after each successful ambush of the fat bastards.

Jonas slung them into the sun's light and the corpses turned to ash before they hit the ground. He got the most kills that night which he wore as a badge of pride and took as a sign of good things to come.

I couldn't see how the job of glorified pest control was something to be bragging about. But I thought back to some wise words I'd heard from a former boss. "Every job has its importance in our system. Much like every species has its place in nature"

I wondered if he was aware of how dangerous some of these species got? Did he know that these mythological beasts existed? Was it common knowledge that I missed out when I dropped out of school? Or was I getting a peek behind the curtain of the world that only a select few got to see?

Jonas distracted me from my thoughts when he kicked the barrel over spilling the gross bloody contents onto the snowy ground.

"Dodger, make sure these get ashed before we leave. I will see if there's anything worth confiscating," he said with a chuckle and went back into the barn whistling a merry tune.

"Ashed?" I asked looking to Sylvia.

"The bodies of creatures without souls turn to ash when they die and are exposed to sunlight," she explained. "It's the only time you can be sure you've killed it."

"Oh," I asked and picked up half a gremlin by its long naked tail, its guts spilled out onto the furry backside of another and I looked to her. "I'm pretty sure it's dead." I tossed its body onto the sun-kissed snow.

"With the right conditions, it could come back to life." She kicked another body into the growing pile of ash that had once been creatures.

"What conditions?" I asked.

She shrugged, and we continued ashing the bodies. I wondered what other creatures the war had brought to life.

We were lining up the barrel to get cleaned out by the rising sun when a POP came from the barn.

"Son of a bitch!" I heard Jonas scream. A few more pops confirmed it was gunfire. Not the loud boom of Jonas rifle. Something smaller like a handgun.

We dropped the barrel and ran for the barn. Sylvia was faster and threw the large door back. I watched Jonas collapsed to his knees. He clutched his stomach, blood poured past his hand. He pointed his other bloody hand to the back door we'd nailed shut that now swung loosely.

"Zakeem." He coughed and blood ran from his lips. I saw the other patch of blood on his chest. I looked for the Rifle but didn't see it. I hoped it got tossed behind a crate in their struggle.

"After him Peter," Sylvia said as she shoved past me. "I've got Jonas."

"R-right." I ran out of the back. Fresh tracks in the snow leading away from the barn and into the forest. I pulled out my handgun and ran after him. He wouldn't get away from me this time.

I ran into the forest with an eye on the tracks and ahead of me. I knew I could handle a regular round, but Jonas had made special rounds. I didn't want to run headfirst into an ambush.

I slowed my pace because it would be easy to track Zakeem in the snow and it didn't look like he headed back to enemy territory. It was alarming how quiet the forest was; the stillness made me nervous. I tried to convince myself it was because of the snow. A distinct CLICK told me just how wrong I was. I froze in my tracks.

Zakeem had doubled back without me noticing and I was square in his sights. I could see him from the corner of my eye. The long Rifle's barrel pointed out from behind some snow heavy pine branches.

"You really must stop being the wrong person to show up all the time, Shield." Zakeem's voice came from behind the wall of trees.

"What do you mean?" I asked and brought myself to face him.

"Nothing important for you. I just wanted to conclude a contract and give my thanks." Zakeem stepped forward, the snow fluttered around his white cloak. What did he mean? Who did he want to thank? The dark double barrels pulled my attention back to the situation.

"Drop the gun," Zakeem ordered.

"So you can shoot an unarmed man?" I replied.

"If I wanted to do that you'd have been dead in your tent the first night you showed up," Zakeem said. "I want a test." He hissed the last word.

"A test? Of what?"

"Relics, Can I kill you? Or can you get to me first?"

"What's wrong with you?" I growled and clenched my hand around the gun and shield.

Zakeem laughed and moved his arm under the rifle to pull his scarf down and reveal his torn-up face. "Many things. But I've wanted to test these two Relics for thirty years. Now I have the chance.

You can indulge me, or I can see if I can finish that worthless fool off from here." He pointed the rifle up into the air.

"Wait." I clenched my jaw. I didn't like Jonas, but I also didn't want him to die. "Fine." I tossed the gun into the snow and raised my shield. He was maybe three dozen yards away, I could make the sprint.

Zakeem grinned his wide twisted, nightmare grin. "So gracious of you. I might actually miss you Shield." He hissed his laugh and aimed it at me. "Whenever you are ready."

I braced myself to make the sprint and waited for the right moment. I wasn't sure what exactly that would be. Honestly, I hoped Sylvia would burst out from a tree and cut him down. But as the seconds ticked by I realized that wouldn't happen.

"If you are too scared to make the first move," Zakeem started "I'll be the one to-"

I lunged at him before he could finish speaking and before I got my second step, he fired. In the forest's shadow, I saw the orange tail coming straight for my shield. I tensed for the impact but it zipped around and came for my side. I spun and tucked the shield to my side just as the round hit.

The bullet exploded and sent me off my feet. I tumbled through the snow several yards.

Zakeem hooted and tried to whistle in amazement. "That fool knows how to make impressive rounds." He said and reloaded as he spun the barrel.

I was on my feet before I stopped moving. The impact hadn't hurt one bit. Though the explosion made my ears ring. A few more steps and he'd got another round off. This one had a green tail. It slammed into my shield head on with enough force to stop me in my tracks. I pushed on but the round came back at a different angle, I couldn't get my shield in front. I thought about taking the hit, but instinct took over and I dove out of its way. On my knees I batted the bullet away from its next strike, then lunged for Zakeem again. But had to dodge away from the bullets next pass.

Zakeem laughed at my efforts. He hadn't moved, and yet I had only made it halfway. I picked up the pattern of the bullet and swatted it more often than I dodged while I made slow progress.

"Let's see how you do with two." Zakeem asked and fired another green tailed round.

It halted my progress as I couldn't do more than dodge and block now. If I made any other moves, the bullets would hit me. I wasn't sure the Relic could hold against another Relic, but I knew I couldn't keep this up forever.

I swatted them both free and made a dash for Zakeem who was doubled over in laughter. He fired a round straight up. I couldn't see it, but raised my shield overhead and reached for my pocket. If I could get one round off.

The explosion slammed the shield against my head and dropped me to my knees. I skidded to a stop before Zakeem. The green-tailed rounds both slammed into my back, I clenched my jaw wincing in pain. It burned, it stung, it felt like they'd punctured my lungs and were about to burst out my chest. My back arched, I threw my head back out and screamed in pain before I fell to my hands.

Zakeem cheered and pumped the rifle over his head. He jumped and spun to celebrate his victory. I expected him to click his heel, instead, he kissed the rifle and praised it in his native tongue.

I knelt at his feet on my hands and knees breathing hard, but steady. My first day I'd seen a man die of a chest wound and he'd struggled to breathe with ragged breaths and coughed up blood. I wasn't doing any of that. It hurt like the dickens but I was okay.

I pulled the pocket pistol free doing my best to not make it obvious. Zakeem seemed to think he'd won. I didn't want him to realize his mistake yet. I acted like I was on death's door with ragged breaths. I moved sluggish in the snow. I tried to push myself up with the shield arm but made it tremble. I was laying it on thick but Za-keem believed it.

"Oh, don't worry little Shield. I won't let you suffer too much." He pressed the barrel of the rifle to the crown of my head. "You may not like me, but I am not that cruel." He laughed. "Though I ask you to look me in the eyes when I kill you."

I looked until I could see the barrel and burst to my feet. I slammed the shield into the rifle. It went off. He grabbed the shield and tried to pull it free from me. I jammed the pocket pistol into his chest. He had just enough time to realize things had gone wrong before I shot.

POP.

His eyes widened, he lurched. POP POP POP. Three more rounds and he hunched over. I finished the last few shots before I shoved him back into the snow. He crumpled and curled to his side.

"H-how?" He sputtered.

"You failed your test," I growled. More angry at myself than him. I glared at the pocket pistol gripped in my hand. What I did was right. So why did I feel so wrong? I flung it off into the forest as Za-keem wheezed his last breath.

Chapter 17

Wisdom and Strength

S ylvia met me halfway back to the barn. Blood stained her uniform.

"How's Jonas?" I asked.

She searched the snow for the words, but I could tell by the amount of blood on her, he hadn't made it. I clenched my fists and that tightness in my stomach loosened. I *did* the right thing.

"Zakeem's dead," I replied and put a hand on her shoulder before I tugged at the collar of my uniform. It had warmed up this morning, and I was finding it too hot with my thick winter uniform on. Sweat beaded on my back from the fight, I figured once I cooled down it would be all right.

"Really?" She looked surprised and almost smiled when I nodded. "What about the Relics?"

"Oh," I sighed and rubbed at the side of my head. "I was so wrapped up in my thoughts that I forgot about them. They're probably still on him." I said and pointed back where I'd come from.

"Peter." Sylvia shook her head. "Let's go get them," she added. I nodded and turned to head back. It looked much further than I thought and I dreaded going back. *It's just another body* I told myself *One that deserves to be there.* That did little to ease the tension in my neck.

"My god." She gasped and brushed a hand over my bareback. I winced and pulled free from her touch.

"Ah, what?" I asked looking at her over my shoulder.

"You've got two giant welts on your back." She tried a more ginger touch, but it still stung.

"Yeah, got hit. But it's not serious." I shrugged it off, though the pain was giving me a headache.

"With what? An anti-tank rifle?" She asked. "You're bleeding," she said and dug into the bag at her side "Let me patch you up."

"After we get the Relics," I said. "There is a stump I can sit on there." I trudged back the direction I'd come. Despite the trail, I'd left it felt much harder to go back this time. I was starting to sweat, my feet were heavy and were it not for the gear I'd likely have fallen on my face.

We returned to the scene of my struggle to find the Relics and Zakeem's body were missing. I walked over to where the packed snow marked where he fell. There was no blood in the snow. I looked at the single tracks that lead away from the imprint.

"Fuck!" I kicked at the snow, threw my shield down, and shrugged my jacket off. It had gotten too hot out for it and I couldn't stand it any longer. I tossed my jacket away and paced back and forth. "How the fuck did he survive? I had him. The barrel was against his chest. I felt the impacts. I saw them." I panted and sweat dripped from my chin.

"Peter, let's get you patched up," Sylvia said trying to calm me.

"No. I want to know, what the fuck happened?" I ran my hands through my sweat-slick hair. "He had a contract with someone? Do you know about this?" I asked.

Sylvia shrugged. "We can discuss it back at the grove," she said. "But for now, calm down."

I couldn't catch my breath and could see the flush in my hands. They tingled with the heat from my fury. Or was it my fury? I'd never been this mad in my life. I tried to calm down but my chest heaved and the icy morning air was the only thing keeping me from burning up.

"Some... somethings... wrong." I gasped out and tore my shirt open. Steam wafted off my chest as I fell to a knee.

"Peter." Sylvia rushed to my side. "What is it?"

"Too... hot." I grabbed a handful of snow and rubbed it over my face. It stung in the best way and I grabbed more to rub over my chest and arms. My arms trembled as the snow fell from my hands. I collapsed face down into the snow with a satisfied groan. I gasped lungfuls of the cold air.

"Pepper!" Sylvia shouted and shook me a few times. "Pepper! Hold on, Please. Just hold on." She ran off.

I groaned in pain as my insides began to burn, the fire coursed through me like petrol hot and gross. I ate what snow was in front of me and rubbed my face to the forming puddle.

Sylvia returned after a moment and use the shield to shovel snow on top of me. I winced and sighed when it melted through my shirt and sizzled against my skin. She buried me and slipped the shield under my arm.

"Please Pepper, don't leave me. I can't be the last one." She knelt by my head. I shivered despite the heat. She rubbed snow over my face and piled more under my head.

I tried to tell her she was strong and that she could handle whatever came her way. But between mouthfuls of snow, it only came out in jumbled nonsense. The world became a blur and though Sylvia continued to call to me, her sweet voice muffled as the world went black.

I AWOKE LATER BACK in my tent. A wicked headache that made lights danced before my eyes when I opened them. My throat cracked and my muscles felt like they'd rusted in place. I had to put effort in to take a deep breath which made me cough. I rolled to my side despite the pain and coughed out an orange fluid onto the ground. It tasted like horseradish and vanilla.

A hand rubbed at my back and brought a cup of water to my lips. "Welcome back to the land of the living Pepper." Lady Therese breathed.

I gulped the water down; it did little to chase the taste away, but it was still a relief.

"What-" I tried to piece my thoughts together, but they were sluggish.

"Happened?" Lady Therese finished.

I nodded.

"You were poisoned." She said and sat on the side of the bed. "We almost lost you. Here drink." She brought a small glass to my lips and tipped it back. My mouth flooded with fresh horseradish and vanilla. I pulled away and tried to spit it out. "It's medicine. Drink it." She encouraged and held me steady. I swallowed the concoction that I felt rumble its way down into my stomach.

"Ugh, I need something to wash the taste out," I begged after she gave me another sip of water.

"Here," She handed me a piece of bread that I wolfed down. Sweet jam spread helped clear the taste from my mouth. I laid back in the bed to appease the protests of my muscles. After a dozen ragged breaths the pain subsided enough for me to think clearer. I remembered my fight with Zakeem, news about Jonas and the burning, I felt like ice now compared to how hot I was before. I remembered nothing about Lady Therese being at the front again.

I looked at her sat at the table beside my bed pouring over documents and reports with her hand. "How did you get here so quick?" I croaked out and grimaced when I turned to face her. Bandages still wrapped her face and went under her hair. Her jacket hung off the back of the chair, new General stars sat on her shoulder straps beside an arrow and sword pin.

"You've been out cold for a fortnight Pepper. I had plenty of time to get here." She said without looking in my direction.

"A what? Fortnight?" I had to think back to the last time I heard that. How long was it? A month? No, that was too long, ugh. I didn't have the brainpower for this.

"Two weeks." Lady Therese said. "Sylvia didn't leave your side until I got back two days ago. Things... are a mess Pepper." She sighed and pushed the report she held to the side. She turned to face me after slipping a blue gem behind one of her bandages. It took its place in front of her eye socket hidden from view.

"The Russians have been advancing, we've lost several trenches. It seems Zakeem has taken to hunting us again. I haven't heard from Rheiner since the letter. There was a gas attack two days before I got here. We lost a few but most of them got you and Sylvia to safety." Her head hung as she spoke. "I don't know if we can recover from this."

I searched for words of comfort, or advice to bring about a change in perspective. Nothing came to mind. So I closed my eyes and laid there in sheepish silence.

Footsteps in the snow outside the tent encroached on the silence before the tent flap opened.

"How is he?" Sylvia's tired tone reached my ear.

"Ask him yourself." Lady Therese replied.

"Peter?" She asked and peaked past Therese's shoulder.

I held a grimace back and spoke. "I am awake." I opened my eyes.

"Oh, thank god." She said and sat on the side of the bed. Her hand brushed across my face. "I was worried you'd never wake up again." Her fingers ran through my hair.

I leaned into her touch despite the pain. "What happened anyway? Lady Therese said I was poisoned?"

"Jonas was using forbidden tonics to enhance his rounds. The rounds that hit your back would have made a regular man explode.

The shield was all that kept you in one piece." Therese said and motioned to the end of the bed. I felt the shield sitting under my calves. I shifted my legs and winced. "At least until we got you back here and administered an antidote." She pointed to a bottle of orange liquid on top of the desk.

"Thanks." I managed a smile.

"You aren't in top shape yet," Therese said. "But I'd say you are out of the woods. Now, if you two will excuse me," she stood up. "I would like to get the latest news from the front and pray for a miracle." She finished and put her feathered helmet on before she left.

Sylvia's eyes lingered on the tent's exit.

"You should go with her," I said after a moment. Her eyes fluttered to mine.

"What? No, I should stay here with you." She patted my chest with a smile.

"You want to go with her, though." I smiled. "It's okay. You've been by her side for years. I get it."

"But I want to be by your side now." She said as she locked her eyes on mine.

"There are better options out there." I motioned to the tent door.

"I think the best option is right here." She brushed my chest.

"Why's that?" I asked but had already figured the real answer would relate to the shield.

Sylvia's eyes bore deep into me, deeper than ever before. "Have you ever killed someone?" She asked.

I hesitated for a moment and looked to my rifle resting against the armoire. "I have... I think. It's hard to tell if it's been my shot or one of the countless others that are firing. I've never been up close and personal as you have." I admitted.

Her eyes beckoned mine back and bore deeper into my own, invading my soul and my cheeks flush, but I couldn't tear away. Hers shone with intelligence yet were as comforting as a clear day. Her full pink lips pursed into a line and her eyelids narrowed while she examined what she saw.

"Hmm," She said after a moment.

"Hmm? Hmm, what?" I asked desperate to know what she saw.

"There is a lot of good in you, Peter," she said with a smile and brushed my cheek. "I want to keep it safe. Because I worry that you don't have the wisdom and strength you will need to survive."

"It's hard to have the wisdom when I've only been doing this for a few months." I sighed.

"That's not what I am talking about." She corrected and reached to the bowl that sat on the table. I examined her face as she stirred the stew slowly, searching for her words.

"What... what wisdom or strength are you talking about?" I asked after a minute.

"The wisdom to shroud yourself in darkness when the time is right, and the strength to pull yourself back into the light. I don't want to see the good in you get lost in the mire of this war." She blew steam off a spoonful of stew before offering it to me. "You'll need your strength, so eat up."

Chapter 18

Loss

I spent the next couple days recovering from the poison Jonas had prepared. Had I known he was using such cruel methods. I like to believe I'd have done something. But I think back to Sylvia's words and I'm not sure I would have.

Lady Therese came to visit me again shortly after I could sit up on my own. She had re-assumed command of the Knights and another company.

"Pepper. I have a favour to ask you." She said in a formal tone. I hadn't seen her without her helmet on since the day I awoke. The feathers gave her a regal, almost mythical appearance.

"Ask freely," I said eager to be of help.

"It's not something I ask lightly, and I ask that you take some time to answer it." She'd turned the chair at my desk to face me and I felt her gaze lock on mine. It dried my throat, and I swallowed before nodding to her request.

"I would like to use the shield again. I feel it's a necessity on the battlefield."

The answer in my mind was yes and came instantly, but I held my tongue and thought about it. Why did I think about it? It was a chance to be free of the damn thing. Sure it was powerful, too powerful. The responsibility had been too much for me. I couldn't be the one to carry it.

Yet, could I really give that to someone else? Someone who'd carried the weight that shouldn't have been hers to bare. Sure she'd done it for almost twenty years. But could she keep doing it? I looked where her eyes should be to assess her. A slow smile crept across her features.

"Why the smile?" I asked.

"You've felt its weight." She said with an approving tease in her voice.

"How-"

"You worry I won't be able to handle it."

"I-I didn't say that." I tried to explain.

"You don't have to. It's exactly what I thought about you." A smirk crossed her lips as a snort of laughter escaped.

"And you were right." I sighed. "It's better in your hands," I admitted and pulled the blanket back to expose the sheet of steel still nestled by my feet.

She didn't move and it was hard to see if she was looking at the shield or examining me. She shook her head after a long still moment.

"Pepper, I am not taking it. Merely borrowing it. The Relic has made its choice clear." She pointed to her eyes.

"Or was that a warning? I couldn't help you then, save Jonas, stop Zakeem. I've done nothing but fail."

She snickered and used a hand to cover her mouth.

I frowned. "I fail to see the humour," I said as her laughter cut deep.

"You echo my exact sentiments when I first got the shield." She smiled and stood up to put a comforting hand on my head or perhaps it was belittling? "You've used it a handful of times Pepper. God has a plan for us all and wouldn't put you on this path if it was too much."

"Do you really believe that?" I asked. I'd heard something akin to that before but I couldn't believe it when I was taking care of my mother. Things had been too much for her.

"I do." She nodded. "I have to." She added in a tone so quiet she must have assumed I didn't hear it. I wanted to say something, anything, but my words failed me. I just looked up at her with a sad smile and nodded. She took the shield and left without another word. I'd later curse not having said anything.

Sylvia returned to the camp most mornings to check on me and help with my recovery. It was embarrassing having her care for me but I was thankful for the hand as the poison sapped my strength. It would have taken weeks or months to recover from were it not for Stephan's special concoctions. Each viler than the previous and I detested him every time he brought them around. But I couldn't argue with the results.

The time I had to myself should have been a blessing but it felt more like a curse as I wasn't able to help. The orderlies wouldn't let me cook, or help clean. I had nothing but a deck of cards to distract my mind and that only lasted so long before they became the focus of my frustration. I swatted the table away after losing another game, Though I knew the anger was at myself.

"Well," Stephan said as he jotted down some notes a week after Lady Therese took the shield, "I think you should be ready to rejoin the effort tomorrow night." He said once he finished. "I'll let Therese know."

"Thanks," I said and buttoned my shirt back up. "How have things been?"

Stephan stood and leaned over the table with a sigh. "Not good. Be thankful they can't over-run the grove."

Sylvia had told me about the grove's runes while I was recovering. It was "a pocket of the world outside the normal world." as she said. I didn't get it but I also didn't question it.

"How much ground have we lost?"

"Too much." He sighed and left the tent.

I got dressed and stepped out too. I wandered over to Therese's tent to look over the maps I heard she brought back the day before. The battle lines were different now. The allies had retreated, and they had etched new defensive lines across the old ones and newer ones beyond that. I did my best to make sense of it. I wondered how much had changed since she got these maps. Surely we'd re-taken some. Was Paris really within striking range now?

"Stephan!" It was Sylvia shouting from outside the tent. "We need you!" She added in a panic amidst groans of pain and hurried footsteps. I stepped away from the table and pushed the tent flap back. A gruesome sight greeted me. Orderlies in a varying state of disarray and dismemberment. Most uniforms splashed with blood, from spray, or a personal injury it was hard to tell. I searched the faces for the one that mattered most to me.

"What happened?" Stephan asked as he rushed forward and pulled a bandage back to examine the first patient on a stretcher. A healthy splash of blood shot across his crisp white uniform. "Fuck." He wasted no time getting to work. Medical tools came out from his pockets as they walked back to the Medic tent.

I searched the returning group who's heads hung low, those who had no injuries were in tears as they walked by. I saw Sylvia carrying a severed arm in one hand while she dragged an unconscious orderly back into camp. I rushed to her side.

"What happened? Are you okay?" I asked and helped shoulder the man's weight.

"Ambush," Sylvia grunted with tears pouring down her cheek. "They set us up. Lady Th-" her words hitched in her throat and she almost dropped the arm.

"It's okay," I brushed a hand along her back. Though I had no idea if it would be.

"No, it's not Peter." She said when we made it back to the tent. Other orderlies hurried about with bandages and more of Stephan's concoctions. We got the one-armed man into a seat and Sylvia set his arm on his lap. The cries of pain and suffering felt amplified inside the deceptively large tent. I didn't think everyone would fit in it but there looked to be room for more.

Sylvia dropped her armoured glove and snatched what I thought was a bottle of blood. But as she poured it over her bloody hand, I realized it was too deep a red. She hissed and clenched her teeth as the liquid sizzled and fumed from the stumps where her ring and middle finger had been.

"Sylvia, what in god's name..." I couldn't get it out. The bottle dropped to the floor, she gripped her arm as it trembled and jerked. She finally looked at me and I saw the pain in her hand was nothing compared to the shadow that tortured her soul. She tried to hide it with flames of rage, her jaw clenched and lips pursed so tight they trembled. Her cheeks streaked with tears and blood.

"She's gone." She finally got out and the rage in her died. Her legs buckled and I reached to help her to her knees as she sobbed.

I knew who she meant, but couldn't accept it. "Who is?" I knelt beside her and wrapped my arms around her. She pressed to my chest and sobbed the answer I was dreading.

"Lady Therese. She's dead!" Sylvia said. She gripped my shirt so tight I thought it would tear and sobbed louder. I pulled her close as reality knocked me on my ass. I looked around at those that could still stand. I tried to fight the tears that welled in my own eyes, but they were inevitable. Therese hadn't been in my life long, but she had become a mentor for me. I could only imagine what she was to Sylvia.

Some orderlies helped us to our feet, and we made room in the infirmary as they set another bed up beside us. I nodded and guided Sylvia back to her tent. It was like mine but more lived in. I sat with her on her bed and rubbed her back. I felt like I should say something, fix the situation. I remembered how my mother would get worse if I tried. Back then I realized that sometimes you can't do anything. I could only be there for her.

"I'm here," I whispered. She cried into my shoulder through the morning until she cried herself to sleep. I stayed with her for as long as I could.

———●———

I JOGGED DOWN THE DARK path from the grove, the stars above my only light, to find a farm with lights on inside at the end of the forest path. The new command made the best of the situation they got shoved into. I heard gunfire crack and explosions rumbled like thunder in the distance. I prayed it was the counterattack. A successful push back would make my night's task easier. I followed the gunfire and found allies on the defensive. There wasn't much I could do as I was. One rifle wouldn't be the salvation needed for these men.

I pushed on, down the fresh muddy trenches, passed the injured and dying who cried out for help that might never come to them. Or for someone to be merciful and end it. Something I learned command frowned upon my first day when they hung a man for ending his commanders suffering in the trench.

Until I stumbled across a familiar face with the stripes of a Captain. He huddled with a half dozen men under the shadow of a destroyed armoured car. A crystal hung beside his dog tags and illuminated a map in his hands. He heard my slowed approached and looked up.

"Pip?" Captain Theirs said. "What in blazes are you..." His eyes widen seeing the crest on my uniform.

"Captain," I said with a nod once the other men looked up. A few faces I recognized but most of them were new. Had they lost their units tonight? Or were they from other regiments that had merged into a new one since things had gone to shit?

"You know why I'm here?" I asked. I now knew that everyone above Lieutenant knew about the knights. Though Stephan told me we're supposed to keep our flashiness to a minimum. Lady Therese had thrown that rule out long ago.

He nodded and his men gave him a questioning glance.

"Where is it?" I asked. Just as a large form limped down the trench behind them.

"It's a suicide mission. Even for one of your kind." He said with a shake of his head.

"Pip!" Leon shouted from behind. "It's so good to see you alive. I heard you got transf-"

A rifle blast from inside the tank cut him off. It reverberated in my bones and made me jump. Most of the other men jumped too. It echoed out into the air and sounded like the Rifle. I wondered for a second if Zakeem had found me already. I patted my hands over my body just to be sure.

"Fuck, Nora! Give a warning." Leon shouted and slammed the underside of the armoured car and wiggled a finger in his ear.

"Not wasting a perfectly good shot," Nora replied and poked her head out of the tank. A dark blue woollen hat sat low on her head, streaks of grease ran up her nose where she kept pushing up her glasses. "You'll just have to be a man- Oh hi Pip, fancy seeing you still alive." She waved and leaned back into the broken machine before I could wave back.

"You're gonna stick out too much." A man said from inside the armoured car, soot around his eyes and oil streaks through his hair. "Take my coat." He said and slipped the oil-stained Khaki jacket off his shoulders. It too had Captain's stripes that glinted in the red glow of the crystal. "We'll provide cover." He added and tossed me the jacket.

"Thanks, but you don't have to do that," I said and set my rifle down as I took off my coat and swapped it for his.

"As much as I would like to let you bugger off and get killed," Theirs said as he stood. "Having a Knight around is our best shot of getting out of here alive."

"I just need you to show me where it is," I said as I slipped the worn jacket on.

"Where what is?" Leon asked and rubbed at his thigh.

"He's here for the Relic that went down with the other Knight, right?" Theirs said.

I pursed my lips and sighed with a nod. Theirs never kept a secret from his men.

"The woman who saved Leon?" A new face said with a french accent.

Leon snapped his fingers. "I knew she looked familiar."

"Whatever you do, you better do it quick. Command said they are sending in more armoured cars led by a Baron." Andrews said as he ran up the path I'd come from with papers in his hand.

I closed my eyes for a moment. They were sending someone special. I wondered if it was Zakeem, or was it just some poor soul that would guard Lady Therese's body until the rat could show up to gloat?

"They'll need almost as much help as you," Theirs started. "If you hope to get to the shield alive." I opened my eyes. The red glow from his crystal gave everyone's face an ominous look. "They lost three tanks trying to get to her," Theirs said and unfolded the map pointing to three pencilled dots. "A few of the crews have survived and set up a perimeter they are waiting for something" Theirs continued

"Wait, her? She's still out there?" I asked.

"Yeah, No one can move her." The man in the armoured car said.

"Some tried," the Frenchman added said. "But-"

"No one can lift it." I sighed. This would be more than a dash and grab. I wanted it to be a recovery too. "Looks like I will need that support," I said reattaching the buckle on my belt and picking up my rifle again.

"Told you," Theirs said with a smirk as he pulled out his covered pipe.

We gathered others who lost their units and formed a small haphazard company of allied soldiers, most barely spoke enough English to understand the importance of getting the shield. Gunners battered an area away from the broken-down tanks. I hoped the shelling would make the Baron reconsider his advance and buy us more time.

Whistles blew and shouts came from the trenches to draw the enemies' focus to an advance that wouldn't come. While the enemies waited, most of the company moved and repeated the whistles and shouting. It was loud enough I thought a few soldiers would be hoarse for a week.

Meanwhile, the squad Theirs had sent with me crept quick across the open field towards the tanks and the handful of guards. A Scotswoman named Ava with enchanting eyes, according to Leon led us across the field. I thought he was just infatuated with her until I saw them for myself. Her pupils thinned to slivers when we met and they shifted to movement around me as I explained the situation. It made it very hard to concentrate.

She waved us down, and we hit the dirt and waited for her to wave us forward. I wished Leon could have joined us, but his prosthetic leg squeaked if he squatted so he kept watch of our advance with a Vickers behind a bush.

Ava waved us forward again and after another minute I saw the outline of the first tank in the dark. I heard men speaking beyond the busted wall of steel. Though it wasn't German.

Ava dove to the ground a few feet from the tank, the rest of us followed suit. She didn't stay flat long; she crawled through the dirt and sat up against the side of the tank and waved the first of us forward.

It was slow going and before long I could hear the distant growl of large engines accompanied by the squeal and clank of approaching tanks. I wanted to jump up and run for the shield but knew I wouldn't make it. I still didn't know where it was exactly.

I looked around to see the shifting eyes of the others. Each searched for someone else to offer a word of comfort or reassurance. More and more of their eyes settled on me. I gripped the icy dirt tight and tried to think of something good.

"Hold." Was all I dared to whisper out. They believed and obeyed me, that weight sat heavy on my back and made the crawl up to the second tank hard. What if I'm wrong and they should retreat? How many lives am I going to cost? How many can I save? I settled my back to the tank and watched the last few soldiers crawl up. They were so young.

The flash and distinct pop of a gun went off on the other side of my tank and interrupted my thoughts. A man scrambled back. Screams and shouting filled the night air.

"What the Fuck Charles?" The man beside me growled.

"Fuck off Hensen. He pissed on me!" The man who scrambled to cover said as gunfire erupted at that side of the tank.

Ava's group returned fire from behind their tank and a few more screams filled the night. A flare soared into the sky and lit everyone up. A man with Ava jerked back and fell dead. Charles returned fire until he got hit in the side. I peeked out the side of the tank. There were four men between two hastily dug positions.

There between the two positions I saw Lady Therese's body. Sunk into the earth's embrace, shield held tight to her form. Gravemarker, the name rang in my mind and sent a shiver through my body. She almost looked peaceful if you ignored the bloody hole in her helmet. One side of the feathers had been blown away. I wondered if they had been collected or had the soldiers disregarded them when they dug in. They dragged other bodies away from her and stacked them up to shore up the defence for their position few men.

My eyes shifted back to them as one aimed for me. I pulled back just as a bullet zinged through the space my head was a moment before.

My heart sank as I realized her death was my fault. I leaned back against the tank as the firefight went on. I'd let her take the shield and lead like she always did. Knowing that Zakeem, that son of a bitch, was out there.

The pit of despair seized my soul until Hensen yanked me to my feet and brought me back to the moment. The rumble of the tanks was louder now. Their lights bobbed in the distance.

"We're here for you!" Hensen shouted. "Do something." He shoved me back and helped Charles patch the wound.

He was right. I couldn't let myself get lost in things that have happened. I have to focus on the now. I peaked out for a second this time, ignoring Therese's body. There were three left and one of them was helping pull his comrade back into cover. I pulled out my new pistol and whistled to Ava and with a few motions she understood I needed cover fire.

An explosion rocked the furthest tank and made us all duck. We were in range of the tanks.

"Now!" I shouted and ran around the tank. One man saw me and turned his rifle to bare. I shot first and hit a body they used as a sandbag. It spooked him and he flinched. I heard the bullet collided with the tank. Ava and her remaining men opened fire and caught him in the head. His comrade duck behind cover as I cleared the distance.

Another explosion landed closer this time. Several more erupted around me and I felt their heat against my neck and face. I leapt for the shield. More explosions ripped through the remaining husks of the armoured car and sent shrapnel flying. I felt the Shields metal slide over my palm and gripped its edge.

I shoved off the ground by her corpse and ran back for the cover of the tanks. More explosions ripped through the surrounding metal. I felt pieces hit my helmet and clip my leg and stumbled to the ground as the pounding continued.

Chapter 19

Hammer

My ears rang like a bell. Smoke billowed out from fires inside the tanks as the dirt settled to the ground. What lingered in the air made me cough while I got to my feet.

"Is anyone alive?" I shouted, though it sounded muffled. I stepped forward dreading the carnage that awaited me on the other side of the tanks. I stepped past and stared wide as the smoke blew clear.

Charles nursed the injury at his side and Hensen sat up and scooped his helmet off the ground. A piece of metal lodged several inches into it. He rubbed at his head where the metal should have been to find a small cut. Blood trickled down the side of his face but it wasn't the fatal wound he should have gotten.

I turned to see Ava getting to her feet and patting herself down. Another soldier held up the torn sleeve of his uniform.

"How are we alive?" She asked. "I felt a shell land beside me."

I didn't know. I had tried to get back to them and get them to retreat. To save their lives, but it seemed pointless.

The tanks stopped their advance, A hatch squeaked open and after a moment a figure stepped in front of their lights. His silhouette was large and imposing. Barrel chested and broad shouldered he held something large on a stick in his hand and charged us.

"Get behind me," I said. Hensen pulled Charles back behind the tank and I raised the shield and stepped forward ready for him or the tanks to shoot again.

He roared out a laugh before he slammed his weapon into my shield. I thought it was a brick, but it was a hammer. A solid steel hammer with a Celtic knot on one side and a bull on the other. It slammed into my shield, I shuddered and my heels dug into the dirt as it pushed my arm back.

I could tell by the man's furrowed brow that he hadn't expected that. I pulled my sidearm and aimed it for him. He swung again and hit my hand. The gun turned to splinters and crumbled out of my hand. I pulled back as he swung again. Something was up with his hammer and I didn't want to risk the Shield. My hand stung from the impact and I flexed it a few times behind my shield before I pulled out my belt knife. Maybe I could get a lucky swing?

"You are Knight? Yes?" The man spoke with a deep rumble to his voice and an accent so thick I could barely understand him. "Ah, One of... Order from Rome?" He asked and clanked the hammer into his metal gauntlet. Now that I got a good look at him he was clearly Russian, The black wool hat and double eagle buckle on his brass buckle were enough to tell me the origins of his accent had his uniform not given it away.

"No, I'm not," I replied to him.

His head tilted, and he sucked on his teeth. "I think you lie. I dislike lies." He growled. "Come, Test your Relic. Which stronger. Shield, Or Hammer?" He hefted the hunk of steel in his hands. It looked heavy, but he moved it around like it weighed next to nothing, like the shield.

"We don't have to fight," I said. I wanted to get back, take Therese back. This was an unwanted distraction.

"Yes, we do." The man said and lunged at me. I dodged back. He stepped and swung wide, Ava took a shot at him and he caught it with his metal gauntlet. He looked surprised and glared at her. He spat something in Russian and pushed past me. I slashed at him with the knife. It cut through his greatcoat and into the flesh of his leg.

He growled and swung back at me. I ducked, he connected with the tank.

My eyes went wide as the whole tank shuddered a foot across frozen dirt. The hammer shattered a wagon wheel sized hole in the metal structure. Splinters broke off and a large piece sat flattened beyond the hammer's face.

Gun fire barked from the bush where Leon sat and sparked against the tank before it swept towards the Russian. He dove and bowled me over getting to cover behind the tank. Leon turned the gun to a group of advancing soldiers that came with the tank and cut a few down before the rest got to cover behind the tanks or in shell holes.

"Ava, get everyone out of here," I said as the flare from earlier hit the ground. Darkness shrouded them but the lights of the working tanks crept past the corners of the broken ones and gave the Russian and I enough to fight with.

"Cowards." The Russian spat and hefted the hammer into his metal gloved hand and advanced. His swings came wide and predictable. But they were fast, and I ended up blocking more than I dodged. He caught the shield and swung past it. It caught me in the side of the head like a slap. I lurched back, more stunned than hurt. With a growl, I slashed his arm, and he released the shield.

I stepped back and kept low. I didn't want the tanks opening fire again if they caught sight of me.

"You are like rat." The man spat after examining the injury. "Frustrating, and weak." He raised the hammer and leapt to bring it down. I raised the shield and stuck my blade into his thigh when the hammer hit.

He grunted and stepped back. His leg gave way, and he fell to a knee. I swung the shield and clipped his knee cap. A sickening pop followed. He shouted in pain and fell to the ground clutching his knee.

"I told you, It didn't have to be like this," I said.

"Fuck you." He spat at me but missed.

The light of tanks turned away. I hurried to peak around a broken tank as the Russian cussed me out. He struggled to get to his feet, but I'd seen enough injuries to know he wouldn't be getting up for a while, and if he did. He'd have to worry about all the blood he was losing in his thigh.

The tanks turned and advanced on the pockets of resistance the allies had formed. Shells blew the ground up around the tanks but only a few received more than a glancing blow.

What could I do? They were tanks. All I had left was a knife. I glanced back at the Russian who gripped the hammer tight and still struggled to his feet. Foam around his mouth as he spewed his string of meaningless insults.

"Don't suppose you'll let me use that hammer?" I asked.

"Fuck you." He spat again. It seemed to be his only English insult.

I shrugged and poked my head into the tank that got hit the least. Maybe there was a shell I could carry or some grenades or a working pistol I could salvage.

Footsteps came up beside the tank fast. I spun ready for another fight. Bring me something good. I thought and got my knife ready.

"Pip?" Leon's voice hissed before his rifle poked past the side of the tank. His prosthetic squeaking with every other step forward.

"Leon? Jesus." I said. "You gave me a heart attack."

"Me? How do you think I felt when Ava came back without you."

"I told her to go." I looked him over. "You got some grenades in your pack?" I asked.

"You know it." He said and eyed the cursing Russian with suspicion. Leon always kept extra grenades in his pack. He usually managed to grab more because of his giant mitts.

"Give em here, and your pistol," I said.

"What happened to yours?"

I merely pointed to the Russian who got to one leg. He hopped around like his one legged-ness made him a threat again.

Leon pulled the pistol from his side and shot the Russian. His metal glove sprang to action again and caught the round, but it sent him off balance. He fell back into the dirt and resumed his swearing.

"Uh, here," Leon said and handed me his pistol and two mags of rounds with a confused look on his face. He unslung the bag from his shoulders and handed it to me.

"Thanks." I grabbed them. "Head back and tell everyone to wait for my signal," I said before I headed off after the tanks.

"What signal?" Leon asked. "What am I to do with him?" Leon asked his rifle now levelled at the mud and blood stained Russian.

I shrugged. "Capture him or kill him. But don't let him keep the Hammer." I said as I rounded the last busted tank and broke into a sprint. I tried to think of what signal I would use when the tanks opened fire. "They'll know it when they see it," I shouted and redoubled my efforts.

I wouldn't have been able to make much headway were it not for the boots. The ground was so loose and pocked by shell holes with muddy embankments. I ran to the first tank and lobbed a grenade by its tread. It blew up, and the tank didn't get much further before it could only spin. The gunner popped the hatch and pointed his machine gun at me. I raised the shield; the rounds bounced away harmlessly.

A few rounds from my pistol and he flinched to grip his shoulder. He ducked back into the tank. I scrambled up it before he could pull the hatch down. It slammed down on my hand and I winced expecting it to hurt. But it felt like a child trying to close the door on me.

I flung the hatchback and aimed my pistol at the man's head.

"Give me your flare gun," I ordered in German. He looked confused as blood stained the arm limp at his side. "Flare gun. NOW!" I shouted. He hesitated, and I fired a round beside him. It was loud and bounced around inside the tank. He complied with my request in a hurry. I tucked the box of flares into the bag.

"Now get out and run," I ordered him and pulled out a grenade. He shouted to the other men who screamed and left out the back of the tank in a hurry. They didn't make it far before being gunned down by Russian forces who advanced now that the tanks had attacked.

I spun the tank's machine gun and sprayed the other tanks until the box ran dry. The first tank stopped and spun to address me. I leapt off the tank as it opened fire. The shell hit the first tank and the blast carried me forward. I hit the ground and rolled into a sprint right for that tank. The other tank also stopped its advance and turned. *Yes. Radio for help. Radio what you see.* I thought and reached for the flare gun. A round caught the side of my head and I almost fired the flare off in the bag. I quickly pulled it free, I needed them both.

I turned to see the Russian infantry advancing faster than I expected. Their roar was almost as loud as the tanks. But they looked young, fresh faced and ready to break at the first sign of things going wrong. I bit the handle of the flare gun before I threw my shoulder into the second tank. It shuddered, I grabbed ahold with both hands. If Lady Therese could lift that boulder surely I should be able to lift this tank. I grunted and heaved.

More bullets sprayed against me to no avail. It was so damn heavy. But I put all I could into it until the metal beast rose off the ground. With a roar of effort, I pitched the damn thing on its side.

I prayed Leon would forgive me for what I did next. I pulled a grenade pin and unslung the bag from my shoulder. With a quick spin, I flung it under the next tank. The grenades went off with a mighty boom that lifted the tank into the air and brought it crashing down. Its treads destroyed and its cannon bent to the ground. The flares from the box burnt bright as they flew and skipped across the battlefield.

I fired the flare into the air and prayed the allied listened to Leon. Because I didn't stop to check. I ran, right for the Russians. Those kids who had seen what I did turned and ran for their lives. Those that hadn't opened fire. Each bullet that got past the shield felt like a child flicking my skin. I pulled out my pistol and opened fire.

I ran into their ranks and they continued to fire at me. Rounds ricocheted off the shield and caught their allies. But they kept coming. A shotgun made me stumble, but I returned fire before he could reload. Before long I ran out of ammo and grabbed a rifle off the ground. Someone thrust a bayonet at my side and it snapped off. I caught him in the jaw with the butt of my gun.

I couldn't make progress, but I could hold them here. The longer I fought the more that reconsidered putting up a fight. I knew it wasn't enough. No one man could swing the tide of this war. Not alone on the battlefield.

Bullets flew around me and the Russians fell. I heard the whistle blow and another mighty roar as the allied troops charged into battle with me. The Russians opened fire and cut down many allies, but they kept charging and crashed into the Russian line with a ferocity I thought the war had sapped from everyone. Like seasoned troops that knew what horrors they were about to see and commit fueled by the vigour of a recruit that had never known them.

I prepared to see the bloodiest battle of my life as the men caught up to me. The Russians were as thick as fleas on a pig in July. That didn't matter we fought and pressed on. Just when we thought the battle was won, more Russians showed up to counterattack. But they broke upon us like water and we took the position they'd come from. This went on over and over throughout the whole night. By sunrise, we had beaten them back. Re-taken miles of land and even captured a Russian general. He didn't look like the kind to talk but that wasn't my business.

By midday, the command had re-issued orders of advancement and were talking about medals and bonus rations.

I knew the rations came because we'd lost so many. It wasn't as bloody of a battle for me because of the shield. It kept my allies safe but its reach could only go so far. It spurred others on by the sight but that didn't keep them safe from the bullets.

I handed my ration of captured beet soup and sausages, to a wounded soldier and made my way back. Back over the blood-soaked and corpse scattered field where bodies laid as they fell, or crawled to their last breath. It felt like miles of death, a glimpse of hell with no reprieve in any direction. Carrion called from above while others squawked compliments and pecked morsels free from their human lunches.

I was tired, too tired to bother scaring them off, and there was still something important that I had to do. I walked alone across the open field. Back to where the night began, Nestled between three long broken husks of metal I found Lady Therese. Other than some dirt splashed across her she lay untouched, almost peaceful. Like the world knew how precious she was and refused to tarnish her any more than it already had. Her peacefulness reminded me of when I returned from work to find my mother dead.

I knelt beside her and brushed the dirt off. The memory choked the words in my throat as I searched for what to say. What was there to say? "I'm sorry." I echoed as the memory played out again, and held her cold stiff hand.

Chapter 20

Last Knight

L eon had followed me back and helped me fashion a stretcher from two broken pieces of Fence and our jackets. He was a good man and didn't deserve what he got.

"I'm sorry about your bag," I said and grunted as I lifted my side of the stretcher covered in a tattered, muddy blanket. It wasn't right, but it was better than nothing. The shield sat on top was the only clue to who was underneath.

"Think nothing of it Pip. Ma will love to hear the story of its demise." He said and his newly acquired metal gauntlet clanged against the tank as we walked by. I'd never mention a word about it. But looting the dead left an uncomfortable feeling in my stomach.

"What happened to the... uh"

"Russian?"

"Yeah?"

"Put up a fight, so I shot him," Leon said in a plain tone.

"Oh." I hadn't been serious when I told him that. But it's war and what is one more life? Even if he was a Blessed.

"Yep, he was ready to listen after that."

"But I thought you-"

"No, I didn't kill him. Left him with a limp, but he'll recover. He was ready to follow along once he stopped screaming. Christ, the lungs on that man. He whimpered the entire way back to command. I'm sure they're putting the screws to him as we speak."

I laughed. Of course, Leon wouldn't kill an unarmed man. Though he had the frame of a bear and unless fly tried to abscond with his food, he'd wave it off. The night's events must have weighed on my mind too much to think clearly.

"What about the hammer?" I asked.

"Oh yeah," he said. "Just a second." He put his end down and walked over to the bush he'd set up in the night before. It wouldn't have done its job in another few days, the leaves were already piling up around its base.

With a grunt, Leon lifted the hammer from under the Vickers. "It's rather heavy." He said and hefted it a few times as he walked back. "I don't know how he could swing it without dislocating his arm."

"Can I see it?" I asked and put the stretcher down to hold my hand out.

"Sure," he said and left it drop and swing before he lifted it for me. "You might want two hands."

I brought my hands under it. Leon set the hammer down and hesitated before he pulled his hand back.

The hammer wasn't nearly as heavy as he said. It felt like a framing hammer. I tossed it up with one hand and flicked it to the other. "You playing a game with me?" I asked with a chuckle. I looked to see he was definitely not. He stared wide eyed and slack jawed at the hammer.

"How... You... What in god's name?" He crossed his arms and looked me in the eyes.

I tried to fight my smirk before I hooked the leather loop at its handle on my belt. "It's why they transferred me."

"Think they'll take me too?" Leon asked, and we picked the stretcher up again.

I thought about it and the horrors I'd seen in the few weeks I've been part of the order. What others awaited me. The end of the war wouldn't be the end of fighting for me.

"I... I'm not sure," I replied. "I don't know how they choose recruits"

"Oh. Well do me a favour and ask all right?"

It's more of a favour to not ask. I thought and continued on the way back.

———◆———

I FILLED LEON IN ON what had happened to me as we made our way back to the grove. He sounded rightfully in dismay over some details. But I told him if he wanted to join he had to know what he was getting into. It was more than I got.

I tried not to think of how heavy Therese was by the time we got to the runes. During the day the transition was a little more noticeable. The trees shifted shape and fog surrounded us, the sound of the wind died off to a soft murmur. Replaced with the crackle of a distant fire and the smell of burning.

I groaned at the thought of a burnt breakfast. Just what I didn't need.

"Hey, Pip," Leon said. "Uh, is it supposed to smell like this?" Leon said and wrinkled his nose. He gave a snort and breathed with his mouth.

"No, I think an orderly must have burnt breakfast," I replied.

"Did they burn themselves too? Because it smells like burnt hair."

I turned back to look at him. He was right. It was burnt hair and what I thought was fog was smoke.

"We have to move," I said and set the stretcher down and ran for the camp.

"Hold up," Leon shouted.

But I couldn't.

I ran ahead first with only one thought on my mind. I almost tripped over an Orderlies body on the path. Another lay behind it clutching to the first's pant leg. Both had a large hole in their chest, where their heart was. I didn't stop.

I stumbled forward and ignored the bodies that had fallen into the fire. The sickening scent of flesh crackling made my stomach want to heave. But I didn't have time for that. No one moved. I panted as I pushed myself harder. Maybe, maybe I'd be in time.

I charged into the tent I'd left Sylvia in the night before to find her bed empty. Maybe she got away? But there was blood in the cot, so much blood it dripped to a pool underneath it.

The world fell quiet and my legs gave way. I gripped the bedsheet and held it tight. Was this how Lady Therese felt? Helpless, lost, broken and alone?

Leon told me later I'd let out an almost inhuman cry before he found me in the tent. Though I don't remember it. The next thing I remember was Leon leading me from the tent and I heard someone call out.

"Stephan?" I hoped it was Sylvia, horse from the smoke. "Stephan?" They shouted louder, it was a man's voice. A man I recognized.

The life that had threatened to leave me a moment before rushed back with a vigour I'd never known and a furry that would later scare me.

I snatched the shield from Leon who had the smarts to bring it when I panicked. I clutched the hammer in my other hand and ran for Rheiners voice.

"You, where is... Hold up I'm only here for." Rheiner got out before I collided with him. We tumbled to the ground and wrestled for control. He was bigger and ended up on top first.

"Listen to me," he growled. "I didn't-"

I clocked him in the side of his helmet with the shield. He fell to the side; I climbed over and raised the hammer. I wasn't in the mood to listen. I swung, and he moved just in time. He twisted my hand. I lost my grip and pulled the shield back to crush his skull.

An arrow shot out of the smoke and broke against my shoulder. It caused me to pause for a second and search for my next target. It wasn't long, but it was long enough for Rheiner to get his luger out and press it under my jaw.

"You know that won't do shit," I growled.

"Maybe." He said with a groan. "Maybe a blessed round will knock some sense into you."

"Is that what you used on the people here?" I growled.

The bolt of a gun clacked and Leon spoke, "I got your back Pip." He'd grabbed an orderlies rifle and levelled it at Rheiner. A break in the smoke let me see the german woman crouched and aiming her next arrow at Leon.

"Let's all try to get along," Rheiner said and pulled his gun back from my jaw. He looked to the woman and nodded. "Wenn der große Kerl etwas versucht, töte ihn." She nodded and kept the arrow notched but relaxed a little. Her eye's set sternly on Leon.

"Do it, and I'll crush his throat," I said to her in German. Her eyes widened, she glanced at Rheiner who looked just as startled

"You-" He started.

"Yes. No secrets. Now talk. Why are you here? Did you help do this?"

"No, of course not. I heard Zakeem had found the grove. I came as fast as I could, I wanted to warn Fraulein Therese. To... to set up a trap for the bastard."

"She's dead," I said.

"I know." He replied crestfallen. I tensed up, did he have a hand in that? "I saw her body when we arrived. I worry now for-"

"Stephan," I said and leaned back off him and gave Leon a nod to relax. He was hesitant but lowered his rifle after a moment. Though he didn't point it too far away from Rheiner.

"Have you seen him?" Rheiner asked with desperation in his voice. "He's fragile."

"I haven't checked the Medic's tent yet," I said while I got to my feet. "It's the big tent in that direction." I pointed him in the direction I thought it was, but the smoke made it hard to tell. I didn't want to see how bad it was in there. It was too quiet to have any injured still alive.

"Rheiner?" A voice called from that direction. "Is that really you?" Stephan's voice coughed.

"Stephan!" Rheiner ran off into the smoke.

I was amazed anyone was still alive. I was sure they'd killed everyone. So I wasn't the last of the order. That silver lining felt worthless without Sylvia. The German woman slung her bow but kept an arrow in her hand as she followed her commander.

"Keep an eye on her," I said in a hushed tone to Leon.

"Sure thing," Leon said and moved to follow her. In my numbness, I almost missed the smirk on his face. I felt like I should warn him that fraternizing with the enemy was quite against the rules. But at this point, I wasn't sure if they were the enemy.

I wasn't sure who I was supposed to be fighting or what I was fighting for anymore. I thought back to Sylvia's idea of running away. We could have done it. Last night we could have packed up and run away. Could have got so far away. Who'd stop us? Now... maybe she was with Stephan?

I couldn't bring myself to hope for it. Besides, there had been so much blood in her bed. But what about the body? Did Zakeem take it as a sick trophy? Or was it scattered among the others? Could I handle finding it?

I walked over and set the shield beside a knocked over water barrel. I saw the person who knocked it over a few steps away. A woman in her thirties, terror etched around the hole in her lifeless face. I wondered why she joined as I got a cup of water. Why did any of them join? The blessed seemed strong armed into their positions, but the orderlies were regular people.

I looked around at the tents that smouldered and the ashes of the orderlies belongings and took a few gulps of water. Why had they come? Their lives were spent like change for something I couldn't grasp and wasn't even sure mattered. With a handful of water, I washed my face and neck of the ash and nights grime, the blood from my hands and the grit from under my nails.

Another gulp of cool water and the world stabilized, yet still made little sense. Would it ever again? I glanced at the shield that sat gently, untarnished and ready for action.

"Impossibly heavy." I uttered the words Lady Therese's once said. She was right. I wondered if I'd be able to pick it up again. I didn't want to. Was this what Sylvia meant when she said the wisdom to shroud myself in darkness? Or was this when I needed the strength to pull back to the light? What light was there to pull back too?

"Pepper," Leon muttered before his hand set soft on my shoulder. "You okay?" He asked.

I took a breath. "Yeah, what's up?" I turned to him forcing as natural of an expression as I could. The concern in his eyes told me I didn't do a good job.

"They've called for you. You didn't answer... uh," He dug into his pocket and pulled out his handkerchief. "Here."

"Oh, sorry I was uh, lost in thought," I excused and waved his offer off. "It's all right, the water feels nice."

"You still might want to wipe the tears away," He said, still holding the yellowed cloth out.

I brushed my fingers over my face to find hot tears pouring down my cheeks. I hadn't even realized it.

"Oh." I took the cloth and sniffled while I wiped my face. "It's just water... I splashed some to clea-" I grunted as Leon gave a slap to my stomach with the back of his hand.

"Cut that shit out, Pepper," Leon said as he looked out into the forest. "We've all been there. Take a moment. We'll still be in the Medic tent when you are ready." He said and headed back. After a moment I heard him talking to others not too far off.

I sat back on the barrel and hung my head in my hands, trying to keep my sobs to a minimum. Exhaustion from the night compounded with the losses and the weight of everything tore through me. I wasn't sure how much would be left by the time I was done.

I cleaned my face off and picked up the shield. I knew I'd need it for whatever was coming. I walked over to the medics tent and pushed the flap back.

Stephan was stitching up his own leg while Rheiner brushed a hand tenderly over his loves back. I didn't believe the stern german commander was gay when Therese told me. But seeing it now it felt natural. Another time and I might see the worry on his face and the softness in his otherwise Icy blue eyes as endearing. Now it was just a painful reminder of what I'd lost and I hated them for it. Even if I couldn't admit it to myself.

"Pepper," Stephan said before grunting when he jabbed a black needle into his leg for another stitch. "Glad you could join us." He grunted again.

"What happened?" I snapped in response to his shortness.

"What do you think?" He growled back.

"Zakee-"

"Of fucking course it was Zakeem!" Stephan slammed his fist into a tray and scattered the utensils. "Fuck." He clenched his teeth as tears welled up, his hands trembled as he finished stitching his leg. Rheiner quietly picked up the tools and walked them over to a station to clean.

"He took her, we need to get her back," Stephan said and wiped the blood from his leg. A thin healed scar remained of the wound he'd just stitched.

"Who?" I asked and narrowed my focus on his face. Beads of sweat dotted the pale features.

He looked at me then furrowed his brows at Leon for a moment. "Sylvia, Zakeem took her in the attack."

My stomach dropped at the thought of Zakeem dragging her body away from camp. I didn't dare think beyond that. "Her body, you mean? I saw the blood in her tent."

"No, I mean her. He didn't kill her. Though he had the chance. The blood was from Philip over there." He motioned to a bed with what I thought was a body. There were half a dozen extra beds from when I left. "I managed to seal the wound but it'll be up to him if he lives."

"He... didn't kill anyone in here."

"Zakeem is a monster. But he's not inhuman." Stephan said.

Rheiner let out a huff and shook his head. "If you say so."

"So... she's alive?" I asked still in disbelief of what I heard. It didn't mesh with the reality I let myself fall into.

"For now," Stephan said as he slipped off the bed. "He wanted you though," he added. "He wants payback."

I almost didn't hear the words. She's alive. The world swept back under my feet along with all the dread of losing it I'd only had for a terrifying moment.

"Payback? For what?" Leon asked.

"Pepper almost killed him a few weeks back," Stephan said.

"Why didn't you finish the job?" Rheiner asked when he returned to Stephan's side. His stern expression had returned as he locked eyes on me.

"Did he tell you where he'd be?" I asked Stephan. I didn't have time to explain something I didn't understand.

Stephan nodded. "But you can't seriously think of charging in there."

"That's my choice. Tell me where." I asked barely keeping some composure over the question.

"Pepper, listen to me. It's foolhardy to-"

I kicked over a stand and scattered the medical tools. "Tell me!" I yelled. What little restraint I had snapped. Fear and fury ran wild with the chariot of my soul, and I wasn't sure I wanted to reign them in.

"Control yourself," Stephan ordered. I glared at him with a heat that made Rheiner step between us.

"Tell. Me." I managed through teeth clenched so tight I thought they might break. Rheiner puffed his chest, daring me to make a move. I glared back and glanced at the scattered utensils on the ground. Could I use one?

Leon backed up a step or two as the tension grew. "They said he went to the Ethereal Circle," Leon spoke up after a moment. It earned him death glares from the others. I relaxed and clasped him on the arm.

"Thank you, Leon. You are the truest friend a man could ask for." He smiled but I could tell he was nervous. "That's where we first met?" I thought out loud and didn't even glance at Rheiner as I headed to the exit. The woman unslung her bow and Rheiner grabbed my arm.

"Just listen, you damn fool." He growled and hauled me back almost off my feet.

I spun and swatted his hand away only to find his Luger was in my face again. Even with the shield, staring into the dark barrel of a gun that closes gives a man serious pause.

"You don't know what you are walking into. Fighting in the Ethereal Circle is prohibited for a reason."

"I don't care, and you can't stop me," I said and stepped back the woman had an arrow in her hand her blue eyes zeroed in on me.

"It could kill you all," Stephan said and pushed Rheiners arm down. "Talking with hostile intents is a risk there. Fighting will bring demons for sure."

"I don't care!" I said again and turned to leave.

"The demons are why the war has gone on so long." Stephan blurted. "Therese worked for decades to seal them away. What will Sylvia think if you ruin that?" He shouted before a coughing fit took him.

"At least she'll be alive," I said under my breath.

Chapter 21
Lies

L eon was right on my heels as I left the tent and helped me search for supplies. It took me longer than I would have liked to find a new pistol and a couple of extra mags. I thought about a rifle but decided It would only get in the way. Leon took a couple of grenades and tucked them into a satchel he found.

"I think I'm better off going with you." He said and handed me another satchel.

"You'll be the first to die," Rheiner said a dozen paces away. He glared from the medic tent, watching us scrounge through the burnt remains of the camp and set the bodies we found in a more peaceful manner than when they fell.

"Oh yeah? How do you figure that?" Leon asked. He sized Rheiner up as he stood tall. They were both towers of masculinity. Though Rheiner had more defined features.

"The Ethereal Circle is a place only for the Blessed. If you aren't driven mad. You'll surely be killed." Rheiner explained and approached us.

"Well, I'm not staying around here with some Krauts," Leon said and spit in the fire.

"Trust me, Tommy, the feeling is mutual," Rheiner said in a hushed tone as he got closer.

I picked up another two mags from a fallen orderly and ran my hands over his eyes to close them.

"We'll take care of the bodies, but Pepper, you need to listen to me," Rheiner whispered just above the wind that picked up.

"I don't want to hear it. I've made up my mind." I said and stuffed the new mags in pouches on the satchel.

"God damn you fool. Shut up and listen." He hissed through clenched teeth. His fists tightened at his side.

Leon reached for his rifle but I waved him off. I knew Rheiner couldn't do much to me.

"I understand why you are going. This is why they have rules against this sort of thing." He grumbled.

"Do you?" I glared. He didn't seem supportive before.

"Why do you think I am here? Instead of with my company preparing them to be meat shields for a bunch of incompetent Russian dogs?"

I hadn't thought about it. "Okay, I'm listening," I said. Though I scanned the camp for some medical supplies, I didn't know what shape Sylvia was in and I wanted to have something encase things got bad.

"Whatever you do. You cannot kill Zakeem in the circle. Fighting is bad enough. But murder is the worst thing you can do. I'd like you to bring him here so I could have the honours. But I have a feeling Sylvia won't wait that long. Nor would I ask you to."

"Fine," I said once I spotted a first aid kit. I walked over to grab it.

"I'm serious Pepper," Rheiner growled and stepped after me. Leon cocked the bolt on his rifle and Rheiner stiffened.

"Huh, guess I did have a bullet in the chamber," Leon said casually and picked the discarded ground up. Rheiner's lips pursed his lips and took a deep breath and let it out slowly.

"Just... keep it in mind." He said and held out a stone no bigger than a child's palm carved with runes. "Here."

I took the stone and looked it over with knit brows.

"It'll get you to the German trenches closest to the door we use," he explained and turned back to the medic tent. "The brighter it gets the closer you are to the door. It'll flash when you are there," he added. "I hope you are strong enough to make the right choice."

I tucked the stone into my pocket. It was an easy choice. Zakeem had to die. He'd caused so much pain and misery and wanted to continue it. I didn't see a way that this could end without Zakeem as a corpse. No good way at least.

I looked to Leon who smiled with such an infectious shitty smirk, I fought a grin of my own.

"She would've killed you." I motioned to the german woman standing by the tent behind him.

"Nah, she wouldn't. We've got a connection." Leon said and turned to wave at her. She tapped the arrow in her hand against her calf. Her stern expression didn't change as she watched. "I bet she has the voice of an angel."

I shook my head and stuffed the stone into a pocket. "You should stay here."

"You can not be serious?" He said and slung a bandolier over his shoulder and sat on a chair while he worked some mags into it.

"I am. You want to be here. Away from the front, right?" I said as I double checked the kit, bandages needle, thread all there.

"Not when I'm outnumbered by Kraut," he replied.

"I'm serious Leon."

"So am I. I'm sticking with you through this." He said and looked me in the eyes. I saw the ferocity behind his determination. I knew nothing short of detaining him would keep him away.

"Why?" I asked with a raised eyebrow when I snapped the kit back together.

"Because you remind me of my little brother and I don't want to lose him again." Leon replied. There was a pause between us as we both took a moment to let that sink in.

"Um.." I didn't know what to say.

"Why the fuck did I just say that?" Leon said, bewildered by his own words. He cleared his throat. "What I meant was, I don't want to lose-" He stopped himself. "I want to see you live on in his-" He let out a frustrated grunt. "What's going on?" He growled and looked around like someone cast a spell on him.

I recognized the chair he sat on and smirked. "I get what you mean Leon. Honesty Seats are a pain in the ass."

He blinked a few times and stood up. "Oh, you cursed thing." He kicked the chair over and turned back. "We have little time. So let's go." He huffed his face a deeper shade of red than normal.

Though it was a nice sentiment, now I had to worry about Leon too. I didn't know how I kept going. I'd seen men break under less. We jogged from the camp our gear rattling as we moved. I slowed for a moment seeing the stretcher we'd brought in. I refused to bring back another one, especially not her. I gritted my teeth and continued forth.

"If we get in a firefight stick close to me," I said to Leon just before the forest turned white. We walked into snow up to our knees.

"Uh, okay," Leon said looking around. "Is this normal?"

"I'm not sure," I said and checked the stone. It slowed lightly, so we were in the right area. We followed the tracks that led away from where we'd come from to the edge of a forest. I saw tents set up and trucks rumbled by. I pulled the stone out, the glow was barely visible. I had to cup my hands around it to see it. We'd gone the wrong way.

"Let's backtrack," I said and swept the stone back and forth.

"What?" Leon said surprised.

"Back." I hissed louder and motioned the way we came and pointed to the stone. Leon nodded, we headed back along the path. Though eventually, the stone dimmed, and we headed off the beaten path. Making more noise than I'd have liked. I heard the roar of planes and before long the forest gave way to an airfield. Russian planes came in to land. Most of them had a few holes. One burst into flames before it could stop. Crews ran out to throw snow and buckets of water as the pilot struggled to get free.

I looked at the stone again and it glowed stronger when I pointed it down to the far end of the field. I motioned to Leon in that direction and we made our way only ducking low when a patrol walked within earshot. We didn't see them but we heard them talking. They laughed at something as they passed and I reached for my pistol. This was a waste of time and I worried Sylvia didn't have the time to spare.

Once they were out of earshot we continued to skirt the airfield and go deeper into the forest. We crossed a downed aeroplane suspended in the thick brush. The snow that coated the machine's corpse felt like a foreboding warning of what would happen if we failed.

I checked the stone once the plane was out of view; it flashed after a few steps.

"We're close," I said. Though with a glance I couldn't see anything but forest.

"Close to what?" Leon asked and kicked some snow off a rock. "Freezing?" He blew on his hands and pulled out a cigarette.

I walked in a circle and shuffle the snow around. "A door."

"A door? What kind of door?"

"A regular wooden door," I replied.

Leon looked around and threw up his arms. "A door in the forest? Are you having a laugh? That feels like the start of a joke."

"Leon, I'm still new to all this. I don't know what I'm doing only that I have to. If Lady Therese were alive..." I choked up and swallowed the lump in my throat. "Then we might have other options. But for now. Just look for a door."

Leon pulled a granola bar from his front pocket and bit into it while he looked around, I shuffled through the snow. I kicked at it hoping to find it under the snow. I pushed large rocks over and scared a few hibernating animals from their homes.

After an hour of kicking around the snow, we found the door under a large rock, just like the first one had been. Once the stone was clear Leon pulled the door handle up to the annoyance of some mice that scattered.

"What the hell?" Leon said and dropped the door. "A fat lot of good this does us."

"Maybe regular folk can't open it?" I suggested and reached for the handle.

"What do you mean regular folk?" Leon asked with an indignant tone.

"There is so much to fill us both in on Leon. When I get back, we'll both get all the answers we can. Okay?" I turned the handle and heard a click. With a flick of my wrist, the door lifted to reveal a dark tunnel straight into the ground.

"My God," Leon said and stared down. "How many of the myths are true?" He asked me. I shrugged and looked around. It was quiet except for the odd buzz of aircraft.

"Are you still set on accompanying me?" I asked. He gave me a deadpan looked in the eye. "Just making sure," I said and hopped into the hall, ignoring the swap in gravity that flipped my stomach. I skidded to a stop a few feet in and turned to Leon. "Don't forget the door."

"My ma didn't raise me in a barn." He said and stepped hesitantly into the hall. His shoulders heaved fighting back the lurch of his stomach no doubt. "That's so weird." He said and pulled the door closed.

"When we get there Leon, I want you to focus on getting Sylvia and getting her out of here," I said as we headed down the hall. Torches popped to life and died off behind us.

"Oh? I thought you wanted to be her hero?" Leon teased. We rounded our first corner, and he looked back. "Uh, there's only one way back right?"

"As far as I know," I replied with a shrug. "And no I want her to escape. I don't care who gets it done."

"All right," Leon replied, and we continued down past the automatic magical lanterns slow step by slow step. I wanted to run, but I remembered what happened when I rushed after Zakeem. So I kept an eye out and held the shield high around every corner. Leon stuck behind me and kept quiet.

The air in the halls was dusty but vibrated with a feeling that tensed my stomach. I worried that it was worse for Leon, he seemed pale when I looked back at him. But he didn't say a word until the torches came to life on either side of a large bronze door.

"Finally. I was beginning to wonder if there was an end to this tunnel." Leon said with a sigh.

"It can be disorienting" I admitted and let out my own sigh. We made our way over to the door and I gripped the handle and paused. I opened the snap of my holster and slipped my fingers around the handle. I looked back at Leon as he set his rifle against the wall and rubbed his hands before he nodded to me.

With a twist of my wrist and shove with my shoulder the door shuddered and heaved open. The room was lit well by extra pyres. Two people sat in the centre of the circle one in a large chair the other on a box. Both jumped at the sudden intrusion. Sylvia was in the chair, bound and gagged with blood streaks on her face from a gash on her forehead. I pulled my pistol free from the holster and aimed it at the other figure.

Zakeem jumped to his feet and had the business end of the rifle pressed to Sylvia's face before I could pull the trigger.

"Stop right there," Zakeem said. Leon and I froze in our tracks. I shifted my gun over the edge of my shield to stabilize it.

Sylvia cried out from behind her gag and struggled against the ropes that held her arms, her legs kicked free but the chair was too high and they didn't reach the ground.

"You brought a friend. How touching." Zakeem said with a chuckle. "Someone to die with you? Or carry the body back?" He sneered his inhuman half faced sneer.

"I'm to help clean your brains off the wall," Leon said with a smirk. He grunted and dropped to his hands and knees.

"Ah, a peasant. For a second I was worried." Zakeem laughed. "You've just condemned that man. Are you happy with yourself?"

I knelt beside Leon with my hand on his back. "Hey, Leon. Come on. What's wrong?" I shook him and he rolled onto his back and cried out. His eyes bulged and turned red as his back arched and he thrashed about. I tried to keep him steady. But he was too strong and shoved me back. Blood seeped from the corners of his eyes as his eyes darted about like mad.

I levelled my gun back at Zakeem. He pressed the rifle closer to Sylvia who was in tears as she watched Leon kick and cuss.

"What did you do?" I growled.

Zakeem hissed a laugh and shook his head. "Nothing. He did it to himself coming here with hostile intent."

"Yeah? Well, I have pretty fucking hostile intentions right now. Why isn't it happening to me?" I asked and got to my feet.

Zakeem sighed and hung his head a moment. "Are you sure nothing happened?" he asked with a raised eyebrow. I noticed shadows shifting and grabbing at the gun in my hand. A voice whispered in my ear but I ignored it and focused on Zakeem. "Besides you are Blessed." He shook his head and looked at Sylvia. "Is stupid really your kind? Had I known I'd have sent over some Russians to warm your bed."

She narrowed her eyes at him and I stepped forward.

"Ah," he pulled the hammer back on the Rifle more. "Don't test me. I can kill your friend and be ready to kill her faster than you can make it here." Zakeem said and took a step back. The Rifle now sat nestled in Sylvia's black hair and pressed against her skull. "Want to test me?"

"No" I pulled the gun back and held my hands up. The whispering grew loud enough I could hear it urge me on. "What do you want?"

"I want a re-match. I applaud your underhandedness from last time, but it won't happen again." Zakeem sneered from behind Sylvia. I looked her in the eyes. She shook her head and I could practically hear her telling me not to do it. Her silent request was barely louder than the whisper that urged me to violence. I knew what was at stake. Now that I saw she was all right. I should have had time to think or plan.

Leon fell still for a moment and I thought it was over until he had another fit. Foaming at the mouth as his body jerked and spasmed.

"Seems like he doesn't have much time left," Zakeem said.

"Fine. Let's do this." I said. "Stop holding her hostage coward." I spat.

"Drop your gun first. I wouldn't want this to be unfair." He taunted.

Sylvia kicked more and Zakeem hit her head with the butt of his gun. "Shut up. The only reason you are alive is because you were helpful." He growled and pointed the gun back at her listing head. She wasn't out cold but she was having a hard time focusing.

"Kill." The whisper said in a loud guttural inhuman tone and fell quiet again.

I tensed, and almost tried to take a quick shot at him. But he was too close to Sylvia, and I was too bad of a shot. His words were lost to me for a moment until Sylvia shook her head and re-focused on me.

I held her gaze, and she shook her head. I glanced back at Zakeem.

"Kill." The whisper said again.

"Fine." I dropped the gun to the side and clenched my teeth. Was that whisper my inner thoughts or something else?

"And the other one," Zakeem added.

I pulled a new pocket pistol out and tossed it to the ground too.

"And any others."

"That's all. I've only got my knife now." I replied and clenched my hands and teeth.

"Really?" Zakeem stepped clear of Sylvia. "I suppose I should be sporting. You can keep it." He pulled the Rifle away from Sylvia's head.

I lunged after him and pulled the knife from my belt. He fired, it clipped the shield and glanced off my shoulder. I spun the blade in my hand just as my arm dropped and a searing pain shot from my shoulder. I stumbled to the ground as Zakeem jumped back.

I looked in disbelief at the blood soaking the sleeve of my uniform. The shield had a chip in one corner. I lifted the shield and a sharp pain pulsed through my arm. It wasn't a deep wound. But it was a wound. It was everything I'd been waiting for since I picked up the shield and had forgotten about it.

Zakeem laughed his hideous snake like laugh. He doubled over and clutched his stomach.

"The stupid look on your face." He finally got out. "You had no idea that magic doesn't work here." He wiped a tear from his eye.

"Kill him." The whisper ordered. I clenched my jaw tighter and got back to my feet and rolled my shoulder. It hurt, but I could handle it.

"That means your rifle won't always hit," I growled.

"I suppose you are right. Good thing I'm the best sharpshooter in the war. I've trained for this." He grinned a toothy evil smile. It made the bile rise from my stomach.

I tried to wait and see what he would do next. But the whisper reminded me I had no time and urged me on. I dashed at him again and he fired. I raised the shield and saw the dent form on the steel. It was thick enough to handle it.

"Shit." Zakeem spun the barrel, but I knocked it away and thrust the dagger at him. He stepped back, I missed. He slammed the side of the rifle into my face. The crack made me sneer and stumbled. Blood poured from my nose, but slashed at him and caught his arm. He grunted and lowered the rifle at my stomach. I spun quick, he fired. The round slammed into the shield and I winced as the dent pinched my hand against the handle.

Zakeem grit his teeth and swung the butt of his rifle over the shield, it caught me in the forehead. I stumbled back a few feet into Sylvia's chair. Red coursed over my nose and I felt the gash burn. The whisper had become a loud growling voice, like a wolf hungry for blood and amused at my efforts. It stoked my rage with mocking words.

I looked at Sylvia for a second and the voice fell back to a whisper. Her eyes pleaded with me for something I didn't know if I could stop anymore. But I could give her an escape. I slipped the knife to her hand and shook the pain away before I advanced again. I didn't have time to debate.

Zakeem reloaded, but I slammed the rifle down just before he fired. The round caught my calf. I slammed the shield up under Zakeem's jaw and he stumbled back against the wall. I thrust the edge of the shield intending to crush his skull as the whisper ordered. He ducked the blow and levelled the rifle at my stomach again.

"Checkmate." Zakeem laughed. I swung and caught the rifle as he fired. The bullet tore into the side of my stomach and I wanted to writhe with pain. But I had the rifle. The barrels burned my palm but I wouldn't let go.

I swung the edge of the shield again and this time I connected with the good side of Zakeem's face. He dropped to the ground. I tossed the rifle free and knelt on his chest. My own burnt with a consuming fire as I raised the shield for the final blow. Shadows swirled around us and pushed me to crush his face as he spat out bloody teeth and cackled.

"Pepper, stop!" Sylvia shouted. Her voice was louder than the whisper and I froze. The shadows hissed at her as their grip fell free. She freed herself and cut the last restraint and got to her feet. "It's what he wants. We can't kill him here." She said and stumbled as she rushed over to us.

"Don't interfere you, stupid bitch!" Zakeem shouted and caught me off guard as he pulled a handgun out from inside his jacket. The gun went off and a scream filled the air as I slammed the shield into Zakeem hand and shoulder. The sickening crunch was oddly satisfying. He whimpered and tried to cradle the wound but I wouldn't get off him.

Sylvia dove at the sound of the shot, but the round bounced harmlessly off the wall. She scrambled over to us on her knees and went to work tying Zakeem up. I gripped the back of his head and pushed off it to stand up but fell back to the wall. The shot that hit my leg wasn't a graze.

"We need to get you out of here Pepper," Sylvia said cut a strip from my pant leg to tie above the wound.

"I agree," I said and stood up again leaning against the wall. I tried to put some weight on my leg but it wouldn't handle it. "Can you help Leon?"

"Yeah, but you're bleeding really bad," Sylvia said.

"He needs to get out of here," I said. "I'll keep an eye on this." I motioned to Zakeem laying face down with his hands bound behind him. "Take the Rifle with you," I said and sat on the ground beside

Zakeem. She grabbed the Rifle and her Sword before she handed me my pistol and gave me a peck on the cheek.

"I'll be back quick as can be." She said before she dragged Leon's still body out of the room. I wondered if he was still alive. But there was something else I wondered about more.

"What did you mean when you said she was helpful?" I asked once Sylvia had rounded the corner, and the tunnel went dark.

Zakeem laughed and winced. "You have no idea? She's better than I thought."

"Spill it," I growled and aimed the gun at him.

"Do it." The whisper spit in my ear and I felt my finger tense on the trigger.

"Go ahead, You'll be doing me a favour." He said with a grin. I kicked his shoulder instead and the whispering voice hissed in feverish rage. Zakeem cried out and pushed his head against the stone floor as he sputtered words I didn't understand. His feet kicked as he dealt with the pain.

"Try again," I said.

"Ugh, she helped me get the Rifle," he said and winced. "I couldn't have gotten this far without her help."

"You're lying."

He laughed. "Am I? How do you think she knew Daniel's name?"

"It's her burden. She keeps parts of them, their memories and such."

"Hah, is that what she said?" He chuckled. "Nah, she lied. I told her. Why do you think she wanted to come back to the front once that fucker Jonas got the Rifle?"

Dread filled my soul as he continued. How much had he been responsible for? "Did you orchestrate the attack against the bunker?" I asked.

"Fuck no." Zakeem spit a bloody loogie onto the stone. "I'd never work with scum like that. If I knew they were in Rome, I'd have killed em myself." He laughed, a hyena like laugh. "I'd have loved to put a bullet in each of those stuffy council members though."

"That was just a coincidence?" I asked.

"Unfortunate for the people. But it hurt no one worthwhile during the- AH FUCK!" He screamed as I dropped the heel of my boot on his shoulder. The whisper cheered me on and urged for more. "What do you want?" he snapped through clenched teeth

"The truth." I snapped as I fought the urge to pull the trigger.

"It is the truth." He hissed through clenched teeth. "Ask her yourself when she gets back. If you can trust her." He laughed and winced.

Chapter 22
Laid Bare

Sylvia patched up my leg with the first aid kit and helped me out of the tunnel. I limped over to sit against a large rock with her help. Leon groaned and sat up, blinking as he wiped the bloody tears from his eyes and looked around.

"What-" He croaked out and rubbed his throat trying to swallow. His hands trembled like mad as he reached for his pack of cigarettes.

Zakeem sat against a fallen tree glaring at Sylvia. He'd stopped talking but had occasional laughing fits. The whispering had stopped once the door to the Ethereal Circle was closed.

Sylvia patched my side and arm up now that we were back in the real world. The sun had begun to set by the time she finished.

"We'll need to get moving before the light is all gone." She said and packed the kit back together.

"Yes," Zakeem spoke. "Don't want to get caught out in the dark." His laughter grew sharp and loud.

Sylvia shoved off the ground and drew her blade as she stomped towards him. I reached for my pistol and checked the chamber with considerable effort. I had lost a lot of blood.

"Oooh." He taunted her when she pulled the blade free. I watched and cold realization swept through me. It chilled my bones and steadied my breathing. She stabbed the invisible tip into his stomach. I slipped my finger into the trigger as he winced and groaned. "Go on. Do it." He grinned. "I'll make sure I stick around for a looong-"

A crack rang out in and Zakeem's head lurched back. His blood and brains splattered down the log and his mouth set in a twisted silent wide laugh. The forest fell silent again and Sylvia turned to look wide eyed at me, pistol still smoking.

"Thank god," Leon said.

"Pepper... you..." Sylvia said stunned.

"Had enough." I sighed. I had just killed a man, actually cold blooded killed him this time, a real son of a bitch. He'd been unarmed, bound and distracted. That didn't sit right with me even if I knew it was the right thing to do. His last warning rang in my ears as I looked at Sylvia, the finger still on my trigger.

"I barely knew the bastard, and I was already sick of his laugh," Leon said. His voice stirred something inside me and I tucked my gun back in its holster.

Leon looked around. "How did we get back outside?" he asked.

"It's a story for when we get back to the grove," Sylvia said and put her sword away. "How do you feel?" She was looking at me, but I knew she was asking Leon. I stared back as she searched my eyes.

"Like everything been torn out of me and stuffed back as horse shit," Leon replied.

Sylvia gave a soft smile and looked to Leon after a moment. "You are lucky to be alive." She said and went about explaining to Leon about the spirits that had almost killed him.

I wondered how much of what she said was true as I wiggled my hand free of the shield and flexed it. Did the shield really have any effect? Or had I been the one who'd been under a spell?

"Peter?" Sylvia's voice interrupted my thoughts.

"Hmm?" I looked up. Leon leaned against a tree with one arm and the other held a new-lit cigarette against his lips for a long drag. It did little to steady his trembling. Sylvia's held her hand out.

"We best get back." She smiled again and held her hand out. This time I smiled back, I hoped it didn't look as hollow as it felt.

"You're right," I said and took her hand. She pulled me to my feet and wrapped an arm around me as I stumbled.

"You okay?" She said with a laugh. I nodded, and she leaned in to give me a quick kiss on the lips. The spark was there but Zakeem's warning dulled it. I leaned into the kiss, hoping to overpower his words, but it only enforced them.

She broke the kiss and smiled. "Thank you," she said and stepped back. She walked over to Zakeem and tugged a silver circlet from around his neck, rifled through his pockets and patted him down. She pulled the pocket watch I'd first seen him with and tucked both away. She searched the rest of his pockets and pulled his rings and dog tag off. She pocketed the rings and a pouched of billed before she pulled her blade out to cut the dog tags up and toss them around.

"There, now we have five Relics," she said as she tucked her sword away again.

"Six." I corrected as we started walking.

"Did you get another?"

"The Hammer," I said. "It's back at camp."

She laughed and shook her head. "You've tripled the Relics we have in a month, Peter. You are amazing." She grabbed the rifle and joined us on the long walk back. Leaving Zakeem's body for whatever animal would satiate their hunger with his flesh. It still felt too good for him.

THANKFULLY, SYLVIAS was clear-headed enough to follow the path, because Leon and I were in such unstable states we wandered off the path a few times. More often to rest against a tree or rock, but with Sylvia's insistence and a reminder of being behind enemy lines, we'd be back on our way again. It was well after dark by the time we got back to camp.

Rheiner was still there along with the other German Knights. One a large skinny black man with two silver circles on his hips. Another was a stout young man who spoke with a Turkish accent that made him hard to understand. And a woman that looked so frail I took her for a ghost as she walked between the beds of the medical tent.

Stephan took his time to stitch me up properly complaining about the bad field dressing. He also warned me how close I'd come to death. Leon sucked on cigarettes the entire way back and was onto his second cigar by the time Stephan finished with me. His hands still trembled, and he coughed now with each puff.

Stephan walked over and asked him to lie down. Leon took a final drag and put out the cigar in the pile beside the bed and did as instructed. Stephan whispered a soft chant and waved his hands to either side of Leon's face. I caught glimpses of a shadow around Leon. Stephan hooked his fingers around it and snipped it free with a pair of silver scissors. Leon jolted at the snip then fell still.

Stephan leaned on the bed as a coughing fit struck him. Rheiner rushed over to guide his love to a seat. I found my hate for their affection absent now. They were enemies and loved each other all the same. Should I be using them as a model?

"You're a mage" Leon coughed in amazement and held his hand steady as could be. "I've never met one in person before."

"Nor are you likely to ever again. We keep to ourselves. Our benefactors keep us quite secure." Stephan said and gave Rheiner a pat on the shoulder. "I'm fine."

I wondered how they did it as I got to my feet. Stephan warned me against exerting myself for the night. Had I not been up for two days it may have been a viable concern. But all I could think about now was sleep.

I left the medical tent and tried to get some sleep. But Zakeem haunted my dreams, His laughter, his warning, his face splitting open from my shot. It rocked me from sleep a few hours after I'd put my head down.

I tried to get back to sleep again when someone walked into my tent as I was about to doze off. I reached for my shield tucked between the bed and the tent wall.

The person sat on the side of my bed and ran their slender fingers through my hair. It was Sylvia. I faked waking up slowly and turning to see her.

"Hey," I whispered and cleared my throat.

"Are you okay?" She asked in a hushed tone.

I nodded and reached for her hand. "I am." I croaked out.

"Peter. Please don't lie to me." She said with such hurt in her voice. I found it disgustingly ironic. "What is bothering you?" She gripped my hand and locked her eyes on mine. The absence of her fingers was off-putting at first, but I gave her hand a squeeze and stared back. Her eyes sought answers but for once I didn't feel like an open book to her.

I sat up in bed and took a moment to find the words I wanted.

"How..." What would this do to us? "How did you really know Daniels name?" I asked and with a breath, I turned to look her in the eyes. Her beautiful green eyes that normally sparkled with life now widened with realization.

"I... I told you," she said and looked away. "It came with the memories." I gripped the bedsheets.

"Sylvia," I said her name rougher than I intended. She struggled to look at me. "Please. Don't lie to me."

"But... I can't stand the thought of you hating me."

"Why would I hate you?" I asked.

"For all that I've done." She choked up and tears formed in her eyes. "For the lives, I've cost."

I wanted to reach for her hand and comfort her, but I didn't know if I could offer that right now. It was taking too much of me to keep my composure.

"I need you to tell me everything. Be honest with me. Trust me with that, and I promise to be understanding." I offered. I couldn't promise I wouldn't hate her. I already felt it growing inside of me. Cold and calming, like when I pulled the trigger on Zakeem.

Sylvia wiped the tears from her eyes and nodded.

"Promise to hear me out?" She asked.

I nodded and made room for her to sit on the bed.

She shifted to sit across from me.

"Zakeem told me of Daniel. I knew he was out there the night we took you to the circle. I knew he was Blessed. Zakeem wanted me to kill him. I didn't want to. But Zakeem knows about my family. He found them and sent me a picture with them. He'd have killed them if I didn't listen to him."

I nodded and felt the hate in my heart soften. "Why not tell us about this? We could have helped."

"I did. This isn't the first time Zakeem tried. Last time I told Lady Therese, and she moved my family into Rome with guards to watch over them, but that didn't help. My youngest brother passed away three weeks after the move. It was a fever. But Zakeem said he poisoned him." Tears flowed freely down Sylvia's cheeks. I got off the bed and grabbed the handkerchief from the pocket of my dress jacket. She took with a trembling smile.

"I knew I couldn't defy him again. So I did as he asked. I insisted that Jonas get the Rifle, that we go back as soon as possible. He said once he had the Rifle my family would be safe."

"But he said nothing about the rest of us."

"I knew he held a grudge and I should have known she'd be the first he'd go after." She got out between sobs. "Pepper. I swear. I didn't want to. I didn't know what else I could do. I tried to protect her."

Her sobbing grew louder, I pulled her close. She sobbed to my shoulder and hugged tight as if I might run away if she showed any doubt. I brushed my fingers through her hair and rubbed her back.

The darkness that had hung on after Zakeem's warning melted away. She was no more at fault than the soldiers that ran across the battlefield at their commander's bark.

"This is why I wanted out. Why I still do." She mumbled after several minutes.

I leaned back and looked her in the eyes.

"Come with me, Peter." She smiled. "I've saved up some money and I'm going to relocate my family. We'll find someplace safe."

I smiled at her. It sounded like a great idea.

"I can't," I said with a heavy heart.

"What?... of course you can. If you come with the shield. No one can stop us. Please Peter. I don't-"

"It's Pepper." I corrected her.

"I know. But I thought you wanted to change it." She looked hurt by my sharp tone.

"I thought I did too. But... It's the last thing I have to remember my mother over. It just doesn't feel right to go by another name" I explained.

"Pepper, please don't make me leave on my own. I want you to come with me." She held my hand tightly and rubbed her thumb against the back.

"I dodged the war for so long. It's not right for me to leave. I want to see the end of this. With the other Knights, we have a real chance to do that." I took a knee before her and looked up into her eyes. "Lady Therese might be gone. But her dream for the end of the war is still alive."

Sylvia shook her head as I explained. She wouldn't even try to hear me out.

"I can't Pet- Pepper, I can't anymore. I'm done." She pulled her hand free of mine and my heart fell apart. "When things are finished. I hope we cross paths again." I stood before her and silently begged her to reconsider. But I saw the determination in her eyes and knew it would be a waste of my breath.

She wrapped her arms around my neck and I held her tight. I swayed us into one last dance, the wind and rustling of the leaves our only tune. She gave me a final kiss before she left my tent.

I didn't see her the next morning and by afternoon I realized that she'd left in the night with her sword. I wanted to mourn her loss, chase her down and run with her. But Rheiner had information on advancements and supply lines that we needed to get to command. And I was the only one left that Allied Command trusted. Stephan introduced me as the latest Knight.

I looked at the others and was thankful I wouldn't be the last knight.

Epilogue
Five years later.

I finished writing a letter and walked down the quiet halls of the Orders newest branch in New York. It was housed in a four-storey brick apartment building. I looked to the clock on the wall and realized I was due to meet a recruit that a local Bishop suggested, but I had to stop by the armoury first.

I rounded the corner and paused as I caught Leon pressing his wife, Lara, up against a wall in a passionate embrace. It wasn't the most compromising position I'd caught them in. I learned shortly after Zakeem's death that Leon was right about the connection he had with the German Knight of the Bow. She was soft-spoken but had looks that cut deeper than steel. She threatened to cut out my tongue if I mentioned what I saw to anyone then, and I kept my word to this day.

I cleared my throat, and they separated in a jolt.

"Headmaster." Lara nodded and excused herself with cheeks flushed crimson. I shook my head at Leon's wide smile after she left. He limped back to the desk and cleaned her lipstick off.

"She brought lunch." He explained with a shrug and held up a metal container from his desk.

"Mmhmm," I said and walked over to his desk. "Got the compass ready?"

"Oh, right," he said. "I got a little distracted." He admitted and headed into the lockup.

"Don't you two have enough kids yet?" I asked and leaned on his desk looking over the pictures with him and his growing family.

"She's only pregnant with number four," he said from inside the armoury. "I had that many brothers and three sisters." He finished and walked back out with the compass nestled in a box.

"You know you won't catch up to Dani and his wives right?" I said and picked up the Relic and tucked it into my shirt pocket.

"Maybe not, but I can try," Leon said with a smirk and a wink.

"I'll pray for your wife," I said with a shake of my head. "Any word from Luka?" I asked.

"The shields due tomorrow. Turns out the man was a con artist." Leon shrugged and sat at his desk to open his lunch box.

"I thought as much. Lots of those since the war. Stephan was right about keeping a low profile." I admitted.

"Good, we got a request for help way up north. Turns out there is some wolf-like creature taking Inuit hunters out." I said and tapped the latter against his desk. "I'm having Sam scout ahead but I'd like to be there myself to establish relations with the Elders."

"Like a werewolf?" Leon asked.

"Not sure. I tried to look up some information but it could be a red haired werewolf, a whale wolf or just a giant wolf," I shrugged and turned to leave. "Hopefully this child the Bishop suggested isn't a false lead too." I finished and pulled out an envelope from my jacket pocket and put it on his desk.

"What's this?"

"A letter I found in Lady Therese's things. Addressed to a Mr. Hamilton. It was someone who served her when she was younger. I hoped you could see if we can get his last words home." I pushed the letter to him

"That'll be near impossible." Leon said and picked up the envelope and looked the letter over slowly.

"I know, but if anyone can do it I know you've got the connections" I smiled at him as I left for my meeting.

We'd gathered a few more people since the war ended four years ago. But we still didn't have all the Relics available. The Spear and Horn had gone missing after the war. We presumed that the Russians hid them, though they denied it.

Rheiner kept people looking for them as Head of the Council centred in Rome. His portrait sat on the wall in the foyer where I walked in to meet the possible recruit.

Sam Logan was there chatting up a woman. The Canadian sharp-shooter was our Knight of the Torc. It glinted around his neck like a silver bowtie and I wondered if the suit he had on was real. He got the best intel during the last months of the war. Though he'd taken to spying for his home country since and I was a little hesitant to have him around our offices. We rarely dealt with anything on a national level, but still.

"Headmaster." Sam clicked his heels and stood straighter as I ap-proached. I gave him a knowing smile. He was also quite the playboy.

"Sam." I nodded and turned to the familiar looking woman. "You must be the boy's mother," I said and offered my hand.

"Yes, a pleasure to meet you. I'm Melissa." The woman said and shook my hand. She paused, her eyes examined my face. "Have we met?" She asked and cocked her head.

"I was going to say the same thing." I chuckled and looked into her eyes. She smiled but her eyes darted past me.

"There you are, Nathaniel. Stop wandering off." She said and let go of my hand. She waved the boy over and with a quick dust of his shoulders and straightening of his golden hair presented him.

The boy had grown quite a bit since I last saw him. Now in his teens, the blonde boy with the innocent blue eyes showed signs of manhood and I couldn't help but chuckle.

"Ah yes. I remember the train ride, five years ago." I said with a nod. Melissa's eyes widened.

"Oh yes. You found Nathaniel and split your head open." She said with a soft giggle. Nathaniel giggled too. Sam smirked, I narrowed my eyes and handed him the letter so he excused himself.

I spent some time chatting with them and checked the Compass while we spoke. Each time it pointed straight for Nathaniel. I read up on all the Relics and knew that the Compass's chosen had a tendency to wander, so after a while I let Nathaniel try the compass. He was a natural which gave me hope. Perhaps we could find more Blessed and fill our ranks so the burden of protecting people could weigh less on the few Blessed that we had now.

I asked that Melissa bring Nathaniel back to meet with Rheiner in a week to confirm my suspicions and wished them a good day as they left.

It had gotten late and with no more appointments, I headed for home. I stopped in front of a flower shop on the way and looked over the roses. My mind drifted until I felt a tiny hand wrap around my fingers. I looked down to see my three-year-old daughter, Therese, smiling up at me. I knelt down and picked her up to kiss her cheek and hugged her tightly before I smiled wider when I saw Sylvia carrying a bag of groceries a few feet away.

"Were you going to buy more roses?" she asked with a smile and shook her head. "You know the last ones you bought are still fine." She added.

"Just checking the prices," I said and walked over to kiss her lips. Sylvia had left the order that night, I didn't see her again until the war was over, almost a year later, at Leon and Lara's wedding. I worried too much time and space had come between us but we rekindled the romance that night and well into the next day. She kept the blade when she found out she was pregnant. She doesn't go out in the field much though, preferring to stay at home unless the Sword was necessary. She disliked that I went out frequently but understood and supported me. I couldn't have asked for a better wife.

Made in the USA
Monee, IL
22 April 2021